THE HIDDEN HAND

Books by Carroll John Daly:

THE HIDDEN HAND

THE SNARL OF THE BEAST

THE HIDDEN HAND

CARROLL JOHN DALY

HarperPerennial
A Division of HarperCollins*Publishers*

To
MY WIFE
MARGE DALY

Contents

1

The Man with the Gun

To simply say that business was dull would be the height of optimism. To say that my bank account was low would be to agree with my bank balance. To say that all the crooks in the city had ceased work would not be the truth. But to say that those unfortunate people who now fell victims of earlier indiscretions did not come to me for help would be wholly the truth. Business was dull.

"Private Detective" best describes me to the ignorant and those who have not had use for such animals. The words themselves are not so bad but I don't like the music that most detective agencies set those words to. There are honest private detectives, of course—but there are honest politicians, too. Get the point? Something like hen's teeth—very scarce, indeed. But I just don't like the label. RACE WILLIAMS— PRIVATE INVESTIGATOR is smeared in big, gold, unashamed letters all over my office door. The "Private Detective" appears on my license only. Nice distinctions are not drawn by civil bodies.

People—especially the police—don't understand me. And what we don't understand we don't appreciate. The police look upon me as being so close to the criminal that you can't tell the difference. Oh, I've got my pride like the rest of us. I'd like to be famous, but I guess, after all, I'm only notorious. Every cop in the great city has my reputation hammered into him as a gun and a killer.

No use to go into detail on that point. I carry a gun—two of them, for that matter. As to being a killer, well—I'm not a target, if you get what I mean. I've killed in my time, and I daresay I'll kill again. There—let the critics of my methods paste that in their hats.

Now, with business dull and a strong dislike for private detective agencies, I was thinking seriously of accepting a position from one of these very agencies. It was an open and shut affair that had been offered me the night before by Gregory Ford, a well-known operator. He just spilt his story and named his figure as he stood in the doorway.

"It's a dull season," he said. "A cold winter and your chance to go South. The State's paying me well, time won't hang heavy on your hands—and if we can pin these crimes on McCleary, I'll give you a handsome piece of change." And when I would have refused, just on general principles, he held up his hand. "And that isn't all of it, Race Williams—not by half, it isn't. This will turn out the biggest grab in the country. The feared name of McCleary is built on blood and murder—but mark my words: He'll turn out to be a pawn in the game. If we can make him holler, buy him, or knock a squeal out of him—we'll lay our hands on the biggest brain that ever backed a crime ring. The business of robbery and murder is simply petty larceny to some of the things those boys in Florida are pulling off." The hand he waved in the air turned into a fist now. "If we catch the big gun behind McCleary, I'll cut you in for ten per cent of the melon, and there'll be a hundred a day in it for you while we're warming up."

I just shook my head. I don't like to work with private detectives. I always play a lone hand.

"Times aren't so good for you, Race." He jerked his slouch hat down over his eyes like a stage detective. "The police in the city are beginning to watch your stunts. Take a few months off—give them a chance to forget you. I'll tell you—if it's you that knocks McCleary off his spot I'll add in one grand as a bonus." Gregory Ford swung on his heels, called once over his shoulder—"If you change your mind give me a ring in the morning. I'm sailing in the afternoon on the *Cherry* to Miami."

And that's the thing I had on my chest as I walked through the lobby of the hotel and entered the dining room for lunch. I could think better on a full stomach, and I have yet to see the day when I couldn't stick my hand in my pocket and wrap my fingers around a hundred or two.

I sat with my back to the wall. Put it down to fear of drafts, if you like, but it's the best medicine I know of as a preserver of health—at least, my health. There are too many boys who'd be glad to put a bullet in my back.

It was just my pride that kept me from working with a private agency. And Gregory Ford—well—he wasn't the worst of them.

I looked suddenly up over my coffee and saw the man crossing the dining room. Somehow, I got the impression that he didn't belong. The neat fitting blue suit and the flashy tie didn't help him any. It's part of my business to study faces, and I marked this boy for a lad who had a date with the undertaker. The pasty yellow of his sunken cheeks stood out vividly on each side of the hollows which held the dead eyes. The walk, too—his knees had a give to them as if he walked a tight rope. But he acted quickly enough as he jerked sideways and flopped into the seat across the table from me.

I smiled over at him. Here was a client. Here would be a case that would keep me from feeling bad about turning down Gregory Ford's offer. And the man spoke.

"You'll keep both your hands on the table." He fairly

gasped the words. "If you move a finger I'll shoot—there's a gun covering you from beneath the table. I care nothing for my own life."

His eyes burned across at me now. The left hand, which he laid upon the table, trembled and the fingers twitched spasmodically. My left hand slid further back beneath the napkin it held. My right hand clutched at the fork. I had sized up this bird as a client—and now he turned out to be the heavy villain in the piece.

I had not seen the gun as he slid into the seat. Now, I put my feet close together and raised my knees noiselessly beneath the table, protecting my body from the lead if the fingers of his right hand closed upon the trigger. It was ten to one that he wouldn't miss. He wouldn't kill me though. It don't take me very long to reach, draw and shoot. But he certainly would cripple me for some time. This wasn't any bluff of a cheap gunman. The set, dry lips and sunken cheeks told the story. He had entered that dining room and dropped into the seat opposite me for one purpose. To kill me. The flickering lips and trembling fingers upon the table were of excitement, not fear. This was a dangerous man.

But he wanted to talk—and now his quivering lips found it hard to form the words. The game was new to him. Yet, instinctively, I knew that he was determined to see it through nevertheless. So I ran in a little conversation of my own. Time was the thing! This wouldn't be the first lad who'd talked himself out of digging my grave.

"You want to talk to me—to be sure I'd listen. That's the reason for the gun—isn't it?" I'd help him talk. And get time to figure out the best way of disarming this emaciated, disease-racked boy.

"Yes, I want to—to talk." He coughed, a rattling sort of cough that shook his whole body. My eyes narrowed. If he did that again I could reach out and—But I dismissed that thought.

"I am a dying man." Upper teeth bit into a lower lip. "A few months at the best. I have a wife—a child. Will I die and see them starve?"

I moved my right hand slightly toward the edge of the table. Those burning eyes detected the movement.

"If you do that again," and his voice was strangely calm, "I'll fire." My hand remained motionless. The youth nodded. "That I can possibly escape has never entered my mind—but I should like to talk to you a moment. Many men would sacrifice their bodies for those they love," and his eyes glowed while he spoke—but always they were on me, "but few would sacrifice their souls. I have been offered money to kill you—much money—that they, my wife and child, will have. God forgive me, but—"

It was an interesting moment. I half braced myself for the shot that would come. And I was strongly tempted to go for my own gun to make sure he would get only one shot. But that he would shoot was not certain yet—wouldn't be certain until I heard the roar of his gun. And the flickering lips told me the reason he waited. Murder was new to him. He wanted to talk up his waning courage—wanted to excuse to himself his deed of violence. Nice pleasant party! But once I moved my hand he'd press the trigger. Slowly my hand hidden beneath the napkin closed into a fist.

"Call it murder if you will," the youth leaned across the table, "but you've killed in your day. There'll be money for them—for them."

"If the money is contingent on your killing me—why—you're out of luck." My voice was calm—calm enough anyway to startle the youth, for he raised his eyes slightly to mine. "Your shot beneath the table will at best strike my legs—and before you can get in a second one—but you must understand that. You don't expect me to sit peacefully here while you empty your gun into me, do you?"

He smiled rather sadly.

"I think not," he said slowly. "I understand guns. The shock of the first shot will give me time to lift my gun above the table for a second. But enough, Race Williams. It's murder. I know that. I can't help it. I—" His voice was getting louder as his eyes narrowed. A sort of reckless courage and the false feeling that he was sacrificing himself to help others were driving him on.

2

The Hotel Murder

Would I lurch forward across the table and take a chance—or would I try the half-formed scheme that had been in my mind ever since he first sat down? And I decided on the latter. This lad was weak—very weak, both mentally and physically. Action generally comes before diplomacy with me, but this time—well—I smiled across at the youth—I'd try diplomacy.

"You haven't long to live," I said. "To wound me will evidently do you no good. You have heard that Race Williams hasn't any heart. To-night you will learn differently. I am going to let you go—to die with your wife and child—if you hand me that gun you've got under the table. Quick—you fool!" I snapped out the words now. "Did you think for a minute you could play any such game with me? Why, I've had you covered since the very second you entered the dining room."

His head jerked erect. His burning eyes sought mine in wonder and alarm.

"Look down at my left hand—at the napkin." And there was a cold steadiness in my voice that sent the blood to his pasty cheeks and put the fire in his eyes. "There's a gun beneath that napkin. And it's pointed straight at you."

His lashes flicked and his eyes dropped. Beneath the napkin he saw—or thought he saw—the nose of a gun pointing toward his pounding heart.

I didn't give him a chance to digest my threat. I came slowly to my feet, leaned forward and stuck my free hand across the table and down beneath the edge of it. It was a touchy moment—there was a thrill to it. For this kind of a menace is more dangerous than the real killer of the underworld. You can't tell what'll run through such a diseased brain. My words were still cold and crisp as I kept my eyes on him.

"You say you don't care if you die," I cut in when he would have spoken. "Just keep hold of that gun of yours a minute longer and I'll oblige you." There was a quick intake of breath, a convulsive jerk to a scrawny neck, and a nickel-plated revolver slipped quickly from my right hand to my coat pocket.

"Now you keep your hands on the table." I put hard eyes on his bewildered wandering ones while I talked to him like a Dutch uncle. "If you want to spend the few days you've got left with that family you'd sacrifice your soul for, and not in a damp, rotten cell—tell me the name of the man who sent you to knock me over."

When he didn't talk I dropped back into my seat and laid it on thick. The room was pretty well deserted. My waiter had been removing dishes in a distant corner, and the jerk of that gun from beneath the table to my pocket had been no more than a movement. If I get a gun out fast, I park it fast, too.

"A fine husband and father you are," I sneered. "I don't know how much your child would come in for—but it would take a pretty penny to pay the price of being pointed out as the child of a murderer. Better take this chance to spend your declining days robbing poor boxes. Build up a reputation your family will be proud of. Come—do you tell me who sent you here or do I call in a harnessed bull? It's your show, you know."

8

"I don't know. I don't know." He gasped out the words as his head sort of fell forward on the table, and I raised my hand for the waiter. The youth braced up a bit after a drink and stared wonderingly as the waiter left the table. Then his eyes widened as he saw me crumple up the empty napkin and toss it onto the table. He made no objections either when I helped him from the dining room and placed him in one of the big chairs in the lounge room. He was muttering, dazed and uncertain. I stood looking down at him.

"Well, my fine killer," I said slowly, "which is it?" And I jerked a thumb toward a convenient cop who had parked his broad back against the window.

"I can't tell. I've sworn an oath. I can't."

"All right." It didn't take much force to jerk him to his feet. "I'll hunt up that wife and child of yours and tell them what a nice 'poppa' they've got."

If I had expected results from that I got more than I hoped for. He went limp in my grasp, and not to attract attention I had to push him back into the seat. He couldn't talk at first—a thick, dry tongue ran over drier lips. And I was through. There was no real danger from this youth. I couldn't browbeat and bully him. No doubt he had been picked up by some cheap gang and given a few dollars in cash and a few thousand in promises.

"All right, Kid." I tried the other side of him. "You have a new suit and a pocketful of money. They gave you something anyway."

"Nothing—nothing. I'd get it later," he said brokenly. "I was a fool—money of blood for my wife and boy—but they won't know. And now—to end it all in jail—in jail. If you'd only shot—only killed me! There would be the insurance—double for death by accident." And he was coughing and beginning to draw the attention of the clerk at the distant desk.

"Jailbird?" I asked him.

"No—no. Army." And he let it go at that.

9

There are some things we can't explain. I won't make excuses. Put it down to weakness. But I ducked a hand into my pocket, fished out a half dozen bills and shoved them into his boney hand. Then I turned toward the door.

Somehow he came to his feet and overtook me, the money still clutched in his hand.

"I don't know. I can't help you. Don't go South. Don't leave the city. Your life is in danger."

"It always is," I encouraged him. And then the significance of his "don't go South" struck me, and remembering my talk with Gregory Ford I gripped the youth by the shoulder. "Who sent you, Kid?" I shook him gently. "It's not your game. Play it with the right people. Tell me the truth and you'll earn real money—clean money—for the wife and boy. Money they won't be ashamed to touch."

"I can't. I'm afraid," he gulped. "But you—watch for the Gas Man—especially at night. Silently he does his work. There, I shouldn't—"

"But who sent you, Kid?" I kept my eyes straight on him. "There's the wife and—"

I stopped and stared into that face. The sickly white was turning to a ghastly, pasty yellow—the sunken eyes seemed to slip forward, even bulge in their sockets, and his breath came in great gasps. The next instant he had pitched himself forward and was in my arms—his hands clutching at my shoulders, tearing at my coat, his nails biting into my flesh. There was fear and terror, even horror in his face. He screamed—shrill, piercing, like a hysterical woman. And I saw that his eyes were not on me, but past me—fastened on something behind me—some one behind me.

I swung quickly as the clerk ran from behind the desk and the elevator starter darted across the lobby. A woman screeched, a man called hoarsely, and a bell rang sharply. And as I spun around with the youth in my arms he opened his mouth and barely whispered a name.

"McCleary—" he said—and again, "McCleary."

10

And that was all. There was a shot, the spurt of orange-blue flame from between two curtains less than ten feet away, and a convulsive upward jerk to the man in my arms. A single moan, the flicker of blood from a lip that hung low—and I knew I held a dead man.

Things happened quickly after that. The lobby, which had been deserted, was alive with people; uniformed boys who ran about, hysterical women who got in one another's way, and the constant ringing of bells and the calling of the clerk who had gone back to his place behind the desk. And I—well—I stopped halfway to the curtains and let my gun slip back into my pocket. A harnessed bull stood in the lobby—the same one whom I had threatened the boy with. The assassin of the youth had escaped long ago, I thought, for others were coming through those parted curtains now—people who formed in little frightened groups and looked at the boy in the chair.

As for me, I must think of myself. I knew the cop and he knew me. I had not moved from the room. I didn't give the officer a chance to frame the words his accusing eyes warned me of. I spoke first.

"You'll frisk me, Beagan." I nodded. "This man sought me out for some purpose and was shot before he could explain. You'll see that my guns are fully loaded—and you know that I have a license to carry hardware."

It wasn't the time for sentiment. The boy was better off dead. I shrugged my shoulders as Beagan went over me. In case of accident there would be double insurance for the widow. After all, the youth's family had gotten the breaks. I mentioned the matter of looking after the insurance to the doctor who rose and pronounced the man dead. Funny, how solemn the doctor was. As for me, I knew the lad had been kicked over at the first jump. I've lived too close to death not to know the feel of it.

And I knew something else. McCleary wanted me killed. Why? Just one reason, and a flattering one. He somehow knew that Gregory Ford had spoken to me, and he thought that I had jumped at the chance to run him down. And what's more, he knew I didn't go into a game just for the money; that I kept going until I got my man. Now, had he fired the shot that killed the youth? Had he meant it for me? Was it to get me out of the way or to silence the would-be killer? It didn't matter. Much as I disliked private detective agencies it would be better for me to be paid to hunt down this feared McCleary than to simply go after him under the head of pleasure. It's business with me. I'm no amateur.

3

The Coming of Howard Quincy Travers

It was well along in the afternoon when I reached my office. There was no reason why I should get into trouble through that shooting. I'd gone along to the police station with Officer Beagan and given my version of the killing to the district attorney. Just the simple statement that I had met the youth at lunch; that he was in trouble, as all my clients are; that he had not told me anything, but was about to when he got shot. I know my stuff. I had wasted some time, but I didn't want the thing to pop up later. That I hadn't mentioned McCleary's name was not through any desire to protect that gentleman. But he had enough of a reputation in Florida without my advertising him in New York.

Besides, McCleary didn't know that I knew he sent the youth. He had either shot to silence the boy or to put me out of the running. He could only guess that the youth was about to open up. And he had shot in sudden impulse. He hadn't planned to do me in himself in the first place. It was only when his tool failed that he took a chance himself. But it didn't matter. There were two sides to the game now.

McCleary wanted to get me—and I wanted to get McCleary.

So I sat in the office nodding to myself as I decided to go into it. Perhaps Gregory Ford had not sailed yet. My hand was already on the telephone, the telephone number on my lips—when I set back the receiver and leaned slightly forward on my desk. The door knob of my inner private office was turning slowly. My hand slipped to my pocket. I smiled grimly. Was McCleary a fool? The catch snapped and the door opened. I half raised my head, and lowered it quickly. I had a visitor.

There he stood, framed in the doorway. Big and slightly stooped, he looked at me through heavy rimmed glasses which were parked to his vest by a thick black ribbon. Brown eyes looked vacantly at me out of a round blank face. Then he smiled. I stiffened slightly. I had thought I had a client. Now, it seemed as if I were about to be approached for the starving heathen in Africa. Benevolence just shone like the rising sun from his kindly, good-natured face. All but his eyes did their stuff, and they remained blank and inexpressive. Brown, I said. I didn't know exactly then; perhaps they were brown—a reddish-brown or even a grayish-brown. Damn it all—their very vacancy held me; their vacancy and lack of definite color—though they had a color.

His age—thirty-five, forty-five, or even fifty. You've seen the kind I mean—nothing definite in the age line.

"Mr. Williams—Mr. Race Williams." He coughed once and ran a thick hand with peculiar, long, delicate fingers across his generous mouth. Then he stepped into the room, laid his cane against the wall, and closed the door tightly behind him.

"It is with considerable pleasure," he spoke as he removed light yellow gloves, "that I meet you—you who stand without a peer in the tracking of the criminal." And he stressed the word "criminal," his thick lips closing tightly and the brown eyes—or whatever the devil color they were—taking on a distinctly reddish tinge. "It is indeed a pleasure. I must

14

grip your hand—I must indeed grip your hand, Mr. Williams."

And he did. I looked up at him as he pump-handled me. If we can believe that each man's life is stamped upon his face, then here was a lad who had spent his days helping old ladies across the street and opening tins of sardines to feed starving kittens.

"You are a busy man, Mr. Williams," he went on, not dropping my hand but placing it carefully back upon the long flat desk, as if he expected to have need of it again. "And I am— or have been—a man of leisure; a man whose time hung heavy on his hands, until— But life and hours and minutes— all time—is reckoned in dollars and cents. I am about to take some of your time. Here," he ran a hand inside his tightly buttoned coat, brought out a huge wallet and extracting from it three packages of new, crisp bills, laid them upon the desk, "I would interest you from the beginning, Mr. Williams. May I sit down?"

And he could. The bills still bore the bank labels, and if he had not slipped out a century note or two the three piles totaled twenty-five hundred dollars. Almost sadly I looked at the money. Pride—conceit—just the boyish itch to get even? Call it what you will, but my fingers closed tightly. Come what might, I was going to take a crack at McCleary. No lad could send out to have me killed and expect me to—

And I looked again at my benevolent visitor. As those generous lips slipped over strong white teeth I, too, fell into their mood, and smiled. Perhaps it was his personality; the contagiousness of that beaming face. Or perhaps again it was simply the three stacks of bills. But the point is—I smiled. Decidedly, I was interested. I had fleeting visions of that money taking wings and flying away. I wondered if after all McCleary couldn't wait. But, no—I knew he couldn't.

I wondered, too, what had brought such a man as this to my office. There was nothing of the fear and horror that is

15

generally found in the faces of my clients. The heavy-rimmed glasses were now beating a tattoo on the fat palm, held tightly in those peculiar, long slender fingers that looked so out of place on the fat hand.

"Your courage, Mr. Williams," the man was talking low and soft, with almost a musical note in his voice, "and your integrity are undisputed, and your reputation as a relentless, fearless hunter of men is even grudgingly admitted by the police. I am here to try all three of those virtues and pay well for them."

"You are in trouble?" I asked. And the surprise in my voice was real.

"Only the pricking conscience of one who has reaped but has not sown. I have ventured into charity, to find that I have spent a fortune in unworthy causes. I have built only temples to Mammon when I would have built temples to God. I have tried to be constructive—to build up. And now, Mr. Williams, after years of fruitless effort in constructive work, I have decided to be destructive—to tear down; not to encourage good, but to destroy evil—that good may rise of its own accord. I— Do you follow me?"

I looked at the bills and nodded. Then, growing bored at the leisurely way he ambled along with his story, I tried to jar him up a bit.

"What's on your chest?" I asked.

He didn't turn red; his eyebrows didn't rise in displeased surprise. His mouth simply widened—and he laughed, low and soft, like his voice. But his eyes remained the same—searching, yet vacant and unexpressive; childish—wondering, too.

"How quaint—how decidedly characteristic!" His round smiling face puffed. "But it was as I expected—and what I would have, Mr. Williams. Have you heard of the McCleary gang, of Florida—of McCleary?"

I jerked erect in my seat. Old Man Benevolence had scored first blood. And I thought of Gregory Ford—the dead youth in my arms—and the flash of orange-blue flame from between the curtains.

"I interest you, I see." And the lips flicked back and the white teeth flashed; and the eyes—well—they were just eyes, nothing more.

"Go on," I said. "You were speaking of McCleary."

And my visitor was talking, leaning over the desk—a crispness to his words, a new life to his quickly moving lips—but the same deadness to those eyes.

"It is perhaps a strange story. When I failed at charity, I spent much time about the prisons—trying to help the criminal, to study him—to get at the peculiar mental twist in man that makes for bad instead of good. And my study left me with the firm belief that criminals are made—not born. Not the product of environment, as many would have us believe—but the product of a stronger, a more determined character than their own. The unfortunate, the weak, and the bitter are dragged into the net of crime by shrewd grasping men—who plan, and profit on those they inveigle. They— Mr. Williams, do you believe in organized crime?"

"Decidedly!" I nodded quickly. And I thought of Gregory Ford and his words of the day before. "Go on—what of McCleary?"

But he raised his hand.

"You must let me proceed slowly and in my own way. We shall get to the point quickly enough. A rotten apple destroys many good apples—an evil man many good men. That is a page from the book of life. To my mind, McCleary is an evil genius. I would destroy him. I was about to give all the evidence I had gathered about him to the authorities—about him and a few others. Then I learned a startling fact. McCleary, Stinnes, Beekman, and the giant Swede, Olaf Sankin—all big criminals—all desperate, clever men, were but tools in the hands of one man; a genius, a devil, a shrewd calculating murderer who controls the great criminal organization that numbers hundreds—that terrorizes Florida and

17

now stretches forth its fingers of blood to the great city of New York itself. You understand me?"

And I didn't—exactly. Here was this somber, black figure; this soft-spoken, almost effeminate voice uttering the names of criminals—two at least of whom were known throughout the country.

McCleary I had heard of often. Beekman for years had been a suspected fence who ran a chain of pawn-shops in New York. Stinnes? His name was whispered among the underworld fraternity. And Olaf Sankin, the giant Swede, I had always taken as more or less of a myth. Any deed of violence which required great physical strength was laid at his door; most unsolved crimes of exceptional brutality were attributed to this giant of the underworld. I never fully believed in him. But McCleary—I believed in him all right!

"Where—" I smacked my lips as I tried vainly to read something in those vacant eyes. "Where do you fit into the picture, Mr.—?"

"Howard Quincy Travers." He tossed a card onto the desk. "Where do I fit into the picture? Let us say—just one who would help others. Just one who would defeat the purpose of these vultures who prey upon society. I have learned much in my innocent way; taken by all as a rather eccentric man who, as a philanthropist, has taken the fancy to study the life of the underworld; the world of fact—not fiction. And they do not suspect. I would break up this one great organization. I would slowly, carefully, and unsuspectedly take off these minor leaders one by one until I reached the head of organized crime."

"And me—?" I tapped the desk.

"You must act as my agent. I have selected you above the many well-known detectives of the great city—for your courage; for your daring; for the fact that you work alone; for the fact that no matter what—what misfortune overtook you, you would not divulge my connection. For the fact also, Mr. Williams, that you carry a gun—and are not afraid to use it."

"Ah—" I thought half aloud. "You would hire me then to kill these men—is that it?"

"Heaven forbid." His eyes closed, hiding any expression that was in them—if there was any expression. "I would order you expressly not to shoot, if I did not know that such an order might—indeed would, mean your death. It is the right of the State to take a life—not the right of an individual. But I would have you track each man down, and make each man pay his price to society—unless—"

"Unless what?" I leaned forward.

"Unless he will divulge to me the name of the leader—that man who is the directing genius that in time will form a trust; a crime trust that will rival in its wealth and power the great industrial institutions of our country."

4

I Join the Man Hunt

Again I asked:

"And where do you fit into the picture?"

"Let us say, Mr. Williams, that I have spent my time and my money, and now perhaps risk my life—that the world may profit. Let us say that I am a man who has reaped, and now would sow. And if you are not satisfied with that—" he watched my face carefully; just a steady glare in those— those—well—brown, red, yellow eyes, "let you think that perhaps I had a daughter—that after all it is just the bitterness of my soul. But let me think what I wish; that I have nothing but the interest of my fellow man at heart." His lips set rather tightly—rather sadly, too, I thought. When he spoke again his voice shook slightly.

"I am not capable of doing this thing alone, Mr. Williams. I have enough evidence now to convict McCleary. I even have my suspicions who the real leader is. But they are only suspicions. McCleary knows—he must tell, or face the electric chair. There are four chances. We must try McCleary first— not because he is the weakest, but because he is perhaps the most selfish. He—"

"Just what am I to do?" I wanted to get to the point.

"You must get McCleary alone. You must get him helpless. You must make him a prisoner. And then you must send for me. I shall confront him with such evidence that will convince him that his only hope is to talk—to tell me the name of the leader. Then I will give him time to leave the country."

"And—" I spread my hands apart, "McCleary is a desperate man, and desperate men sometimes—well—if one of us must die I would prefer it to be McCleary."

He hesitated a long moment.

"I would prefer it so, too, Mr. Williams. That is the reason I have come to you. Let us hope for life, but let us not fear death." He half bowed his head.

There was nothing of hate in his countenance; nothing of hardness in that smooth, soft, clean-shaven face. Yet, there was a twist to his lips—a determination or a bitterness or a secret sorrow. And I sort of cuddled to that half-hinted "daughter" business of his—though I put it down to some other attachment. But he was still talking.

"You must let me plan—and you act. I have money to pay you well. I have information that will guide you. This is not an idea formed in a few hours or a few weeks. I have thought—and now has come the time to act, to strike; carefully, but surely and relentlessly."

There was more, but why let him ramble on? His story was not built from imagination. He might have illusions—but not Gregory Ford. And with the thought of Gregory Ford came the thought that I had wanted to be in the game—that I wanted to get McCleary—and that, after all, our paths might be fated to cross in death. And if it was so to be, why not be paid for it?

"What am I to be paid for this work?" I asked finally, as I looked down at the three stacks of bills. "I am sorry, Mr. Travers, that I haven't got the good of the community at heart as you have—nor," I added significantly, "have I a daughter—or did I have a—"

"That," he said suddenly, "is for your thoughts alone—if

you wish to entertain such a thought. There is only the condition that, come what may, you do not mention my name; that, if you meet me any place you do not recognize me—unless I speak to you first. Let us say then—this twenty-five hundred to see you started—and all expenses, without regard to the amount. And," he stroked his chin a moment, "will you suggest a fee as each individual case is—is attended to?"

"Say—five thousand." I hazarded the amount. "And the completion of each case consists of—the man a prisoner for you to talk to—or—" I watched him closely.

"Dead." He bowed his head. "I don't like the word. But all that live must die. We may condemn the body, Mr. Williams, but we can pray for the soul." His head came erect, his chin set a bit squarely, and his lips tightened but his eyes remained the same. "You either do not appreciate the danger of your task or you do not flatter my generosity. Let us say, five thousand for the first case, and double that for each succeeding one, until the single one who directs murder and robbery and defamation for his own greed faces justice—or his God. When that time comes—when the leader stands at the bar of justice, or judgment, you may name your own figure. I am a wealthy man."

"That's a dangerous offer, Mr. Travers." I smiled.

"But, no." He shook his head. "If you take my all it will not matter. For I shall have no use for money then." And there was a sincerity in his voice, even if there was a smile on his lips. Oh, the thing was deeper than just a desire to help his fellow man. I was sure of that. Perhaps not a hatred, perhaps not a bitterness; yet, I felt that here was an angel of mercy, rather, an angel of vengeance. Certainly, he struck for a good purpose; and certainly, too, that purpose was not entirely an altruistic one.

Our hands clasped and I got a peculiar sensation from that shake. It was strange, hardly explainable. But his hand seemed moist and cold, while his fingers were dry and warm.

Something like holding fish in a paper that had split suddenly at the bottom.

There were instructions to be given me. There was a description of McCleary, which Old Benevolence Travers did well.

"You figure it almost a coincidence—my coming here today, Mr. Williams," he ran on. "But I feared you might take an offer from this Gregory Ford, through the State of Florida. It's open gossip that they have hired him and wanted you. It mightn't be a bad idea to help him at times. He'll think you're working independently, for the State. I'll see to that. It would establish your position, then, with this McCleary and the shadowy hand that guides him—also make my position safer and less subject to suspicion.

"So," he glanced at his watch, "you will take, this evening, a train to Jacksonville—and there board the steamship *Cherry* for Miami."

"But Gregory Ford is on that ship."

"Quite so." He nodded emphatically. "And there is also another on that ship—Jack McCleary."

He smiled once, with his lips alone—turned quickly and was gone.

5

The Green Bag

The southbound steamship *Cherry* had only a gentle roll to it. Not enough to be uncomfortable, but just enough to give the passengers a slight list to starboard as they paced the deck. Gregory Ford winked at me, pulled down his vest and scowled as he passed. All eloquent pantomime. The wink, that he recognized the reason for presence; the scowl, that he resented my working the game through some one else; and the jerk to his vest, that he'd come out on top anyway. He thought, as later events showed, that I had joined in with the officials of the State of Florida for a better price than he could offer.

Then I went to pacing the deck. Not so much for exercise as to give exercise to the one who was following me. For some one was getting my smoke. Crudely perhaps, yet insistently, footsteps beat in with mine. When I went to the rail and leaned over, the footsteps also went to the rail. When I looked along the rail, the owner of the footsteps looked out over the ocean. I got a laugh out of that—death had not been hammering on my trail.

There was nothing of death in the face I spotted beneath the deck light. Everything of life—despite the shadows under the eyes; dark shadows that set off her beauty rather than detracted from it. My shadow was a "she" and a rather beautiful "she" at that. Just a slip of a girl, no bigger than a pint of whisky and not half so strong or so deadly—and I looked down at her hand and wondered about the deadly part.

The green handbag that she clutched tightly was oddly in contrast with the low cut of her red evening gown, the dainty slippers, and the suggestion of bare shoulders beneath her wrap. She had a carriage and a form that— But we won't drag in the sex interest. This was entirely a business trip.

I looked along the deck. She was alone. There was no dark hallway behind her, no darkened portholes for a lad to lean out of and practice shooting. The girl looked suddenly toward me. We sized each other up for a minute. There was no pretense now. I waited until she smiled—then I did my stuff. I slid along the rail toward her. The first word in a conflict is almost as good as the first blow in a prize fight.

"What's on your chest, sister?" I chirped. And my hand shot out and rested on her bag.

She drew up—slightly indignant, I thought. Then she laughed.

"It's better so." Her shoulders shook. "I'd like to speak with you a minute." Her head turned from side to side. She hesitated a long moment before she spoke again.

"You're looking for McCleary, Race Williams. I would like to talk to you about him."

And you got to admit that knocked out the sex appeal. I nodded. She bit her lip, opened her mouth, and closed it. A man came slowly down the deck. A cigar flashed for a moment in the darkness, then popped into the light. It was Gregory Ford. The girl paled slightly and spoke quickly.

"Follow me to my cabin. I have something to tell you." She half ducked her head into her coat, and seeing that Gregory Ford was upon us she turned suddenly and slipped along the deck. I paced a few steps behind her. We turned into a companionway. Once I looked back over my shoulder—Gregory

Ford's cigar was puffing like a furnace. But he didn't follow us. He stroked his chin and jerked at his cap. By the time he thought it over, we'd be gone.

The girl moved quickly but occasionally glanced back. There was a nervous indecision to her lips; a frightened, animal-like fear to her eyes and a hesitancy to her whole body each time she paused to see if I followed. Then she jarred forward again. She wouldn't give me a chance to question her. In a way, then, she must have been glad that Gregory Ford interrupted our little tête-à-tête. Such an interruption might have been planned, to a certain extent anyway, with the girl expecting some one to walk along the deck.

I followed her down the companionway—a sharp turn to the right—and a blind alley. McCleary was on the ship. Was I being led into a trap? But I only shrugged my shoulders. If the girl led me to McCleary I would be satisfied.

She paused finally—before the door at the end of the corridor—pushed it gently open and motioned for me to enter.

"Inside," she whispered, in a high-pitched voice. "I want to talk to you." And when I hesitated, "It'll be worth your while, I promise you—and I promise you that nothing will happen to you."

"All right, sister." I smiled. "Ladies first."

She hesitated only the fraction of a second, then stepped into the cabin.

"Now the light, little one," I suggested. Almost at once she flashed it on. I could see the entire room, except for that portion of it that was behind the door. And I saw that there were no curtains—not a place for a man to hide, but behind that open door.

To say that the idea of a trap never entered my head would be ridiculous. For an assassin to park himself behind a door to crash his victim is the leading requisite of the gentleman thug, in the underworld's Book of Etiquette. It was crude, of course—hardly what one would associate with a criminal such as McCleary. But then, it's just as bad to overestimate your man as to underestimate him.

"Hurry—come inside." The girl called softly as I still hesitated.

I placed a hand on the door and found that it was back as far as it could go, so there was no chance to bang a foot against it and knock over any anxious lad behind it. But the girl wanted me in that room for some purpose—and I wanted to know what that purpose was. And she wanted me to hurry. But I don't think she expected me to move quite as fast as I did.

I just jumped into that room. But I'll give the man credit for being quick. The heavy door swished through the air, brushing my sleeve—then it crashed closed and the lock clicked. I stood staring into the mouth of a heavy nickel-plated revolver. The man behind the door was on the job—when the door missed me, he was ready.

"You're cornered now, Race Williams—ya dirty rat." He cursed. "One move, one shout—and I'll drill ya, if the whole crew are on me for it." And that last crack was comforting. He didn't intend to shoot unless I got mussy.

I smiled pleasantly at him.

"I'm so susceptible to the feminine charm," I told him. "However, my friend, if you'll just lower your eyes a bit you'll see that my artillery is tickling your stomach."

He lowered his eyes quickly, and to add emphasis to his vision I playfully thrust the gun tighter against his breadbasket. Of course I had the gun in my hand when I made the leap.

I got a good look at his face now. There was no doubt that the man was McCleary. But Old Benevolence Travers' description didn't do him justice. He wasn't exactly what you'd call a handsome lad, but his build and his carriage were good. His lips were broad and thick, his nose flat, and his eyes narrow. There was little doubt of McCleary's breed; as he wiped the back of his hand across his mouth I got his

27

number. Just a killer—an underworld type that had risen above his fellows by his own physical ability. Not just brute strength perhaps, but the brute courage and the brute conscience and thoughts. A cruel, ruthless type that would sweep aside those who stood in his way.

I thought, too, that Old Benevolence Travers was right. Here was a lad who'd squeal—not through fear, but through greed.

"Well—" I said, "do you drop that gun or do we find out what you had for lunch?" I dug my gun the deeper into his feed-bag.

But McCleary was not to be taken off his guard.

"I have only ta press my trigger." He jerked his head forward so that his thick lips were close to my face. "And then—"

"Double or quits." I shrugged. "At best you'll be an awful mess."

Maybe it was a ticklish moment, but really not much cause for alarm. I sized up McCleary as one who stuck to the old proverb, "It's better to give than to receive." He'd think some before he'd press that trigger and bury a bit of lead in my head. No—decidedly, McCleary was one who wouldn't hesitate to put a bullet in a man's back—but to face a man; well— I didn't think there was much danger.

I stiffened suddenly. I had forgotten the girl, or most of all I had forgotten the little green bag she carried in her hand. She didn't have to speak. She didn't have to go into detail, and I didn't need the sudden glint in McCleary's eyes to tell me the truth. When a gun is pounded against my back I know the feel of it without any explanation.

"You may lower your gun, Race Williams." And the girl's voice trembled. "No harm is intended you."

"Yeh—drop it!" McCleary shot in, licking thick dry lips. "She's a good kid—she'll plug ya at a word from me."

I gave McCleary one good grinning.

"The situation hasn't changed any," I told him. "I'd just as soon have two bullets in me than one. We can't die but once,

28

you know. Your little lady friend can put her cannon back in the bag or— Come!" I said sharply. "If you want three shots and two bodies—why, tighten your finger a bit." And my gun shot forward.

"No—no," the girl cried hoarsely. "He only wants to talk to you."

"That's right." McCleary nodded vigorously. "I only had a cannon ready in case you didn't see fit to listen." He forestalled the question on my lips.

"And the rope in the lower bunk, there?" I jerked my head toward the end of the thick rope that peeped from under the pillow.

He switched nervously from one foot to the other.

"I wanted ta make sure you—you'd listen." And then in sudden alarm, "They're goin' ta make a pinch at Miami, aren't they?"

And that was news to me. I didn't think Gregory Ford had the evidence—only the suspicion.

"Maybe." I nodded.

"I was a fool to take the boat. I've been led blind." He gulped.

"How's the law in Florida, Mac?" I got familiar. "Do they jerk 'em, or roast 'em?"

"None a that stuff, Williams." He put those narrow eyes on me. "I don't need three guesses as ta why you're on this ship. I've watched ya—and that wax dick, Ford. You're workin' together? What's the racket? Why don't ya make the pinch?" And when I remained silent:

"I'm no rat what breaks down 'cause a couple of hyenas hit my trail. You've got me spotted but you haven't any evidence—nothin' that'll stand up in a court of law. That's it, ain't it? The bulls have been guessin' on me for some time— but guesses don't burn lads. Leastwise, they don't burn lads with money. You drag me in and I'll walk out in two days. There's fall money and a good mouthpiece. I've got friends in Florida. There, I'm givin' it to ya straight."

"Well—if you're safe, why tell me about it? I know what a high class guy you are."

"It's just a warning." He twisted his mouth. "Ya ain't goin' to be in New York. In Florida, you won't walk no back alleys, with a harnessed bull on every corner. I want to warn ya off. I want to know if you're paid ta knock me over. You nor Gregory Ford, nor the whole State of Florida can't ride me—Jack McCleary. Not with the friends I got."

"Not with THE friend, anyway," I said pointedly.

"No—" he said. "You can't."

"All right." I swung slowly around, half backing toward the cabin door. "No tricks, sister." I spoke to the girl. "Drop that gun and walk around where I can see you, or I'll put a hole in your boy friend. My wrist's getting tired."

"That's right—" and the girl's voice shook. "You wanted to talk," she spoke over my shoulder. "Don't go yet, Mr. Williams." And she was around front, her hands empty but for the green bag—and its contents.

"If you want to speak to me further, McCleary, make it snappy. Maybe I haven't anything on you. Maybe I haven't any wife and child, and an insurance policy that will double in case of accident. Maybe—"

His eyes bulged, his gun wavered, his finger strained upon the trigger—my gun jarred against his stomach and my own finger tightened. It was sure death—for both of us, I thought. But it was the girl who broke the tension.

"Don't—don't shoot," she shrieked. "You wanted him here. I brought him. You have the same chance now that—"

He rocked on his toes, dropped his gun slightly—then shot his words through the side of his mouth at the girl.

"Get the hell out a here," he snarled.

From the corner of one eye I saw the girl waver for a moment, and I saw, too, that her fingers were working involuntarily about the catch of the bag. Twice I distinctly heard it snap; then she turned suddenly. There was a draft of air, and the door slammed.

6

Gregory Ford Horns In

I made no attempt to reach up and grasp McCleary's gun hand. It couldn't have been done. I don't think I was ever nearer death than at that moment when his finger tightened upon the trigger. No, I was never nearer death, and neither was McCleary. It was the girl's voice that saved the situation—the danger was over now, if I watched my man carefully.

"Want to talk?" he said suddenly, his lips slipping back over yellow teeth. "We won't get far this way."

"Park your gun," I said—and seeing the uselessness of that suggestion, "We'll park them together."

"I won't be taken alive," he said.

"You won't," I agreed. "Start your gat down—you've got further to go."

"It ain't fair." He hesitated. "You draw quick." Then in sudden determination, "We'll talk as set. Keep your voice low—that dame's got long ears. Now—what did ya mean by that crack? What—?"

I didn't give him a chance to finish.

"I mean this, Mr. Jack McCleary—that your game is up." And I laid hard eyes on him. "I know that you were at that hotel yesterday—I saw you behind the curtains. I saw you murder the boy. And he whispered a name before he died—your name." And seeing the whiteness of his face and the terror in his eyes I made my lie a better one.

"You can't scare off the jury there—they'll get a conviction, and—"

"Gregory Ford—you told him, too?" And his tongue was constantly at his lips now.

"No—I'm working independent. You want to talk to me, McCleary, and I want to talk to you."

"If you knew so much, why wait—why not—?"

"Make a pinch," I cut in. "Not me—you're small fry, McCleary. I want the name of the big gun behind you, and I'm playing you off against him. You know who he is. Give me his name and you can go free. You can't lie to me. You can't get away. You're right about Florida, maybe—they only have suspicions. But I've got facts. Besides," I warmed up to the subject, taking it from McCleary's point of view, "your big friend's days are numbered. And when the show-down comes I'll bet he won't help you any. Also, Stinnes, or Olaf Sankin, or even Beekman may talk. I'm in on the show—the one who outs with your leader's name first, gets the free ticket. It's a cinch, McCleary—the authorities will forget all about you when they get the Big Boy's moniker."

It was with a sudden jerk that he shot out the words.

"I'd like ta think it over to-night." And then, suspicion gleaming in his eyes, "I'll do it, if you wait until we dock. I want to be sure of a get-away."

"All right." I backed toward the door. "We'll take a taxi together when we land. Don't disappoint me—don't try to double-cross me. You're making mud pies on the edge of an open grave. There's some more evidence I've got, that would stand up even in the State of Florida."

"What's that?" he gulped.

"Tell you in the taxi." I swung open the door, and both our guns dropped.

"No one but you knows it—about that hotel killin'—no one else?" His chin shot forward, his narrow eyes were two straight lines.

"No one but me—no one else." I nodded.

"No one else." His whispered voice echoed my words—and there was an ominous ring to them.

Had I done right—should I have forced McCleary's hand right there in the cabin and have carried the name of the leader straight to Old Benevolence Travers? No—for it was Travers' show, not mine. He had his suspicions, I didn't. He'd know if McCleary lied, I wouldn't. Besides, orders were orders—and the pay was big. I was paid to put McCleary in a position to talk to Travers, or—and I stroked my chin. Back to me came the whispered words of McCleary. "No one else."

I didn't pay any attention to the girl who crouched close to the cabin. She was through with me and I was through with her. I went whistling down the corridor as if I hadn't seen her. Then I stopped dead and swung about. Was this girl in the gang, or was she just McCleary's woman? Despite the gun in my back I couldn't put her down as simply a gun-toting moll. And McCleary, too. He had been anything but anxious for the girl to hear our conversation. But that seemed natural—except McCleary hadn't seemed to care until I made that crack about the boy that was shot. Now—I hesitated, and looked back at the cabin.

The hallway was deserted—all stateroom lights but that single one were out. Only darkness came over the transoms. The soft strum of the music, mixed with the throb of the engine, came up to me from the ballroom below. The stateroom door opened, the light flashed, and the girl passed within. The door closed but it did not click.

Could the girl have listened to our conversation? I thought not, but I wondered just the same. I retraced my steps softly, and reaching the door leaned close to it. The girl's voice was very calm—nothing to show emotion or anger but for a sharp, rasping occasional break in it. And it was these breaks that came to me clearly.

"You killed him. I have no proof but your word that you were on the boat. You could have made it. If you did, McCleary—I'll tell all I know, come what may."

"There, there, Tina." I heard McCleary's voice distinctly. "You get wrong thoughts." And then in a hissing sort of note—"I couldn't—but if I did, you're too deep in it now—for yourself—not him—not the dead one."

"And he died like that—to murder a man for money—his life snapped out. Don't deny it." And I could picture the accusing finger. "Jack McCleary, if you did this thing I'm going to give you up."

"You can't." Heavy feet beat across thick carpet. "The silence you kept for him must be kept for others. There's your family. I've watched and learned just as much about you as the Big Gun himself. Tina Sears, your name may be to others. But to me it's Tina—"

I straightened suddenly and lost the name. A huge, shadowy figure stood at the end of the companionway. A black cigar did tricks in a generous pan—and I cursed inwardly. Gregory Ford, MASTER DETECTIVE, was on the job.

Did Ford know that McCleary was on that boat? Wouldn't he suspect something if he saw me listening at doorways? I wanted to beat him to the catch of McCleary. If that fuss went on inside the stateroom, Gregory would be in on the show. I coughed a couple of times, banged my elbow lightly against the door, and sauntering down the companionway met Gregory.

"Hello," I said, good-naturedly. "Don't you think it's bad policy to be seen together? This 'Me and My Shadow' business of yours is rather suggestive." And I hummed the tune of the song loudly.

"Some one's going to stick a pin through one of them key-holes and put your eye out." Gregory Ford laughed. "I oughta put the cuffs on you for a 'peepin' Tom.' What's—" And he jerked back into the main corridor, pulling me with him.

Footsteps beat quickly—there was a sob, a bent head and small delicate shoulders. The girl known as Tina Sears passed, and casting but one quick, frightened look at us hurried toward the deck.

"Now, that's downright small of you, Race." Gregory pinched my arm. But I didn't laugh with him. I wondered if the girl would tell McCleary of seeing Ford and me together. A nice story that, after what I told him.

"Do you know?" Gregory Ford stroked his chin as I led him away. "That girl—well—I think, if I keep her in sight I'll find Jack McCleary. Decidedly, Race, you're flirting with death, and incidentally with McCleary's woman."

I swung on him sharply—then I laughed. Why should I champion the girl? Perhaps the girl would lead Gregory Ford to McCleary, but that she was McCleary's woman—I doubted. It had come to me suddenly that she was—well—the widow of the boy who had died in my arms.

I let Gregory Ford take me to his cabin, and I was listening to what he had to say.

Ford took himself and his work seriously, even if he did go in for the black mustache, the heavy scowl and the big black cigar.

"Is he on this boat?" he asked.

"Who?"

"Don't come that 'who' stuff on me." His cigar made a race course out of his face. "You know why I'm here and I know why you're here. You pulled down a larger chunk of change working direct for the State of Florida. I'm beginning to think McCleary's on this boat. It may be a coincidence—me being on with him—but not you."

"Where do I fit in? Why tell me?"

"Why not?" he demanded. "Ain't we both in the same game? I'm paid a regular salary, and you—you're probably working on a flat rate for a corpse."

"What do you mean?" I got a little hot. "I'm no murderer."

"I know, I know." He waved a big paw. "But you just natural-like take the bit in your teeth when you go after a man. This boy, McCleary, is a killer. There's enough suspicions and circumstances to fry him a hundred times over. But there's no evidence yet. I'll get that as soon as I hit the State of Florida. This McCleary's only a cog in the wheel—a mighty dangerous one, but a cog just the same. But McCleary's bad. When the State hired you they knew one of you'd be kicked over. Oh, they don't put it that way—but it saves money. Besides, it's the law. We're both sent out to get a man or a body. There's more in it for me with a man—convictions come high. But what I want is to knock a squeal out of this McCleary. I want the name of the man behind him—behind this band of criminals who are terrorizing Florida."

"If he's on the ship, why not make a pinch?" I asked.

He scratched his head.

"They'd bail him out and squelch his activities. I want to scare him into a squeal. He's the weakest link, I think."

I nodded at that. We were both working for the same result.

"How do you know I'm working for the State?"

"Gregory Ford Knows Everything." He flicked an ash from his vest and jerked his thumbs into the armholes. "If McCleary's on this ship I ain't aiming to let him leave it—evidence or no evidence. We do things different up New York way. I'll make him talk. But they say he'll never be taken alive. Stick close, Race—you may get your corpse when I lay my mit on McCleary."

I was more than slightly alarmed when I left Gregory Ford. For all his bluster and bluff he was a first class operative. And I couldn't blame him so much for watching me. He didn't

36

doubt for a minute that I was after McCleary and the leader of this gang. It would have been childish to try and convince him that I was on the ship for another purpose. And then I got to wondering something else. Would Gregory Ford mess up my chances of getting a squeal out of McCleary by following me about so closely?

7

The Warning

It was I who found the girl this time. On the wind-swept upper deck in the shadow of a lifeboat. And she wasn't the same cocksure little dame. She was crying softly. We were alone—the snooping Gregory Ford was not on my trail. This girl had just been accusing Jack McCleary of killing some one. Was it the youth in the hotel? I thought so. And who was she? Well, one gets information from an angry and wronged woman! "You ain't done right by our Nell" should be going strong. I stuck a mit on the girl's shoulder.

She jerked to her feet so suddenly that her head crashed against the lifeboat. She reeled slightly and tumbled onto my chest. I'm not exactly a Lothario, you understand, but I held her the best I could. If it was a plant it was a good one—but before that little head had snuggled against my manly chest I had jerked the green bag from her hand. Maybe the thing was real, maybe she was slightly stunned, maybe she thought it was just a petting party when I half pawed over her for the mate to that gat which the weight told me was still in the bag. But she wasn't sporting any more hardware that I could feel.

"Why the water-works, Kid?" I straightened her up and parked her against the boat. And then getting confidential and perhaps taking advantage of her banged head and uncontrolled sobs, "Why not give the boy friend the air. Work in with me. Why—"

And her head shot up—soft, wet eyes looked into mine; small white hands sought my shoulders and rested on them. There was nothing of badness in that face; nothing of that sinister beauty that is so often found in the underworld type. Yet—she had stuck a gun in my back and—

She spoke.

"What did you mean, below, when you said to McCleary, 'I haven't any wife and child, and an insurance policy that will double in case of accident.' What did you mean?"

And when I didn't answer:

"Tell me the truth. He's really dead, isn't he? You didn't kill him, as you might have. He was sent to his death. You held him in your arms when he died." And the fingers closed and my coat tightened.

"He's dead all right," I said, almost brutally, with the hope that it might jar some hysterical information out of the girl. "Just before he took a chestful of lead, he mentioned a name. He was looking over my shoulder, Kid. There was horror and loathing and deadly terror in his eyes. He tried to scream but he couldn't—and he whispered the name of your little playmate—Jack McCleary."

"No, no." Two hands shot before her face. "He swore he didn't. He couldn't have—or he wouldn't have made the boat."

"It was close to two." I tried to show her that McCleary could have made the boat. "A car behind the hotel, and a quick dash to the deck. Think, Kid—couldn't he have made it?"

"No, no, no—" She gasped the words over and over, while her head nodded "yes." Then with a sudden upward jerk of her head, and burning eyes that flashed into mine:

"Don't trust McCleary. I don't fully understand, but there's to be a taxi at Miami—and somehow you—" She looked frantically about the deck. "He'll kill me—as he intends to kill you."

"Don't you worry, sister." I patted her shoulder. "Cleverer boys than McCleary have had the laudable desire. You don't think he'll come across with the name of the leader behind him and—"

"That—that man." She fairly gasped the words, and her head went around as if it were on a pivot. "McCleary will try to kill you, and if he fails— He's shrewd, but he's selfish and greedy—and fears death. If you can outwit him, why—"

"Want to help me—if I help you?" I said, when she didn't speak.

"You can't help me." And the look in her eyes was one of hopeless resignation, mixed with fear. "I envy you your strength and your courage, and your will to kill."

"Why did you lead me to McCleary? You wanted to see me trapped?"

"No—it was entirely selfish. I wanted to save myself and those—I love. I'm afraid. If anything happened on the boat, nothing could save me. If you made a truce with McCleary— why—I might be let slip away—I might hide." And then in sudden impulse, as her fingers gripped the lapels of my coat, "The Hidden Hand, that guides McCleary, has ordered your death."

"You know this leader—this man behind McCleary and—"

"I only know him as the Hidden Hand. Only the fear of death would make McCleary betray him. I think he mistrusts McCleary. I think McCleary knows that, and might— But he would murder you without hesitation to save himself."

"The boy that died in the hotel—he was your husband?" I asked.

Her head came up; her lips framed words that she did not utter. She clapped a hand across her mouth and smothered a screech. I half turned as her hand shot out and clutched at the bag. There was a snap of the strap, and she was gone—running across the deck, the green bag in her hand. Well—she needed it. As for me, I stood peering into the darkness. Had I seen the misty whiteness of a face—a face with thick lips and narrow eyes? But when I pushed between the lifeboats, the deck was empty. That hunched shoulders had disappeared down the steps, forward, seemed certain. Was it the boy friend, McCleary, or my little shadow—Gregory Ford?

The next couple of hours McCleary and the girl kept out of the picture. But twice I had seen Gregory Ford. Was he going to follow me around like a good-natured Saint Bernard? Finally he slipped from the smoking room and sought his cabin. I hung about the deck until his light went out. He had decided to call it a day, I guess.

It was twelve when I hit my stateroom. One quick glance was enough to tell me that no one was hidden there. It wasn't what you'd call an ideal location—unless one contemplated a bit of murder. It was too close to the engine room for comfort. Perhaps not enough to complain of, but decidedly the throb of the engine would deaden to a minimum any sound of a shot—that is, a single shot would be lost in the night.

Altogether, I was rather well pleased with myself. McCleary had proved himself the proud possessor of a generous streak of yellow. He was willing to sell out. Or was he? Was it just a truce, to give him a chance to knock me over? McCleary knew that I held his secret. The girl had told me that he intended to trap me in a taxi at Miami. There was a laugh in that. But suppose the girl was simply a decoy—and led me to believe that McCleary would not attempt to get me until after we had docked! Was it to lull my suspicions? There came back to me McCleary's final words, "No one else." If I died, McCleary was safe, he reasoned. And if I wasn't suspicious, what better place was there for a murder than right on the ship. He'd get off, somehow, in the morning—before the murder was discovered; or—well—he might have the pleasant thought of slipping me to the fish.

I got a little hot. The idea of a little killing had been all McCleary's way. Now—was it my turn? I looked over the situation.

There were just two ways to get into my cabin—the door and the window. The transom above the door wouldn't admit a body, the window would. It was a real window, with a wooden shutter that ran up and down. It opened on the main deck—I nodded grimly. I was supposed to sleep tight, and then McCleary would come to the cabin and do his stuff.

I locked the window and ran down the curtain. I undressed, too, for shadows tell their story. Then I put out the light, pulled up the shutter, opened the transom for air, and left the window locked. It was too cold to have the window open anyway. Too dangerous, too. But the room was dark, the night clear. I could see out the window, while no one could see in.

I hesitated about how to lock that stateroom. There was a bolt on the door as well as a lock that worked with a key. And I decided to just turn the key and leave it in the door. Then— any one wishing to enter could insert long slender nippers, grasp the barrel of the key and snap back the lock. I was holding open house—and I didn't want my expected visitor to have too much trouble. A lad who's planning a bit of murder has enough to contend with without my making the work harder for him. We'll just say that McCleary was welcome. If he intended to knock me over, I wanted to know it.

In the dark, I dressed again—all but my coat and vest. Put it down to modesty if you wish.

So much for that. I had set the stage—now I sized up my berth. I'd have to lie backward in it. Then I could face the window and the transom. I swung the pillow around, stretched out with my guns—one in each hand—and waited.

8

Creeping Death

One hour—two—passed. No chills ran up and down my spine. There was little of a thrill about the thing. That had worn off years before. A man had sent some one to kill me; a man had perhaps tried to kill me; a man had arranged to trap me here on the boat, with the girl as a decoy. Now—I stretched out comfortably and waited. Was that man, Jack McCleary, deserving of and needing one good killing, coming to murder me? Maybe I'd have to kill him—maybe I wouldn't. But if I did, I was already planning my story for the Captain of the ship; the court of law—and wondering if there was any way of horning Gregory Ford in on the show. His agency had a nation-wide reputation, he had the backing of the State—his shoulders were broad enough to carry this killing. And—

The first card was dealt in the game. At my window a blurred whiteness hovered for a minute before the glass. Maybe it was one of those flying fish we hear about, in the Florida waters. But I had more than a sneaking suspicion that the white blur was a face. Fine! I clutched my guns the tighter—and the face was gone. I don't know if

I saw it after that. If I did, it was more distant and indistinct—maybe just the wavering of the clouds, or—

I sat the straighter in my bunk. The knob of the door had turned—hardly a noticeable click, maybe—partly lost in the throb of the engine—but I knew that it had turned just the same. After my first jar erect I pulled the sheet over me and fell back slightly. Surely this bird might, or would, take a look-see over the transom before he entered the room. Maybe he'd just shove down an electric flash and fire, without coming in. But that was his party—not mine. Anything he decided was all right by me.

I lay still and watched the transom above the door. The face that would appear there would be discernible even in the semi-darkness—maybe not enough to recognize it in the dimness of the corridor light at that time of the morning, but discernible enough to pick out a nice spot to shoot at, if the occasion warranted it.

Again I cast a look toward the window. And again I thought that I saw the white face—distant, like the clouds. I wondered if one watched by the window while another entered by the door. But any way it suited McCleary suited me—I'm not particular.

Silence in the hall without! The knob of the door did not turn again, or if it did, it turned in tune with the throb of the engine and made no sound. But no face appeared at the open transom. There came a hand—a hairy wrist—an arm; and I strangled the impulse to put a bullet through that arm. Those fingers opened and something flashed for a moment in the dim light above the transom, then was lost in the darkness of the cabin. But I heard it strike the wall, back of my berth just above my feet and where my head should have been. I sucked in my breath.

There was a tinkle of metal—or was it metal? Didn't it seem more like falling glass? And the hairy arm again—thick, searching, groping fingers—a sudden jar—and the transom was slammed shut. Now, what was that for? Certainly—and I

44

drew in another deep breath. A sweet, peculiar sort of breath—a breath that made me suck quickly again—once more. And then I breathed no more.

I didn't want to breathe. I couldn't breathe. I didn't dare breathe. And my eyes were burning like my throat—a dry heat set into my head, parched my lips and coated my tongue. I put up a hand—a hand that was meant for my face and didn't reach it. Chloroform—gas—ether—something deadly. And I knew the truth!

I knew what had come over the transom; a package—a can—a glass jar—a tube—some damnable thing of—of death. I wasn't dizzy. I wasn't wheedle-headed. I was like a man in a dream—a horrible nightmare. The thing gripped at my body, tightened upon my muscles, brought a sudden sweat through the heat. There was no pain—no sense of something gripping and clutching at my throat, like there had been at first—just a dull listless feeling—a tired, worn-out sort of indifference—but above all, the nightmare grip. Keen senses—a fairly good vision, if a blurred and distant one, and the lack of power to control the movements of my limbs—no coördination between mind and body—no response of the muscles to the sharp quick orders of the brain. Some place in my body the nerve energy had stopped—and I knew what the dead youth had meant when he spoke of the "Gas Man."

My left hand lay upon the sheet where it had dropped from my face. My right hand still clutched a gun—a gun that it could not lift. A finger encircled a trigger—a trigger which it could not press. And through it all was no special fear—just an indifference, yet a knowledge of what had happened, and a terrible straining effort to hold my breath.

It was all clear enough, but distant—like looking through the wrong end of a telescope. And he came—the door opened—broad shoulders—the hairy arm—and a hand with a flash of steel in it. My eyes bulged, popped wide, and the sweat poured down my forehead. There was a sense of fear— a sense of horror that I don't think I ever experienced before.

It was new to me—yet it couldn't be true—for the man who opened the door and was advancing from that great distance upon me, had—had no head.

I tried to close my eyes to shut out the thing that stood in the doorway. I had been poisoned, gassed, chloroformed—but was I going mad? I couldn't even shut my eyes—then came a breath of air from the open door. Like ice it felt, across my hot face—and I think I breathed it in, choked with it, too—coughed, maybe, but I'm not certain. The door closed again, shutting out the apparition—or at least the clearness of it in the distance. Now, just a blurred something, it came toward me. It passed the light from the transom and I saw it again—the headless thing. And I knew.

There was no white face and no hairy head—but there was a head. The man wore a gas mask. Somehow, that gave me relief, and, somehow, my mind cleared—but my body was paralyzed. Still that soft, sweet-smelling death engulfed me. God! how I longed for the door to open again—for another breath that might—that would break the grip upon my muscles. For there I lay with my hand upon a gun, and powerless to use it. Just one more suck of air and—

The man was close to the berth now but at the wrong end of it. I could see the thing in his hand—see it flash up, and knew that it was of steel. Silent death, then, this was to be—with a knife. McCleary had beaten me—and I was tempted to open my mouth and swallow in the sweet, paralyzing stuff, and sleep; go out without knowing it. Not from fear, you understand—not from the horror of watching myself die, as if from another world—but from a certain sense of shame that I had let myself be taken in like this.

Gas man! Gas man! Gas man! I repeated the words over and over to myself. They helped me hold my breath—the thing that was almost driving me to bursting. I wondered if a man ever did burst—and I thought that I might, for I'd die before ever I sucked in any more of that deadly sweetness—and I'd die, too, if I did suck it in. And—

A hand was on my foot. I saw the whiteness of it rather than felt it. The man was feeling for my face, as I should have been lying the other way in the bunk. Slowly the hand ran up my leg, paused at the knee and held it a moment. He turned then—eyes glared at me through misty windows. Eyes that bent forward; eyes that through the gas mask saw the whiteness of my face.

Slowly that hand crept up the length of my body. It seemed a long distance and a great while, though it couldn't have been more than a few seconds. Still I held my breath. A hand was on my face now, and the knife was raised. What a way to go out! Frantically I tried to raise that gun—just an inch—just a fraction of an inch—not at all. If my fingers could only move—if one finger could only close upon the trigger!

The knife started down—and stopped. The man was careful—a thorough man. A light flashed for a moment—shone full upon my face and into my eyes, yet they did not blink—just stared and stared at the light and the raised hand, and the knife in it—the knife that had started slowly down again, like a slow-motion moving picture.

There was a crash—the breaking of glass. And the knife held, the weird face turned to the window. I, too, was looking toward that window, and saw the white blur fade from the glass—the glass—but there was no glass. There was a rush of cold, crisp air from the sea—my mouth opened and my lungs sucked it in.

The figure hesitated between the window and me. Then turned again, raised the knife—and I lifted my gun and pressed the trigger. A stab of yellow, a roar that sounded above the throb of the engine, a falling thing in the moonlight, the thud of a body—and quiet and blackness. Then again, the throb of the engine, the swish of the sea—and I sat up on the edge of the berth, the gun dangling in my hand, a yawn on my lips and my eyes fastened on the window. This time when the face came I knew it was a woman's face—then it was gone, and I heard the beating of feet across the deck.

In a dazed way I knew that the window had been crashed in—that the girl had done it, and had saved my life. Peculiar that—and the door burst open and I swung around, half raising my gun. Gregory Ford rushed into the room. He was talking.

"I was keeping an eye on your cabin and I saw the girl by your window. Then—I heard the glass crash and the single shot. You're all right, Race?" and there was real concern in his voice. "I've come in time?" And stepping forward he tumbled over the body. "Good God! What's this—and what's the damn smell?"

In a moment the door was closed and the lights were on. Gregory Ford jerked the gas mask off the lad on the floor. There was a hole where one of his eyes had been. But I knew him. It was Jack McCleary.

"No polish to your work." Ford rolled the man over on his back. "Think this is McCleary? But he's dead enough." He flopped back one of his arms. Then he looked at me suspiciously. "Well—there's your corpse. I ain't even in on the picnic."

"You can have him," I said wearily. And then warming to my idea I leaned toward Gregory Ford and gave him what was on my chest. "You take the blame and you can have the glory. You see, there's others—and I don't want them to know I'm on the lot."

"You're generous with your stiffs." He eyed me a moment. "But I'll take him. No squawking afterwards—understand. I've got a pretty free hand with the State. I won't have to explain much—if he's the right bird." He compared the face on the floor with a worn picture he took from his pocket. "That's him—that's McCleary." He nodded.

I didn't listen to Gregory Ford's story of the killing that he'd feed the Captain and the authorities. Certainly, it wouldn't be noised about the boat. As for the glory—the very doubtful glory—well, he could have it. It didn't interest me. I wanted to sleep—take it any way you looked at it, I got five thousand. McCleary was dead and—damn it all—I'd of been a mess if some one hadn't crashed in that window. The girl had saved my life. But why? She had tried to take it—trapped me. But then she hadn't known or suspected that McCleary had killed the youth. Yep—it looked like that boy who died in my arms was her husband.

I just staggered down the hall to Gregory Ford's room, found the door open and flopped onto the bunk. I needed sleep—and when I thought of my closeness to death, I hit the hay with an easy conscience. I don't think any one would put up a squawk that Jack McCleary didn't need doing in. But who was the man behind him—the Big Gun—this directing genius who terrorized all Florida and whom the girl had called "The Hidden Hand"?

9

A Surprise Visit

In a dazed way, after my closeness to death, I sat upon the edge of the bunk in Gregory Ford's stateroom, rubbing my eyes. A small lamp, that I distinctly remembered putting out, was burning. I blinked again—then shot my hand beneath the pillow and jerked out my gun. Plainly, before me, were the stooped shoulders of a man. He was bending over the little desk, writing. It was not Gregory Ford.

The man finished his writing, laid down his pen, blotted something upon the desk, and swung slowly around—facing me. My grin was rather a silly one. I was looking into blank, expressionless and colorless eyes. The man at the desk was Old Benevolence Travers himself. The last time I had seen him was in my office in New York.

"What—how did you get on this boat?" I gasped.

"Sit there—collect yourself—rest." He shoved me easily back in the berth. "I was on the train with you to Jacksonville; I boarded the boat with you there. Since then I have kept to my stateroom. I thought perhaps you might corner McCleary and I could talk with him—get him to confess, for his own freedom, the name and whereabouts of this man—this leader."

"McCleary," I said slowly, "is dead."

"Quite so." His head nodded. "It is too bad. But we must console ourselves with the thought that there is one less murderer alive, to prey upon his fellow men. I do not blame you. You could not have acted otherwise. But where we condemn the body we must pray for the soul."

He bowed his head and his lips moved. Then, stretching out a hand, he gripped mine—and I felt again the warm, slender fingers and the cold, damp, fishlike palm.

"You must tell me about it," he said. And when I had finished with the account of McCleary's death and how Gregory Ford, the international detective, was taking the blame and the credit for the killing, Old Benevolence nodded in satisfaction.

"It is good. Continue to use Gregory Ford. You say he suspects you are working for the state of Florida. Encourage him in this belief. At the end we must turn this leader over to him. But—we must forget McCleary. If things go well I should know the name of this leader to-night."

"To-night!" I jarred erect.

"To-night." He echoed my word. "McCleary will be identified as soon as the boat docks. The papers will carry his death across the front pages. Gregory Ford may get the credit there—but this leader will know the truth. There will be panic in the camp of the enemy, and a meeting perhaps—to wipe out the menace that confronts them."

"And this menace?" I asked.

"You," he said simply.

Flattered? Maybe. But I just stroked my chin. Before I got through I intended to prove a menace.

"If you know of this meeting—know the leader will be there—why not tell the police, Gregory Ford; raid the place and make a complete catch?"

He raised his hand.

"Not so fast, my friend. We are dealing with shrewd, as well as vicious men." He ran the names off on those slender

51

fingers. "McCleary was simply a non-thinking, strong-armed gunman, as is Olaf Sankin, the giant Swede. But Stinnes is shrewd—and Beekman, a cunning dangerous man, while back of them all is the brain and power of the leader. To notify the police might be to warn these men, for I firmly believe that their safety so far rests upon a leak in the police department. The leader we may not catch to-night. But Stinnes, we must. I must talk to him. He goes in constant fear and, I believe, will tell me the name of the leader if cornered and aware of the secret I hold. For my speaking out what I know, the electric chair would claim him. For the name of the leader, I shall help him leave the country."

"You would do that? You would break the law?" All along this was hard to understand. His somber attire, his kindly benevolent face, his soft, almost effeminate voice were all strangely at odds with his words—his purpose.

"Too bad I didn't get McCleary alive." I stretched. "I think he was the kind to talk."

"Let us hope for better things next time." He suddenly slipped a check into my hand. "There is your promised pay. I would be an angel of mercy rather than an angel of vengeance. But I must go. Gregory Ford may be here any moment. I would not have him suspect my interest. He is a brighter man than you give him credit for being. The game of life and death must proceed rapidly from now on." He leaned forward, his mouth close to my ear. "Stinnes is here in Miami. The police suspect him. Gregory Ford more than suspects him. That is perhaps why I followed you onto the boat. Stinnes is close to arrest. He has made an error. A well-known jeweler recognized him as the man who visited his shop just before a robbery—and a murder. You understand, then, how important it is to reach Stinnes before the police. If he confesses the name of this leader to them, this leader will know—be warned and escape."

"You're pretty well up on things, Mr. Travers." I followed him into the narrow companionway. "This leader, now—he's called by this fantastic title—The Hidden Hand. And the girl—what of her?"

"There are women as well as men, Race Williams. And they are to be trusted no more than men. Watch this girl—stay close to this girl—for she will lead you to Stinnes. They will wreak their vengeance on her if they know the truth."

"And Stinnes—how am I to find him, and this—"

"Stinnes will find you." He smiled. "Here—you will find me at the Coloseum Hotel when you have him prisoner. Send for me and—" He stopped, listened a moment, and swinging suddenly down a companionway, was lost to view. Heavy feet were beating down the main corridor—feet that paused and turned. I backed into the stateroom.

And I saw the figure; the scowling brow; the heavy black cigar. It was Gregory Ford.

"Things are jake now." Gregory Ford jerked his head up and down as he swung into the cabin. "You've got nothing to explain. I did the talking and the police will handle the matter when we dock. God! man—you're a sight; turn in. I got a description of the other one."

"Other one?"

"Yep—the other one. It'll surprise you, I bet. But we all have our weaknesses, Race. Got to do some 'code stuff' now." He lifted a little black book out of a bag.

"What other one?" I caught him by the arm.

He dug a finger into my side.

"The weeping female, Race. I've got a hunch she's McCleary's woman. We'll spot her when she leaves the boat." And he was gone.

10

The Empty Limousine

I didn't think much then. I locked the door and slept. It was close to nine o'clock when I awoke and jumped from the berth. That "other one" bothered me. And that "other one" had saved my life. Whether because McCleary had killed her man made no difference. She had saved my life. Running back over the years, I couldn't find that that same distinction belonged to any other person. If I explained the situation to Gregory—but I shook my head.

When the boat docked, Gregory Ford was on the job. There he stood at the head of the gang plank, lazily watching the people pass off. I was in time then—the girl hadn't come. Or had he already arrested her and was watching for some one else? Was it possible that my benevolent client had delved so deeply into crime and the activities of these particular criminals that his presence on the boat was known—perhaps, suspected—or—? I stretched my neck and saw him coming. The black coat, the well-creased black trousers, and the somber tie which did not even lend the semblance of color to his person. A steward carried his bag, his cane hung over one arm, and his black fedora hat was pulled well forward on his forehead.

He reached Gregory Ford; almost brushed his arm—then

he passed, and Gregory Ford still studied the passengers. I was nearer now, and there could be no doubt that the one he sought was not a man. It was the women—the young women—whom Gregory Ford scrutinized so intently.

And I saw her. Tina Sears was just ahead of me in the crowd. She carried no suitcase—just the same small green bag that had held the gun, and still held it, I suppose. I shrugged my shoulders. She had made her own bed, let her lie in it. And with that thought came another. I had made my own bed, too, but the girl had not let me lie in it—lie in it to be stabbed to death.

I slipped quickly from the crowd, along the lower deck and under a rope directly behind Gregory Ford. There was too much noise for him to hear me; too much excitement and men slipping about for him to bother—and besides, his eyes never left the crowd. His elbows on the rail, his hands on his underslung chin, and the cigar slipping back and forth. There was no way to tell if she saw him. She must pass close to him, so that he had only to stretch an arm out over the rail. And my heart jumped slightly. That would be Gregory's way. Nothing polished or silent about his work. When he made a pinch, the whole world could be in on it.

The girl reached him apparently unaware of his presence. Her face was pale but her eyes looked straight ahead, and her chin was half buried in the collar of her coat.

I breathed a sigh of relief, and then stepped forward. Gregory Ford moved for the first time—his chin shot out of his hands, his cigar clashed skyward against his broad nose, and his hand came from the rail.

"You put that hand back on the rail." My voice was low and guttural, with a curse in it—and the hard object which he felt against his spine jarred his underslung chin back to where it belonged. "One move, Bozo, and I'll blow hell out of you." My voice was still disguised.

I give Gregory Ford credit for knowing his stuff. His hand clapped back to the rail, the cigar fell forward on a level with his face, and his shoulders hunched slightly. My eyes followed his as the girl reached the dock, crossed into the shadows and was lost to view.

"Don't take it so hard, Gregory," I said in my own voice.

He swung on me, his mouth open—his eyes ablaze.

"Strike a pose, Gregory." I grinned at him. "That girl is going to help us find the Big Boy behind the show. You're a good guy, Gregory; did me a good turn last night. The girl saved my life. When the times comes for a show-down I'll deal you in."

So I faded from the picture. Gregory Ford didn't follow me. He just stayed there, scowling.

I hurried down the gangplank, seeking the girl who had preceded me. Hurry and bustle—kissing and hugging—moving trunks and scattered boxes. Through it all I made my way directly to the exit.

Tooting horns and dashing cabs and porters grabbing at my bag. But no sign of the girl. I shrugged my shoulders and set my bag down. Well—I'd let her go. And there was a laugh in that. As if I had anything to say in the matter.

A hand rested upon my arm—a black, leather-gloved hand. I looked up the brown sleeve to the smart brown coat and peaked cap; then I took in the leather leggings and the man as a whole. A rather spiffy looking chauffeur altogether.

"You were looking for a young lady," he said. "And she is waiting for you. This way, please." Leaning down, the uniformed chauffeur picked up my bag.

The street was crowded; two cops were untangling the traffic less than ten yards away. A trap? Maybe. Then again, maybe not. But traps are interesting studies. I just shrugged my shoulders and followed the classy bus driver.

He led me around to a more quiet street—and by that I don't mean a deserted one. Just a street where there was an opportunity to park a car or a truck—mostly trucks, they were. But one car stood out—a low, rakish limousine where the driver sits in the cold and don't contaminate the air of the mighty.

I smiled good-humoredly as the chauffeur swung open the door and stood aside for me to enter. Perhaps it was just the trained servant. Perhaps there was no sinister purpose in his getting the back of my head toward him. But I had a picture of being cracked from behind and shoved into the car. I never gave my suspicions away. I motioned him to slip my bag in first. If there was any little cracking from behind to be done I'd 'tend to that. The man simply nodded his head and leaned in with my bag.

"The gentleman's bag, Miss," I heard him say—then he jarred suddenly back, turned and faced me. "She's gone— she's not there—she's—" he gulped once and blew up. There was nothing of the actor in this man's makeup. The expression on his face was of fear as his darting eyes ran up and down the sidewalk that was packed with boxes.

Heavy boxes were being tossed about; trucks were backing to the curb; men were shouting to one another. No, it wasn't exactly the place for a bit of kidnaping; yet—

And I thought that I saw her, half a block away. At least I saw a woman, and she was hanging to the arm of a man—or his arm was thrust through hers. Her feet were moving listlessly with his. Was it the girl? If it was Tina Sears, then she was going willingly with the man who clutched at her arm.

The woman turned her head. There was a half block between—moving boxes—hurrying men; but I saw her face, and I knew her. And I read the appeal in her eyes—a hopeless sort of appeal, mixed perhaps with a touch of horror. She didn't cry out. She didn't even beckon or signal me in any way. Just that hopeless, terrible haunted look in her eyes.

"Take your car, turn it around and follow me—and keep the motor running," I called to the chauffeur. I didn't have any set plan; I didn't trust the chauffeur exactly—but his trembling hands and shaking knees and white face all stamped him as the frightened servant who knew too much.

The man with the girl didn't see me hurry along after him. But another did. A well-dressed stranger suddenly appeared from between high boxes and sauntered into the middle of the sidewalk, directly in my path. That he intended to block my passage was certain. How he'd go about it I didn't know. How far he was willing to go I didn't know. It would be easy for him to start a brawl and attract the burly longshoremen from the trucks. Three minutes might be lost; two, or even one, might be too long. Far down, near the corner, I could see a high-powered touring car and a man who stood beside it, looking anxiously up the street.

The big stranger stopped directly in front of me and started talking loud enough for several men to hear.

"So you were with my wife last night at—" he started with a scowl—and that was as far as he got. It was all old stuff to me; good stuff, too, I daresay. A common street brawl; the interference of the men about; an explanation in the police court and a couple of dollars fine for disturbing the peace. Yep—great stuff, as he planned it. But he was working on the wrong lad when he picked me. I busted right in as I came close to him. And my words were hardly above a whisper, but loud enough to be heard by him.

"I'm Race Williams." My eyes met his, my hand jerked up from inside my jacket pocket, and the hidden nose of a gun covered him. "Can the chatter, swing quickly and walk straight down the street—or drop now, with a bullet in your chest. Come! Quick! I don't play with firearms."

He hesitated a split second as his eyes flashed from my face to my pocket. Then his lower lip flopped slightly, words died on his tongue, and he turned sharply and hurried down the street in the wake of the man and the girl.

A lucky break for me? A chance bluff that was put over? No! I wasn't bluffing. I had business beyond that man. If there was any luck it was all his way. He knew me—knew my name—knew what it stood for. I'd of shot or crashed him if he had hesitated even the rest of that split second.

The man with Tina Sears saw the act over his shoulder. He shot a furtive glance toward the distant touring car, realized the uselessness of trying to make it, and jerking the girl suddenly to the left disappeared in an alleyway.

The man who had blocked my path grew panicky, or planned to help his friend, or— But he made the mistake of suddenly breaking into a run and following the man and the girl into the alley. Softly my rubber-soled shoes beat on his heels—just a few yards it was, and I hit the alleyway right behind him.

There was a little door to the side—a door that was closing—a door that the running man was trying to force further ajar and push his body through. He was talking, too.

"It's me, Oscar—I—"

And that finished his conversation. The alleyway was deserted—I just stretched out my right hand, swung it once through the air, and let the barrel of my gun crash down beneath his slouch hat—close behind his ear.

He was an obliging lad—and the fellow within helped, too. For he opened the door slightly and let his friend crash to the floor, blocking the door from closing.

11

Oscar Stinnes

There was a curse from within that room, the muffled cry of a woman, and scraping of feet across wood. That was my cue. I stepped over the prostrate form and squeezed my way within. The other man was at the rear of the large room—his shoulders against curtained doors. The girl was close to him, held by both his arms as he half led, half dragged her to those doors.

"Just a minute, friend." And the gun in my right hand I suddenly shifted to my left. For the room I was in was an office of some sort and faced directly on the street—and what's more, there was a large window running the whole front of the place; a somewhat dirty window, to be sure, but easily enough seen through by any one who took enough interest to look. Occasional figures passed before it—and two men loaded a truck that was backed against the curb.

The man hesitated, saw the gun, caught the movement of my hand, and dropped the girl into a chair. His shoulders twitched. The rough stuff was over. He was going to try diplomacy or bluff, or perhaps both.

"You struck that—that man." He indicated with a jerk of

his thumb the recumbent figure who lay in the doorway. And then looking from me to the girl, "I understand—you thought that he annoyed her. And you are quite correct. She—Miss Sears here is my friend. Won't you sit down?"

"Certainly." I played his game and flopped into a chair which gave me three views. The window, the door I had just entered, and the double doors with the curtains.

"We thank you—Miss Sears and I." He stood before me, both hands at his sides. "She has had some trouble and I helped her—you, too, now—I hope, for the lady's sake, you are not the sort of man who wishes an explanation."

"No," I said abruptly, and then I hesitated. Here was no pawn in the game. I knew from the man's voice—the lack of nervousness in it; the strong dominant chin and steady eyes, that I was facing one of the principals in the cast. Such men as this are rare, in crime, and quickly jump to the top.

Out of the corner of my eye I noted the gilt letters across the window, and as the man went to the water cooler and drew a glass of water for the heavily breathing girl I spelt out these letters and the name that was backwards to me. My lips set hard and I gripped my gun a bit tighter. The name on the window was OSCAR STINNES. I looked at the man again and wondered, as he turned.

"I am afraid," he said in slow even tones, "that our presence here will attract unfavorable notice from passers-by—a notoriety, perhaps, that Miss Sears does not seek. I thank you again, and if you will leave your card—Miss Sears, or one of her immediate family, will give themselves the honor of calling upon you and thanking you in person, I'm sure."

"And you?" I asked.

"I am simply a friend of Miss Sears." He half bowed. Then stepping toward the door, "Now—you will leave, if—" he smiled as he glanced down at the silent form that was hidden from the window, "if you have fully recovered from your—exertions."

I came to my feet and smiled across at him.

"I'm ready—any time Miss Sears is ready."

"Miss Sears—" He pondered a moment as he stroked his chin. "Miss Sears will be staying here for a while."

"I think not." I was just a bit abrupt. "She has an engagement with me." I crossed to the girl.

"Miss Sears," easily, almost gracefully, he, too, walked toward the girl, "is not up to keeping any engagement just now. Under the circumstances I feel sure you will excuse her." His clear green eyes swung from me to the girl.

"The gentleman misunderstands the situation, Tina." He spoke very slowly and distinctly. "No doubt he misunderstands my attitude and interest in you as well. You wish to stay here and have me take you home later—that is it? That is it?" He fairly snapped out the final three words.

"That—is it." The girl echoed his words and her eyes avoided mine—dropping quickly from the man's to the floor.

"Miss Sears," it was rather difficult getting myself between the man and the girl and at the same time keeping an eye on the man, "you come with me. I have things to talk over with you. Come!" I did a bit of the snappy voice and steely eyes stuff myself as I held out an arm.

The girl half rose in her chair and dropped back almost at once.

"No—no," she cried. "I must stay here. I—I wish to stay here—with Mr. Stinnes."

Stinnes! I swung now and gave him the up and down again. Certainly the girl wished to go with me and did not dare. What did this man hold over her? What did this whole rotten criminal society hold over the girl? First, there was McCleary—now Stinnes—and as I looked toward the window the two men who had been loading the truck sauntered toward it and stood looking in. Evil, sinister faces these. Strong-armed men—the cheap, lead-pipe type.

Once his name was mentioned, Stinnes' attitude changed

slightly. The soft, suave manner was there still. The smile, too—but a different sort of a smile, with a hard curve to the lips and a coldness to the eyes when he spoke.

"I am afraid, my friend, that I have misjudged you—and now must ask—even insist—that you leave this office."

"We will hear from Miss Sears again—" I began, but he cut in on me.

"Unfortunately Miss Sears has no say in the matter—she stays here."

Politeness was over. Diplomacy was over. His hands clenched at his sides and his chin shot out. Good enough! I gave him chin for chin and scowl for scowl. I knew who he was now—and I played my cards accordingly.

"Right!" I snapped out the word. "Miss Sears unfortunately has no say in the matter—and neither have you, Mr. Stinnes. Miss Sears goes with me." And this time I fairly jerked the girl to her feet. "If she's a sensible woman she goes quietly. If you're a sensible man you'll let her go quietly."

"No—no," the girl cried hoarsely—but just the same she clung to my arm. Stinnes took a step toward me—spotted the gun—thought better of it and swung toward the phone. Hand on the receiver, he stopped.

"Just what right have you—what right to force yourself in here and plan to take that girl out? Quick! before I call the police."

"I want to question her regarding the death of one Jack McCleary."

"You are a police officer, then—the girl is under arrest?" There was surprise, more than fear, in his voice and I wondered if he knew me.

"About her being under arrest—well—we'll see what she says first—what explanation she can give of her conduct on the ship."

"You have a warrant?" He was going to get legal, so I killed that.

"My name is Race Williams," I told him, and I suspected from his face that he knew that all along. "I'm working up a bit of evidence in Florida. If you want to drag the police in—go ahead. There's the phone! Use it!"

He hesitated a moment. "I think I will use it," he said slowly. And then, without another glance at me he lifted the receiver and I heard him say:

"Police headquarters, please."

Now, police headquarters was the last place that I wanted, and I thought, too, that it would be the last place that Stinnes wanted. But I was into the thing now. I'd have to see it through or bluff it out. I thought of Old Benevolence Travers' last crack about Stinnes and his fear.

"While you're talking to the police," I threw casually at him, "you might ask them about a certain jewelry robbery—and if they intend to consult you about who murdered—" And that was all of that.

The receiver crashed back on the hook, an ashen face turned toward me. The intelligent features were suddenly convulsed in anger, hate, or fear—it was hard to distinguish the emotions that shot across his face. But if I wanted action I was going to get it—get it sooner than I expected it.

"You dirty yellow spy." He fairly hissed the words as he came to his feet and rocked toward me, his hand shooting to his hip. But my raised gun checked him there. Stinnes faced death and he knew it. Just the single movement of his muscles stood between him and the grave. I cried out my warning as my gun jerked up.

You could almost see the will of the man overcoming the passion that shone so vividly on his face. Yes, my gun cowed Stinnes; at least, it made him hesitate and bring his hands slowly up to rest on the desk—empty. But my gun had served another purpose that was not such a good one. It had jarred those two evil faces away from the window. Not that I minded that, but it sent them flying into the alley. I heard their feet beating across wood.

"Get down on the floor behind that chair," I told the girl. Then louder, for Stinnes' benefit, "And stay there till they pull up the dead wagon. Now, Stinnes—if these men come in, you go first."

But those men didn't come in. There was calling and threats and hoarse curses from behind that partly open door. Then there was silence for some time, except for the scraping of feet and the restless movement of bodies behind the thick door, and whispered, hoarse, inarticulate words. So I did some whispering myself—just for Stinnes' benefit.

"Stinnes," I went a bit nearer him, "I want to talk to you alone. I want you to give me a half hour in private, and I'll make it worth your while—worth your life." I bent close to his ear, keeping my eye on the edge of the door, making sure I didn't get within the line of fire.

"About—about the—" he looked from me to the door, and to the girl.

"The jeweler—the murder—yes," I whispered.

"If I burn—if I burn," I barely caught his words, "I'll—but the girl—you'll—you'll lose her and—" His head turned to her. "Remember, Tina—here's your chance to make good."

There was a crash, a flash of light, and sudden blackness in that room—sudden blackness that was broken only by a soft dull streak of light that came through the partly open door.

The thing was sudden and surprising, of course, in broad daylight. It was a new racket on me—but I've been through so much that I don't get jarred into a panic, and I haven't any nerves. I dropped to my knees with the fading light. And I knew, too, just what had happened. A heavy steel curtain had crashed down before the broad window, and the sudden darkness—even if not complete—was blinding, after the Miami sunshine.

There was dead quiet for a moment—no whisper of voices now—not a movement from without the room—not a movement from within. And there was a creaking of a board behind me; a stealthy step and a hand on my arm.

"Come—" The voice of Tina whispered close to my ear. "Don't—don't stay—for—for my sake." There was a sob in her voice as I jerked her aside and back. But no shot greeted her whispered words—no voice called out a warning—nothing now but the sudden breathing of a lad who couldn't control his emotions a moment longer.

12

The Escape

I let the girl lead me from the room—knew that we passed through the curtained doors and that we were still in darkness. The passage was narrow and black, but the girl knew her way. I went with her—not trusting exactly—not suspicious either—just slipping along with my hand on the girl's wrist.

"I don't know—I don't know." Tina Sears clung to me suddenly. "Every exit will be watched. There—" I felt that she was pointing toward a streak of light that ran along the floor in the distance, "that door will be watched."

"How many will there be?" I asked. "And does it lead to a street?"

"To a street—yes." She echoed my words. "There will be one guard there—but—but don't—oh, don't try it."

"One—" I laughed away her fears. "Why, that'll be child's play. Come!"

"No—no," she said, over and over. But she came along with me just the same—her feet scraping, then sliding as she held back.

"Where's your nerve, Kid?" I encouraged her.

She had struck me as a sturdy little thing—used to this

racket and this life, and with not many nerves. The way of women may be to blow up when most of the danger is over— but not the way of such a woman as Tina Sears. She came from a world where death and blood and crime are part of life—or—I felt the warm little hand that clutched mine now—and I thought, too, of the big car and the classy chauffeur. Still—I shrugged—crime runs to big cars and classy chauffeurs to-day—such affluence is no longer the reward of virtue.

We were well down toward the streak of light as I half pulled the girl along, explaining to her how simple the thing was. I would be in the darkness—the man in the light. It wouldn't take but one crack, or—

And the door opened before us. A man stretched himself, looked out on the street and took a seat in the shadows, far back from the sidewalk.

"Don't!" the girl screamed as I slipped forward.

The man had his chance then but he didn't take advantage of it. He wasn't a quick thinker, I guess. The next instant it was too late. My hands shot out, fastened upon his throat— and he was jerked back into the darkness. Handy! Why, if I'd written him I was coming and to make things easy for me, he couldn't have been better prepared. Almost at his feet was a coil of rope.

"Silence is golden, me lad," I told him grimly, as I sunk a gun into his ribs. He smiled sickly and let me tie him up. I suppose it wasn't necessary to fix him tight, but I'm a thorough man in such things. When I got through with him he'd have difficulty in even wiggling his ears. Of course I had the bracelets with me—but they cost six dollars a pair, so why leave them behind?

Then I turned to the girl who was crouched in the corner.

"Come, Kid." I took her by the shoulder. "It's all easy sailing. Look! people are passing on the street—nothing can happen here. I'll go out first and take a slant around—then I'll call you. Just a quick look-see up and down the street."

"Don't—don't go." She leaned back against the wall, her hands over her face. "There's another way—safer—better, and—"

But I was gone. No other way could be safer. I had tipped my hand off to Stinnes. He knew enough to fear me now—thought that I knew enough to send him to the chair. If he was white, he'd bend every effort to kill me. If he was shrewd, he'd try to buy me off. If he was yellow, he'd try and sell the name of the leader for his own freedom. No—there wasn't any time to waste.

Just at the moment I approached the sidewalk the street was deserted. Figures might be lurking outside, their backs tight against the building. But I could step out quickly. In the open street they wouldn't have a chance.

Eyes straight ahead, I saw the ground floor of the building across the street. Then, as I drew nearer—the second floor, and still further—the third floor and the dirty windows, and—I half swung around. I thought I was being attacked from behind. Quick footsteps; heavy breathing; a cry and sigh, like that of a frightened animal. It was the girl.

She slipped under the arm I held out against the wall—passed before me, and, turning suddenly, threw herself into my arms. No—not into them, to be exact—but against my chest. As she hurled me back my eyes rested on that third floor across the street—on an open window and on a long metal cylinder that flashed in the brightness of the Florida sun.

I knew that the metal cylinder was a rifle—that the face behind it sighted it—and I knew, too, that a finger pressed the trigger, but I caught no report of a gun—just a dull whizzing sound of air, the tiniest whiff of smoke—and then the girl went limp, clutched me once, and slumped to the floor.

I didn't need to have a written explanation of just what had taken place. That exit was watched—watched from the third-story window across the street—and watched by a man who held a high-powered rifle with a silencer of some kind.

That it was a heavy rifle and carried a generous chunk of lead I knew from the distinct whir that came to me—and that must have come to others on the street.

I didn't give thought to the reason of it then. As the whir came again, and the tiny puff of smoke—I grabbed at the girl and jerked back into the shadows and out of the range of fire.

The sniper could have gotten me, I guess. It wasn't my quickness that saved my life when I clutched at the girl. It was the hesitancy of the man with the rifle. He was there to shoot down a man, not a woman—and the confusion of the sudden appearance of the girl jarred him a bit, I guess. For a second he wasn't sure just what had taken place. But he tried desperately enough to find out.

For almost on top of his first shot and the falling girl he jerked himself and his rifle close to the open window. Plainly, before that second shot, I saw his face—great matted hair, flat nose and unshaven chin. And I saw, too, the long scar; the vivid blotch of purple that stretched from his mouth almost to his ear.

I might have fired—might have gotten him, but both my hands were on the girl. And the man had lifted his rifle and fired again—fired standing in the window—fired without regard to those who might see him. He had seen me then as I reached for the girl; dragged her back and lifted her in my arms.

There was the thud of lead against wood, a splinter against my cheek and dust in my eyes. So much for that second shot; it was buried some place in the old wooden floor of the musty building. But that first shot! The girl lay a dead weight in my arms. No—she wasn't dead. She was breathing—softly, slowly, and in sharp jerks.

In the semi-darkness I looked down at her face—very white, very pale lips, and heavy lines of blackness beneath her eyes. Other lines, too—lines that were thin and hardly visible—lines that should not have been on that young face for many years yet.

And I saw the streak of blood—the wide, yet not deep wound across her neck. She wasn't badly hurt then—wasn't in need of immediate medical attention. As I hesitated there, between going out into the street or seeking another exit from the building, came the sharp blast of a whistle—the hoarse call of one man to another. And I knew—the police were on the job.

The street, then, was safe for me. But was it safe for the girl? Gregory Ford had wanted the girl before. More so now, when he learned where she was. That is—if he suspected Stinnes, which Old Benevolence Travers had thought more than possible.

The whistle came again—a blue uniform flashed by the long hallway, hesitated a moment, half peered into the darkness and dashed across the street.

"Don't let them get me. Not the police—not the police." The girl opened her eyes at the second shrill blast of the whistle, clapped two arms about my neck and cried out her appeal.

"All right—all right, sister," I told her. "It's your party— where to now—where—" And I hurried back through the darkness. She had done a flop again—a little head was against my shoulder; black bobbed hair brushed my cheek.

After all, I owed something to her. Certainly she had saved my life on the boat; certainly—well—if she had not saved it there in the alley entrance, she had come mighty close to it. And certainly—I got to thinking and trying to look at her face in the darkness. The stamp of evil wasn't there. The lips, unconscious, were slightly parted, but no curl to the corners of them. The tiny lines beginning to form from mouth to nose were of fear and doubt and uncertainty and worry, rather than the cruel hard lines of dissipation.

I pulled up, well back in the dark narrow corridor. There was a door to my right—not that I could see it exactly, but I could hear it and, more so, feel it. The draft of air, the slight creak of hinges as it swung. I hesitated beside it—half pushed

71

it with my foot and felt it give, and felt, too, the strong current of air that came through the opening. Should I go straight ahead or go down that side passage, or wait where I was in the darkness until the excitement on the street was over?

The hall was narrow and long. My position was a strategic one; the door beside me a retreat in case of necessity. Back in the dark hall was uncertainty and Stinnes—Oscar Stinnes, to give him his full moniker.

I decided to hold my ground. Just decided to, when I changed my mind—thrust a shoulder against the door, crashed it open and staggered into a dead blackness, the girl in my arms. For at the end of that long corridor, down which the girl and I had come, a door had opened—a light had flashed, and figures pushed through. Not figures that slunk silently along, but figures that dashed headlong toward the light—the light that came from the street.

They passed on the run, heavy feet pounding over the boards—rubber soles that beat one upon the other. Hoarse breathing—a low question or two, and an answering curse. I set the girl down against the door. I sure was doing a lot for this dame—but then, this girl was to lead me to Stinnes. Old Benevolence Travers had said so. That was the reason I stuck close to her; purely a business reason—and I knew that that was not the reason. She had done a lot for me; the others must suspect her—they were a bad gang. The girl had been the cause of McCleary's death. Did they know it? Did they suspect it? It would be worth her life if they knew. No—I was sticking to the Kid because—well—because the Kid had stuck to me when I needed her.

Tina Sears at my feet, I struck a match. If I had any nerves they'd be doing their stuff now. I had placed the girl down behind me and against the door. Not thinking as much of her perhaps as of the fact that the door couldn't be suddenly flung open and the pursuers trap me. But, if I'd have placed her in front of me I'd of laid her just about twenty-five feet farther down than I intended to—for there was a ten-foot square cut in the floor before us, and that ten-foot square dropped about twenty-five feet—then water. Plainly I heard the water lapping hungrily below us.

13

The Escape—Continued

The feet were pounding back now along the corridor, and I swung about and faced the door. Then I saw it—a second before I tossed the half-burned match away in the rippling water. Just beside me and flat against the damp plank wall was a ladder—a rusty iron affair. But it was perhaps a way of escape from the black dampness and the yawning hole in the floor behind me.

The girl stirred now, and spoke.

"We—you came through that side door?"

"Shs— Right!" I helped her to her feet and supported her as she swayed there. "There's a ladder leading above—men without in the hall. They'll think of this door and—can you climb it? Where does it lead to?"

She held my arm for support as she groped along the wall.

"There's a trapdoor above. Come—I can climb it—I think."

And she did. Pulled herself up rung after rung as I followed her, gripping at the rough rust-covered iron—thrusting up a hand to brace her every step—and wishing I was alone in this game. The old proverb was a good one: "He travels farthest who travels alone." You couldn't get away from that.

"It's locked—bolted." The misty whiteness of her face hung above me in the darkness. "I can't push it up. It never was bolted before. Last time I—" And she quit dead.

"Last time." I thought that over as I drew myself up higher and reached a hand for the trap. Last time! I thought again. So she had been this way before—knew the ins and outs of this old wharf or warehouse, or whatever the devil it was. And the trap gave—groaned. I saw a streak of light.

"Hang so, to the side," I told her. "And grip my arm; not that one—the one on the ladder. There—" I managed to slip up another rung, got a better brace and a shorter reach, and shoved that trap up. It was stuck, not bolted.

It wasn't used much. Musty, damp dirt pounded down in my face, but the trap gave. A minute later I was through and had dragged the girl up behind me. She was sitting on top of the closed trap, breathing heavily. The light from a tiny, glassless window, well up in the wall, shone upon her pale face, quivering lips and searching eyes—eyes that peculiarly enough avoided mine. Eyes that had seen the man with the rifle even before—yes—before the man with the rifle was in line of her vision. And I wondered. Did she know that he was there? Did she let me go—? But I put the question to her straight—suddenly—impulsively.

"Did you know that he was there?"

"Yes—"

I didn't have to explain to whom I referred. She knew, and her answer was no more than a gasp.

"It was a trap then, for me?"

"It was a trap then, for you." She echoed my words and her eyes now came from the floor and looked straight into mine. Brown they were and glistening—not misty exactly— too bright and with too much of a sparkle for that.

"How come?" I stroked my chin. Rather a farfetched trap; rather laid on coincidence and my actions. When she didn't answer, I got a gleam of light of my own. I'm a pretty slow thinker at times, but I don't need a brick wall to fall on my head to wise me up. So I thought aloud.

"When Stinnes said 'Remember, Tina—here's your chance to make good.' The plan was laid then?"

"Yes—then."

"And you knew the man was there—let me go—and didn't tell me. Then why at the last moment—but you did try to keep me from going that way. Why didn't you tell me?"

"Because I was a coward." Her voice wasn't listless now. "I was a selfish coward. I couldn't face the consequences of letting you go free and Stinnes—giving me up. I won't make excuses. I let you go—go to your death—because I was afraid for myself. Yes, I knew of that man with the rifle. He was there before, when I took Sergeant Murdock, of the police department, down that alleyway. I didn't know then. Murdock knew too much—knew about Stinnes and this other—" and her voice lowered. "This Hidden Hand. I thought Murdock was to be—to be let go. But I trapped him—and he was killed. If—if that ever comes out I'll be—held—yes, convicted of murder."

"But you saved me at the last minute—risked your life. Why?" I was close to her now; looking straight into her eyes; holding her arms.

"I don't know." She shook her head. "Something snapped within me. It wasn't reason—wasn't my will to do good. I deserve no credit. I—"

She stopped suddenly, listening. Then she grabbed me by the arm. Men were on the ladder below—feet scraped upon iron—a voice called:

"They're up there—it's bolted."

"Come—" The girl dragged at my wrist. I followed her through narrow corridors; open rooms, twists and turns and walls packed high with boxes.

"We're safe now—there ahead—stairs and an exit, and—" Her head went up sharply—a foot hung in the air and went to the floor softly. We listened together.

There was an open door just ahead of us—and stairs

below—and the tread of feet, and voices. Quickly I crossed the floor, slammed shut that door and turned the big key in the lock. Footsteps were on the stairs—a man's head was even visible as the hinges creaked.

"It's the police," I cried over my shoulder. "Now—" And I turned. The girl was gone.

I looked about the room, spotted the door we came through, saw that it was closed and ran toward it—jerked at the knob as the key turned on the other side.

A laugh greeted my quick question. But it was not a mocking laugh, nor a vicious one—more, a hysterical gurgle in the throat. And the girl spoke from behind the locked door.

"The police are your friends. I can escape, if I have a few minutes. Do that—for me." Light, running footsteps, away from that door—heavy pounding feet at the other door. Feet that kicked against the wood—loud voices that demanded entrance—other feet that beat across wood beneath. Bodies pounded and strained against the heavy wood.

The wood was stanch but the lock was not so good. I faced the door as it burst open. Stood my ground and smiled as the flashing guns and blue-coated figures stumbled in.

"If you move a muscle—" The voice stopped; a face thrust forward; a cigar hung limp, and dropped to the floor. A great hand shoved a brown hat back over a moist forehead, and Gregory Ford pushed his way to the front.

"What the hell kind of a game is this—and what are you doing here?" he demanded.

I simply grinned at him.

"Look here, Race," Gregory somehow got another cigar from his pocket and pointed it at me, "there's been attempted murder in this building—there's been—" His mouth closed like a trap as he turned to the uniformed men behind him. "Here—get out of here—search the entire building. No pull, now—no political friends—no influence, behind this show. You boys get Oscar Stinnes and bring him to me—no guesswork this time. No excuses either. I want him for murder."

When the men had left, Gregory pounded a fat finger against my chest. "Are we at it again? Me after a man—you after a body?"

"I hope not," I said.

"I did you a good turn on the ship, Race." He let the cigar wander indifferently about his face as he eyed me reproachfully.

"And I you." I nodded.

He walked across the room and tried the door through which the girl had departed.

"The dame was here." He turned on me. "You're alone now. Four feet ran over the boards above me—one pair of those of a woman. I'm not a fool. You had her and you let her go—false sentiment, that." He shook his head. "She's close in the thing. Do you know where Stinnes is?"

"No more than you," I told him. "We're working the same racket. You go your way and I'll go mine—until the end. We both want the Big Boy behind the show, Gregory. When I get him—I'll deal you in."

He shook his head as I followed him to the window.

"I saw the district attorney, Race," he flung at me over his shoulder. "Just a minute or two, on the dock. We have the stuff on Stinnes this time—he may squeal when we drag him in. I don't think he suspected—but now—" And half knitting his brows, "The district attorney didn't know anything about your working for the State. But you can't fool me—I—" And again the bluster. "Gregory Ford knows everything."

I turned to the window to hide my smile—glanced out over the Bay of Biscayne and the sparkling sunlight. The glare hurt my eyes at first, then I saw the winding Causeway to Miami Beach and a glittering greenish hint of the Atlantic Ocean beyond. And I saw something else too—distant, flickering—like an old, worn moving picture film.

There was a small building close to the docks, and across the street from where I watched three men and a car. The door of the little building opened. I couldn't be sure at that

78

distance—but I was sure enough. A figure staggered from that doorway; a small, light, girlish figure that was thrust out onto the street.

Just that single glimpse, and she was swallowed up by the three men who crowded about her. Like the vision in a dream; the jostling men as they moved toward the car, and the hint of a struggling figure in the center of the men. And it was over. A racing engine came distantly to me, and the car sped away. But I knew the truth. Tina Sears was in the hands of the enemy.

"I'm going." I turned suddenly to Gregory Ford.

He tried to stop me; wanted to talk—then let it go at that. But he followed me down the stairs, across the floor beneath, through the long corridor and out onto the street.

"What's the next move—what's on your chest? You can't work this thing out alone, Race. Let's get—"

"I'll work it out alone." I nodded vigorously. "It's Stinnes or me—and very soon." And I left him. My thoughts were of the girl.

I walked quickly down the narrow back street for a pace— reached Flagler Street and turned toward the Biscayne boulevard, and spotted the several large hotels that front on that street. The Coloseum, where Howard Quincy Travers—alias, to me, Old Benevolence Travers—had hung his hat, wouldn't do. I didn't think he'd fancy my stopping there—he was willing to spend his money to make monkeys out of this gang but he wasn't anxious to have this gang make monkeys out of him. Fair enough, that. I was being paid to take chances.

I picked out a good hotel with a fancy front, and did myself a room and a bath overlooking the bay. And what's more, I wrote my name on the register as clear as print. RACE WILLIAMS stood out—no alias for me this time. The boys, in general, and Stinnes, in particular, knew that I was in Miami. Now, if they wanted to see me—they could know where I stopped.

14

The Cry of a Woman

It was toward eight o'clock when the phone in my room rang. It was a visitor who sought me most earnestly. I told the clerk to send him up, slipped a gun from a hip to a jacket pocket, and stood ready by the door. Here was a message from Stinnes—a threat about the girl, if I didn't withdraw. Perhaps, an effort to trap me and—it wasn't.

The spiffy chauffeur of that morning stood trembling in the doorway. I let him in—took my bag, which he carried—led him to a seat, and after closing the door gave him a drink. He needed it. I didn't. I only drink for pleasure. This was business.

"It's Miss Tina, sir," he stammered after a bit. "She's gone—some one—something dreadful's got her. It's that HAND she feared. And I—I dare not tell any one."

"But you can tell me." I stood before him. "I'm her friend. Now, tell me."

"But what, sir—what can I tell you? I don't know anything."

"Come—come!" I shook him rather roughly. "You know something. You traced me here and—"

"It's a man, sir—a longish fellow with the queerest eyes

and—them fingers; they just pawed at me, sir—and—"

"Yes, and he gave you a message—come, quick."

He fumbled and shook, but finally got it out. A crumpled bit of paper. I read the scribbled note quickly.

The Hollow—South West 8th Street, beyond Coral Gables. S and the girl. Quick!

And I knew whom the note was from. Old Benevolence Travers had sent it. He didn't dare be seen with me. I was watched then. But somehow he knew where the girl was and where Stinnes was. I read the paper again—burned it in the ash tray and laid a kindly hand on the chauffeur's shoulder. Not much of an ally in a dangerous game—but I needed a car and needed some one to trust.

"Miss Tina—is in danger—grave danger." I looked steadily at him. "Do you know of a place called THE HOLLOW?"

"Yes—a roadhouse—notorious—but it's closed now—after the boom."

"You will drive me there to-night," I cut in. "You'll be brave now—do it for Miss Tina—Miss Tina's life. You won't be afraid—Archibald?"

"Richmond is my name, sir." He corrected me very seriously. "I'll do what you say for Miss Tina, sir—but I'm afraid—terribly afraid."

"That's all right, Richmond. A man who faces something he's afraid of—is a very brave man."

"And you, sir—do you understand? They dragged her away—they nearly killed her once, when she went after her poor—poor—" He stopped, and I helped him out.

"Her husband, Richmond. Eh?"

"Husband, sir! Gawd, sir! She married? I never—"

But there wasn't any time to question Richmond. He was in a nervous tremor already, and I didn't help him any when I jerked a gun from my bag and placed it in his hand. He held it from him as if he expected it to snap down on his fingers like a mouse trap—then he thrust it in his pocket. Yet, Rich-

81

mond would serve my purpose. I wanted a car to find Stinnes—and I wanted a car and a driver ready for a get-away. If I left Richmond in a dark spot he'd be too scared to leave before I came back.

It was just about nine o'clock when we left my room and pulled from the hotel. The Biscayne boulevard is a series of three streets separated by grassy, palm-covered safety zones. In the middle of the three driveways was an empty taxi—in fact, there were several taxis, but I'm thinking of one taxi in particular. Two men hurried to it, climbed in, and rolled along in our tracks.

I didn't wise Richmond up to our shadows until we had crossed the bridge and shot onto the Timiami Trail, which is the fancy title hung on South West 8th Street. I didn't want to put anything else on Richmond's mind in the traffic. He was muddled enough.

Richmond looked back and spotted the pursuing taxi.

"We can lose them easily, sir," he said as he stepped on the gas.

"But I'm not sure that we want to lose them, Richmond." I thought aloud. "I'm afraid, my boy, you're going to face sudden death to-night—and like it. If these lads behind us miss us they may suspect our destination and go to warn the enemy. Pick a side road—a lane—anything, and turn down it. Here—this one will do the trick."

Richmond jerked over the wheel, shot his foot to the brake, and we pounded into a little side lane. I leaned forward and snapped out the lights as we came to a stop. Then I climbed from the car and waited.

There was the roar of a motor, the squeak of brakes, the flash of lights, and the scrape of skidding tires. Plainly through the trees I could see the lights of the car and knew that it was turning around. Slowly it came back along the broad highway. The brakes squeaked again, and the lights went out.

The moon was fairly bright. I slipped along the pines, back

toward the main road. Two figures climbed from the car and stepped into the end of the little lane. One man was talking.

"It's a dead-end street, started in the boom. They'll have to back out. We'll wait here."

"Right," the second whispered. "It's him—Williams, all right. Thought to slip us. You don't suppose he's goin' to—" A pair of guns flashed for a moment in the moonlight—then I spoke my piece.

"Both hands up, gentlemen—drop the guns and HANDS HIGH. So you would—" I fired as one man turned, saw me, and half raised his arm.

I didn't shoot to kill. Just a bullet in his leg, that was all. But he made enough fuss as he rolled about in the sandy road. He didn't seem to be thankful he was alive. It wasn't my big heart that made me play for his leg. When I shot, I wasn't sure of him—he might have been one of Gregory Ford's boys. And he wasn't. At least he made no claim to that distinction.

They were two quiet, well-behaved young men when I got through talking to them and searching them. Richmond finally stuttered that we were miles from town, and after many "For Gawd's sake don't kill them, Mr. Williams," managed to back the car onto the main road.

I know something about engines, and in about three minutes under the hood of that taxi I did enough damage to give some local garage three days' work.

Don't try to come to The Hollow, boys," I called to the lad upon the road and his friend who stood beside him, cursing him. "The police will already be there."

With that parting shot we were off. Speeding along the road toward The Hollow.

I got little information from Richmond. About the girl he would not speak. There was no doubt of one thing. He was scared to death—a pitiful wreck of human emotions. At the same time he had no desire to turn back. He worshipped that girl—shivered and shook, but never wanted to quit.

The Hollow was on the main thoroughfare itself. So we drove right by it without slowing up much. Maybe the road would be watched—maybe it wouldn't. There was no back road.

We pulled the car up in a cut, just around the bend and close to two hundred yards from The Hollow.

"You wait here," I told Richmond. "Keep the lights out; sit behind the wheel and be ready to start at a moment's notice."

"You can't go alone." He followed me from the car and tugged at my coat. "I don't know what it's all about, but I know Miss Tina's in danger. I've come this far—I'm going with you."

"You stay here." I jammed a gun against Richmond's chest. He winced and trembled and slunk back. I hated to frighten poor Richmond, but I couldn't have his teeth chattering beside me.

"It's no use." His lips trembled so that he could hardly speak, but somehow he got the words out. "As soon as you go, I'll follow—something stronger than myself is pulling me on, sir. Miss Tina—like she counted on me—and needed me. I—just got to go on."

Mad? Yes! I was tempted to hit him a crack on the head and be done with him. But I couldn't. I admired the man. I don't know fear myself—but it must be a terrible thing.

"Come on—" was all I said. And a little later I handed him a handkerchief to put between his teeth.

But, at that, Richmond helped. He knew The Hollow—and the rough country around it. Once we stopped, and I questioned him about the roadhouse—the rooms—and how he knew the place so well.

"From driving Miss Tina here. She came often, sir—not for herself, mind. For it's a place of evil repute—but for her brother, sir. Mr. Bob." And this time he put the handkerchief suddenly back in his mouth. Richmond was forgetting himself.

We were close to the house now—a bluish, two-story, stucco affair, it was. One of those many near Spanish houses that went up in the boom. Weird and misshapen it looked there in the little clearing, in the moonlight. The lower part of the house was in darkness—but there was a light above.

Slowly we snaked nearer and nearer to the house. It was tough going in the thick growth. Richmond came along like a sleigh being dragged over dry pavement. There was no hope of a secret approach if any one was guarding the outside of that house. They'd hear him before we got much closer.

It took some little time, but at length I convinced him that it would be to the benefit of the girl if he stayed behind.

"I'll make the house," I told him. "You lie here. Hand onto that gun—and fire a shot to warn me if any one approaches the house. It's best for Miss Tina."

"Yes," he said at length. "I guess it is—best for Miss Tina."

Much relieved, I pushed on alone. There was a little clearing close to the house. In the thick bush I waited for the guard to make his rounds. Just a quick rush forward, a pound of the gun, and—but it's all old stuff to me.

Five—ten minutes passed, and no guard passed through the moonlight. Strange that. In dealing with criminals I've always found an outside guard. Was Stinnes, then, so sure—or had he fled?

I came to my feet—took a chance and crossed the stretch of moonlight and planted my body close against the pale blue stucco. Still no sound—no guard—and then a noise above me—something low and whining, like the wind—but there wasn't any wind; just the still, quiet, warm winter night of the southland.

There was a window to my right. I thrust up a hand—felt for the glass, and my fingers encountered cardboard. I bent my head around—all cardboard in the eight squares of the two frames. I pushed up the window, very slowly. It groaned ever so softly. Still no other sound—then it came again. The soft whine, like the wind or a distant bird—but it wasn't the wind and it wasn't a bird, for it came from within the house.

For the third time it came again—louder now, with a pathetic, appealing note in it. And I knew it was a moan—of a man or a woman. A woman! The girl. Tina Sears!

Was she there alone then? I didn't know—I didn't care. I tore the cardboard aside and climbed in the window, with my gun drawn, my flashlight ready in my hand. Both feet planted firmly on the floor, I snapped the button of the flash. A sudden dart of light; dust, dirt, a cricket that chirped, a moth that flickered through the light—and emptiness. And I snapped out the light. Just before me was the hall and the stairs leading above.

I crossed quickly through the darkness—no beat of my rubber heels, but an unmistakable groan to the worn boards of the floor. At the foot of the stairs I waited.

For the fourth time came the moan—real and loud and fearful this time. But there was no tread of feet above—no movement of a body—no sound of a voice.

15

The Shadow on the Floor

I tried to reason things out before I went up those stairs. Was I acting like a timid schoolgirl? Was I overrating the danger before me? Stinnes had certainly taken the girl. Old Benevolence Travers knew that. He had sent me a message that Stinnes and the girl were here. Wasn't it possible, or even probable that others had been watching my hotel—seen me leave with the chauffeur—noted the direction I took, and notified Stinnes?

Then what? He would do one of two things. Plan to trap me, or flee the house. If he planned to trap me there, surely the house would have been guarded. And it wasn't. If he fled, wouldn't he take the girl with him? Or—and I gulped. Would he kill the girl? She had caused McCleary's death. Stinnes must suspect that. It was a bad gang. Murder was not new to them.

But the moans from above. Surely that was a woman—surely that must be the girl—and surely she must be alone. He had left her for dead, maybe. I sent one quick stab of light up those stairs—jumped aside at the bottom and waited.

No shot—no sound—and then a voice.

"Help—help me." A moan then.

There was no doubt now. It was the girl. It was Tina Sears.

"Tina—" I pushed myself back into the protecting archway which gave entrance to the room across the hall. "Are you— It's I—Race Williams."

"Come then—come. He'll be back—please come." She called from above.

"You are alone—no one else in the house?" It seemed like being a quitter to stand there while the girl who had once saved my life called to me from above—but I couldn't forget the man in the window—the high-powered rifle and the whir of the air gun.

"Yes—Stinnes. He got a message—left suddenly—and— but he'll be back. Please come up—don't be afraid." And there was agony in her voice.

And I came—quickly up the stairs—a gun in either hand. No flash now—just ready to shoot if a gun barked out of the darkness. Halfway up the stairs a light flashed across a narrow hallway. I made my way quickly toward it as the girl pleaded for me to hurry.

I made the stretch of light, skipped through it and was in the room. There she was, directly across from me, a huddled mass on the floor by the window—arms bound and twisted high behind her—ankles firmly held by thick ropes, and a dirty cloth gag that had slipped from her mouth and now hung over her chin.

The room was bare of furniture. There was no bed, no closet—no place for a man to hide. All this I took in in one quick, unconscious glance. It was the girl I thought of. Of that slender body, those delicate arms, and the tiny wrists that were now swelled to reddish purple lumps.

I pocketed one gun, ran quickly across the room, jerked out my pocket knife, snapped it open, and kneeling beside the girl cut the rope that bound her wrists.

She lay quite still now, her cheek on the boards that were thick with dirt, her eyes half open, filmy and swimming. She must have suffered agony there. How long, I didn't know—but she was speaking.

"Hurry—take me away. Stinnes brought me here—questioned me. But I denied it all—about McCleary. He was going to kill me. But he wasn't sure—he had to wait—to hear from him. The Head—The Hidden Hand." And she screamed suddenly—flung her arms up toward me—clasped me about the neck.

I didn't turn my head. I didn't need to. There, below me on the floor I could see the shadow across the light—the outstretched arm. I knew even before the voice spoke. And I cursed myself for a fool—a sentimental fool. I don't think my voice shook when I spoke. If I was to die, I wanted to know the truth before I went out.

"You—knew?" was all I said to the girl.

And she didn't answer. Her eyes were on me with surprise and fear, and then over my shoulder with horror. The shadow behind me spoke.

"You will drop the gun in your hand, Race Williams." It fell to the floor at once. I'm no fool. "And the other one you will take from your pocket—carefully, slowly—and drop that, too." Now the voice went on. "You may rise, walk to the wall and turn about. Really, you're quite a child after all. Strong, foolishly courageous, and with little regard for death. And that, I guess, about describes you—and finishes you. Anything to say?"

I reached the wall, turned and faced Oscar Stinnes.

"Only—that your game is up, Stinnes. The police know and are searching for you now. I can still offer you a chance for freedom, and help you to leave the country—for a consideration. To kill me will not help you."

"Do you know?" he said quietly. "I'm rather proud of this moment. You're supposed to be quite a man—and there's quite a price on your head. Fifty thousand dollars in cash for the man who kills you. Not bad, that?"

"And a seat in the chair—if that man happens to be you,

Mr. Stinnes. But who offers the money? This Hidden Hand?"

"Exactly." He nodded and laughed lightly. "I played rather a clever game to-night. If the girl had cried out that I was here—or suspected that I was here—or if you had come in force, with the police—or Gregory Ford—I would not have run away. I would have offered information for my freedom—to you and the man who hired you—Gregory Ford." And then, leaning forward, with a note of hatred in his voice, "If you'd played the game and kept secret the information you and Ford had about me—that jewelry murder—I'd of sold out to you."

"It's not too late," I encouraged him. "I can still offer you—"

"You can offer me nothing," he snapped. "The Hidden Hand has shown fear. What can you offer me that he will deny me? I'll get clean away—and be worth millions—millions." His eyes flashed. "I shan't trust any one—not any one. But this Hidden Hand—he will send me money—thousands—thousands—to keep his secret. For if I told his name— But, there—you have played the game and lost. I have played it and won. The girl goes first."

His eyes blazed, his lips set. He whipped the gun slightly aside and lower, covering the prostrate form of the girl there on the floor. I bent my knees, braced my feet against the wall for my plunge forward. Not that I could reach him—not that I could hope to save the girl. I knew it was the end. It was simply my animal instinct to die fighting.

I don't think I was afraid. I always expected it. We can't live forever, you know. And Stinnes cried out again.

"The girl first. She did for McCleary—then— Stand back, you fool." He swung the gun toward me.

It was too late then—for me and for him. I was already in the air when his gun cracked. But there was something else in the air, too—a stumbling, screeching, screaming mass.

"Not her—not Miss Tina." It was Richmond, the chauffeur, who cried out. He didn't attempt to throw himself on the man. He simply attempted to throw himself between the girl and the gun. Mad with fear he may have been—but it was physical fear—not moral fear. He didn't have it in him to fight the man with a gun—but he did have it in him to die for the girl.

His body crashed against Stinnes' gun arm as Stinnes fired; and I leaped forward. But Richmond was between us now, and I couldn't pull back. Then the gun cracked again—and the space between Stinnes and me was empty. Richmond was no longer there. He had crumpled at my feet; at Stinnes' feet.

Stinnes fired again, I think—blindly, wildly this time, and he made the mistake of stepping back—being off balance when I reached him. He was a big man; a strong man, I guess—but then, I do six feet myself, and top the scales well into the hundred and eighties.

And I was on him—inside his gun—hands upon his throat—knee into his stomach. He gave ground quickly, stumbled upon the door jamb, and crashed backwards. Pounding knees, tightening fingers in soft flesh, butting head against his face—we hit the boards together.

This was no gentleman's encounter. No heroics about my clean punches. He was a man with a gun. This was a fight for life. Even as we struck, I raised his head from the floor and pounded it back upon the wood again.

I heard his feet click as his knees straightened. Then he lay still, and I heard, too, the dull thud of metal, and knew that his gun had fallen from useless fingers.

When I climbed to my feet, Stinnes lay still—his feet in the room, his body and shoulders in the hall, with his head close to the stairs. I dragged him back into the room.

Then I cut the rope about the girl's ankles, and as she struggled to her knees by the window, gave my attention to Richmond. He was making a terrible row and calling upon his relatives. I went over him as he begged to die "at home." And he wasn't even scratched. He had crashed to the floor in sheer fear. A great coward was Richmond—yes, a great coward—but a great hero, too, if you get what I mean.

I forgot the girl; forgot Richmond, as I looked down at Stinnes. He was there—in my hands. He was alone—and he would talk. And there was a fortune in the talk he could give. And that fortune I wanted. Old Benevolence Travers had said, once this leader—this Hidden Hand—was brought to justice—or death, I could name my own price, even if I took his all.

"There's a phone in the house?" I asked the girl. It was a lonely spot—it might be better to get Travers here than try and drag Stinnes some place.

"Yes," she said, "there is. For Stinnes received a call just before you came—and I thought he left. You—you believe me?"

"Sure—" I answered, without much thought. Bigger things were on my mind.

16

I Deliver Stinnes

It took time to arrange things. If I wished to trust the girl that was my business—but I had no right to make Old Benevolence Travers trust her. She and Richmond would have to be out of the house when he came. She didn't want to leave me there alone, and she had difficulty in walking. Richmond also had difficulty in carrying her.

I pulled out my handcuffs, lifted Stinnes to a big chair that I dragged in from the hall, locked his wrists together behind him with the chain of the bracelets through the back of the chair. His head hung forward on his chest but he stayed put. Then, with Richmond carrying the girl, I followed them down the stairs. I'd see them safely to the car.

We were passing to the front door when I heard it—the heavy breathing of a man—there in the room, the window of which I had opened. I pulled up sharply, stepped quickly back from the streak of moonlight I had just entered, and in the darkness swung toward that room.

"Careful—" a low voice came to me. "You—have won—you have him—Stinnes?"

And I lowered my gun. I knew the voice and I knew the

figure that stepped into the moonlight. It was Howard Quincy Travers, my client, alias Old Benevolence. I rubbed my hands together. Surely this was getting the breaks, the real breaks!

On Travers assuring me that no one lurked without, I let Richmond go out with the girl. She wouldn't go on to town though. She insisted that she'd wait in the car until I came.

"A detective—a friend of mine." I explained the voice she must have heard in the darkness. "Wait, if you must—I'll do what I can to keep your name out of it. But—in ten minutes the name and identity of The Hidden Hand will be known." So I shoved Richmond out the door, watched him stumble across the clearing and disappear in the thick tropical growth. Then I turned to Old Benevolence.

"Stinnes is above. I might have known you'd follow—after your message. I think he'll talk when he comes around. In fact, he said if he was caught he would." And I told Travers of the night's doings. "We'll wait until—"

And I stopped. From above came the curse of a man—the dragging of a chair across the floor and the pounding of feet.

"I must go in to him alone." Travers put a hand upon my shoulder—a hand that trembled slightly, and his voice shook. "In a few minutes, then, I will give to you the name of the man the whole state of Florida seeks. You will go for him then—to-night."

"Ready any time." I nodded. "And the reward, Mr. Travers—that is to be paid at once—when I have this man?"

"At once—and without question—your own figure. If Stinnes talks, and you—you get this—this Hidden Hand."

"Stinnes will talk. I'll wait here on the stairs—and watch the house."

"Good!" A hand gripped my arm, fingers pressed tightly. And he was gone—slowly up the stairs.

I saw his head once as the door above opened and he was in the light. Then the door closed. A long silence—ten minutes passed—the light again—the figure again—and feet in the hall above—feet that came down the stairs—an excited voice close to my ear.

"Quick—the key to the handcuffs." And as I switched on my flashlight I saw that Travers held paper and pencil in his hand, and that his face was very white. And the colorless eyes were flashing vividly—burning, far back in their sockets.

"He will write a confession—give me the name—on my promise not to use the paper until I get him out of the country."

"Has he told you, then? Who?"

"Not yet—not yet. The key, so he can write—and a glass of water from the kitchen. He wants a drink."

He waited there on the bottom step, the key in his hand, until I had found the kitchen and returned with a glass of muddy water from the little-used tap.

"It's a great moment, Race Williams," he said solemnly. "For me—for you—for the citizens of Florida. Wait here."

He turned and went rapidly up the stairs. Below, I waited. Not bad work this—and I wondered just how much I could really charge. Just how much this would be worth to Travers. And I wondered, too, who The Hidden Hand would be. A big name—undoubtedly a well-known name, that would startle the whole state—perhaps the whole country.

Then I went up a few steps. Travers had a gun—I had seen that—but he was to release Stinnes. Would he just release one hand and keep the other cuffed to the chair? Stinnes was a dangerous man.

There was a crash of falling furniture—a cry from Travers—and the frantic twisting of the door knob in that room above. I was up the stairs in an instant, and at the door. It was locked. And Travers was there, screaming for me to open it—yelling at the top of his lungs. Another yelled too. Stinnes—yelled and cursed and threatened as something heavy bounded across the floor—bounced and dragged.

And I thought I knew. Stinnes had suddenly attacked Travers, but he was fastened to the chair. And now—Travers beat at the door—and Stinnes struggled with him.

Once, twice, three times I hit that door—and the third, it gave. There was the splintering of wood, the snap of a lock—and I was in the room.

There was Old Benevolence Travers, crouched back against the wall—his gun dangling in his hand. And there on the floor, writhing in agony, was Stinnes, his left hand cuffed to the overturned chair, his right clenched in pain. And his face—it was screwed up in horrible contortions. Paper was scattered about.

Travers tried to explain—but his voice was thick and I hardly got the words.

"The water; he put something in it when he drank it—poison, I think. Before I got—the name."

"Stinnes—" I went quickly to the suffering man. No time for sentiment, this. Stinnes held the name I wanted—Travers wanted—Gregory Ford and the whole state of Florida wanted.

"Stinnes—the name—don't you understand? Don't be a coward—we'll protect you—save you—get you—"

But it was useless—the man was dying.

"Don't—don't touch him." Travers was dragging at my shoulder. "He took the poison—at the last minute—in fear—fear of this Hidden Hand. He's a loathsome, crawling thing. Come away—come away."

Travers was almost as bad as the man who groveled upon the floor. I shook his hand from my shoulder; thrust him roughly back against the wall. Stinnes wanted to talk—was trying to talk. In death he was afraid, I guess. And he was dying!

I was down beside him now, his head on my arm, his lips close to me, his glassy eyes dazedly searching the room. But he was trying to speak—straining every muscle—frantically trying to utter words. It didn't matter if he meant it—it didn't matter if he was delirious. I wanted that name and—

Stinnes jerked erect. Then his voice came—clear and loud—almost a shout.

"The Hand—The Hidden Hand—he is—Hand is—"

And I let his head hit the floor with a thud. There's no use to question a dead man.

I turned to Old Benevolence Travers, who was crouched in a corner.

"Well—you messed it," I told him. "If you'd opened the door I'd of got—but just what happened?"

He told me the story in jerks. Stinnes was about to write; had the pencil in his hand. His fingers shook—the pencil fell to the floor, and when Travers bent to recover it Stinnes reached for the water glass.

"He must—have had the poison in his hand," Travers stammered. "I noticed the strange color of the water—but it's muddy anyway. Then he smiled slightly, and drank it. Muttered something about being true to his chief—and suddenly clutched at me. It was a horrible sight. His face—those glassy eyes—the foaming mouth. I lost my head—ran to the door—forgot the key was in my hand—and— But now—I've—Yet—"

"I did my part," I cut in. I wasn't going to forget business. "Better luck next time. No fear of the police in this. We'll just leave him here—these sort of birds take care of their own dead." There was no use in rubbing it in on Travers. He wasn't built for the job. I had no kick. If he had of been, he wouldn't have hired me. Slowly we turned from the room and went down the stairs and out into the night.

But who was The Hidden Hand? I shrugged my shoulders. There was Olaf Sankin, the giant Swede, yet to be cornered— and also Beekman. As I had said to Old Benevolence Travers: "Better luck next time."

17

Room 891

Leaning back in the soft-cushioned chair of the palatial hotel suite at Miami, Florida, I looked at Howard Quincy Travers. He turned his eyes from Biscayne Bay and spoke.

"You're not sorry you're in the game—not afraid, even now?" he said softly, those vacant colorless eyes staring at me.

"Fear is like everything else in life," I smiled, "reckoned in dollars and cents. You pay too well for fear. Who's next on the list—Sankin or Beekman? We must beat Gregory Ford to the final curtain."

"Olaf Sankin," he leaned forward. "We must reach him first, for here is a different type of man—a killer. Reputed to be the quickest shot in Florida." He hesitated a moment.

"Florida's a small state." I shrugged my shoulders.

Old Benevolence Travers eyed me a minute and his lips smiled, but his eyes still remained expressionless. Then he spoke.

"Olaf Sankin is controlled by his passions alone. In him the physical rules the mental. He is strong, quick, shrewd and different from the others in that he is known and wanted by the police. There is no secret to hold over his head to force information from him as to the name of this leader. The state has enough evidence now to convict him for any one of a half dozen murders."

"Why not go for Beekman then? If this Olaf Sankin is wanted by the police and I take him prisoner, what can you offer him that will make him talk?"

"His freedom! My money, my knowledge and my help to leave the country. He's a selfish brute. You hold him for me. He'll either talk, or I'll deliver him to the police." He raised a hand when I would have spoken. "The police know him and want him, and now that Gregory Ford is here, will take him. Once in the hands of the police, he will talk. As I have said before, there is a leak in the police department. The leader will know as soon as Sankin is arrested, and make good his escape. We must forestall that. We must have the name of this leader before he is forewarned of his danger and leaves the country."

"This Hidden Hand—" I thought aloud. Then, "You're very well informed, Mr. Travers."

"Better informed than even you think." He smiled with his lips. "So much so that I can direct you to Olaf Sankin—at least, to his haunts—" he leaned far forward now, "and to the girl—his woman—whom he will send out to trap you. But you can buy her to our side; she will have her price. And if my information is correct, she is already tired of Olaf Sankin. Love no longer holds her to him; it is fear now. But all that I shall leave to you. If Sankin once thinks that the girl has betrayed him, and that you are the cause—he will hunt you out, even on the public streets. He is ruled by his passions alone."

"Our agreement still holds good then. The larger fee if I put Sankin, helpless, into your hands and if for his freedom he gives to you the name of this leader—this Hidden Hand. But—" I stroked my chin, "Sankin is a desperate gunman, and desperate men—well—life is full of hazards and such men do not live forever. It's dangerous business, Mr. Travers.

There is ten thousand dollars in it for me if he—should die?"

"If you must kill him—yes. I did not question you before; I shall not question you now. Death by violence is a horrible thing to contemplate—but those that live by the sword shall perish by the sword."

"I guess that goes for guns, too." I nodded. And when he would have given me a description of the man, I cut in. "Beady eyes, matted hair, thick lips, broad dominant chin, and a scar from his mouth up the right side of his face. I saw him. He has already taken a pot shot at me." My lips set, as I remembered the shot from the high-powered rifle and the tiny wound on Tina Sears' throat from the bullet that was meant for me.

"It is good." He nodded vigorously. "This woman of Olaf Sankin's. You would do well to find her at once. The police do not suspect her as yet. Her name is Rosie Sorrelie. There is a hotel at Fort Lauderdale, and—"

"First," I said, "there is a duty to another. Some one whom I wish to take to West Palm Beach."

"The girl, Tina Sears?" He shook his head. "I thought you were above women, Race Williams. When the fancy of a moment takes the place of—"

"The girl saved my life," I busted in. "She's in danger because of that. I have no interest in the girl. But I have a debt to pay, and I'll pay it."

"Careful!" He shook one of those long slender fingers that stuck out grotesquely from a fat hand. "Youth finds it difficult to distinguish good from bad. And the goodness of a face too often hides the badness of a soul. Watch that she does not trap you."

"Of course. But even if it were a trap, I would go just the same. I owe her even that."

"That is like you—very much like you." He stared at me. "It is remarkable that you have lived so long."

"Such an occasion has never arisen before." I smiled.

"Until that night on the boat I had managed to take care of myself."

"An embarrassing situation, but a commendable one. I shall see you at West Palm Beach. I have many friends across the lake, at Palm Beach. And my hotel—you can find me there." He scribbled the name of a hotel on a piece of paper and handed it to me. Again our hands met—again the cold, fish-like palm and the warm slender fingers. "I shall not meet you again—until your task is completed. If I should be seen with you—" he paused, rubbed a hand across his mouth, and smiled with his lips alone. Although his voice was steady, I noted that the corners of his mouth quivered and his fingers trembled slightly.

"They won't suspect us—here?" I asked.

"No—*no*." The second "no" with emphasis. "When you leave this hotel everything will be centered on you—and the dangers you have experienced so far are as nothing compared with what will follow. Mr. Williams, your life is in danger even upon the open street."

Old Benevolence Travers came to his feet and held open the door of his room as I passed out. But he stood well back in the shadows. His precaution, however, was unnecessary; the hotel hallway was deserted. I walked to the stairs, went slowly down the three flights to the eighth floor and straight to room 891. The door opened almost at once. Tina Sears was waiting for me.

18

The Pursuit

"Have you seen a doctor?" I asked, as I looked at her throat, and the tiny scar which was now a yellowish red. Iodine, I thought.

"No—no." She grabbed at both my hands. "It's nothing—and you've come to help me—take me to West Palm Beach."

"Yes." I nodded. "You have friends there?"

"I shall be safe there—if I reach there." She went to the window and pointed out on Biscayne boulevard. "They are watching for me."

I looked down to where she pointed. There was her high-powered motor, the spiffy chauffeur, Richmond, close to the door—and behind the machine a disreputable open car with a man at the wheel and another in the seat beside him.

"We'll have no trouble," I told the girl. "With that boat of yours we'll leave them far behind. Open country to Palm Beach?"

"Open country." She nodded, then suddenly turning and facing me, "Why do you do this for me? Why do you jeopardize your life—your work, for me?"

"You saved my life. I'm paying my debt."

"There is no other reason?" Two little hands went up to my

shoulders, two swimming brown eyes sought mine, and a well-featured face with small lips was braced by a chin that parked itself upon my chest. "There is no other reason?" she asked again—and her voice was very low.

"There is no other reason," I told her, as I lifted her hands from my shoulders—and then, "Come, Tina—why not blow up on the whole show? You don't belong. Fear holds you. Do you know this—Hidden Hand?"

"No," she said, "I don't know him. Only that he is wicked and cruel and merciless—and that he holds my secret."

"How did you come to get into this mess? You had a brother." And when she showed surprise, "Richmond, the chauffeur, gave that away. It was he who was killed then—not your husband?"

"Not my husband," she said. "I'm not married—never was." And then suddenly, "I shouldn't let you come with me. There is no escape for me. The Hidden Hand has only to send for me and I must go to him. But—I'm so—so alone and afraid."

She grabbed me suddenly by the arm and pulled me toward the door. Was I a fool to risk my life in taking this girl to West Palm Beach? Hadn't she already nearly sent me to my death, and only at the last minute regretted her action? Maybe I was a fool. Maybe my ethics are all twisted up, as the police claim they are—but the girl had saved my life and I'd stick to her when she needed me, danger or no danger—trap or no trap!

We took the elevator to the ground floor and passed unmolested to the street. If eyes were watching us I didn't spot the owner of them. Still, the feeling was there that we were at least under observation, if not actually shadowed. But no one interfered with our departure.

Richmond, the chauffeur, spotted us at once and pulled noiselessly up to the door. This was an expensive motor. The shabby car at the opposite curb broke into life—there was no guesswork about that engine. You could hear it a block away and see it shake from three blocks. Not a high class job, this—and I snickered to myself as we climbed into the big car.

The drive out of Miami is straight along the Biscayne boulevard and along the Bay. Great, wide, well-paved streets—and since it was midday, the traffic was heavy. But it was not hard to spot the shabby car as it weaved in and out, ever on our trail.

"We are followed?" the girl said—and it was more a statement than a question.

"For a bit." I laughed. "Give us a stretch of road and in five minutes we'll be alone. Rotten old boat."

But that didn't seem to cheer her up any.

"Why not give the whole show a ride, Tina?" I said after a while. "You must know I'm your friend now. If it's money, come on my side. We've got the money."

"Money!" And her laugh was a deep, unnatural one. "No—I shan't need money. But there's my mother and father. I—" She stopped suddenly.

"Go on—" I encouraged her.

"I will." She nodded vigorously. "There is no use to tell you who I am. I daresay in time you'll find that out. But I had every advantage in life—and threw them over. Not for myself, but my brother. Oh, don't you see? It was he who was killed—he who had fallen in with these people. They didn't want him. They didn't need him. They got him to bring me in. I had—well—they wanted me—and my brother needed me—and he sent for me. I came—and I'm a criminal in fact, if not in spirit. I— Do they still follow?"

And they did. I looked back and saw the car careening along behind us. We were well out toward Hollywood now, and I gave Richmond the office to step on the gas. There was a slight hum to the motor, and the palms along the road appeared thicker. We slowed down a bit for Hollywood, then hit the open country again. Forty—fifty—and sixty, we reached. The rickety car was a speck now—a fast-fading speck. I tapped the girl on the shoulder and smiled.

"Made monkeys of them," I said. "Now—if you feel safe, and can talk."

"We have left them like that!" She raised her voice above the roar. "It seems impossible, if—if they want you. And they do, for they fear you."

"Hick gunmen," I encouraged her. "Look—you can't see even a—" I broke off suddenly and smothered a curse. Surely that moving flash behind us was not the shabby touring! Surely it was just another car bent on speed! And I knew the truth, though I tried to tell myself differently. The dilapidated touring was just a stall—a little bit of by-play to lull my suspicions.

"All she's got, Richmond," I shouted above the wind to the chauffeur, and I realized that the money spent on this fifteen thousand dollar boat we were in was spent for comfort and class, while the people behind had put their money into speed. Yep, we were doing well over sixty—no doubt of that—yet that flash behind us was eating up the distance between us—making feet out of the yards.

And the boys behind had timed it well. Most of the road along the Dixie Highway is lonely enough—but here was a particularly deserted stretch. I knew the make of the car behind now—the fastest stock car in America—and guaranteed to do over a hundred miles an hour.

There was a chance that this was just wealthy youth doing its stuff at America's playground. And lots of youth. Two men in the front—three on the rear seat—and another crouched between the front and rear seats. Or was it another? I got a pretty clear vision—there is no dust in Florida. The thing between the front and the rear seats was not a man— but something covered with dark oilcloth—something high— like a surveyor's instrument.

I looked straight ahead now. Not a car in sight. To our right a slight ditch and heavy tropical growth. To our left the railroad tracks and open country....

"Take the center of the road, Richmond," I hollered. "Give her everything and keep your attention on the road."

105

If this car was on pleasure bent she'd give us the horn now. Man! but she sure ate up the distance between us. After all, speed—like wealth—is only built on comparisons. Five minutes ago we were flying over the roads. Now, although the speedometer made it sixty-five, we were just crawling.

There was no horn from the car behind; just the roar of the motor. Deafening it was as the long black flash drew closer. I crawled up on the back seat, swayed there as with the butt of my gun I knocked out the glass in the small rear window.

The car was very close now. Yet they made no attempt to pass. Too bad, that—if they were the enemy and meant business, and Richmond was half the driver he seemed to be, we'd easily ditch them. Now I tried to make out the blurred faces; the hunched shoulders—but most of all I looked for hands, and the flash of nickel in the sunlight.

I wondered how they intended to play the game. They couldn't pass us and stop us. They couldn't pull alongside and open fire. And to shoot from that speeding car would be tough going. They'd have to lean out the side, against the terrific force of the wind, and fire—or stand on the seat and fire over the windshield. Any lad who tried standing on that seat would suddenly find himself half a mile or so back, on the road.

And we hit a divide in the highway—a one-way road between heavy pines. The flash behind was right on our trail now—the road was narrow and we were right in the center of it. The car behind slowed down to our pace and then men in it came to life. Quickly one flipped the canvas off that "surveyor's instrument." And it wasn't a surveyor's instrument. I knew that before it began to rise—rise slowly above the heads of the men in the front seat.

It was a machine gun, and a particularly heavy and vicious looking one. They didn't lift it up—they cranked it up. I could see it rise in sudden jolts, and I could see, too, the heavy iron supports that held it.

"Duck down in the car, Kid," I said to the girl. "Hold your

nerve and your wheel, Richmond," I cried out to our driver. Then I raised my forty-four; took careful aim through that little glassless rear window at the driver of the speed demon.

There was no doubt now what was in the minds of the boys behind us. They were just going to open up with the machine gun and rake the car with lead. Nothing high class about their work; nothing of the fine touch you'd expect from a high class, much-feared criminal such as The Hidden Hand. But you've got to admit that it would be effective. They wanted me out of the way. I was too close on their heels. They probably wanted the girl, too, or were indifferent to what became of her. Maybe they only had suspicions of her connection in the death of McCleary—maybe they were certain. At all events, one extra death or two didn't matter. Any way you looked at it, these boys meant business.

19

A Pretty Bit of Shooting

I've often said that crooks are like children at play. Here, they had planned the whole thing without taking my actions into consideration. Or had they? The police and the man-hunters of the law generally do not attack until fired upon. That must have been what they counted on now. Counted on me waiting until they opened hostilities—counted on my usual court plea of self-defense.

Yet, what chance would I have once that machine gun opened up and peppered the car with a hundred bullets or more? So I decided to fire first. The distance wasn't great, the road was fairly smooth, and the driver of the car behind crouched over the wheel less than a hundred feet away.

I saw the machine gun swing sideways in the sudden rush of wind as its nose peered above the windshield. Then I saw it slowly begin to swing back again—moved by a mechanism that worked from below.

That was enough. I braced my gun upon the wood and drew a bead on the driver. One shot, and six deaths. I couldn't miss, and if I did I'd have five more tries at it in quick succession.

The driver saw me but never moved—never even

crouched the lower over the wheel—never even yelled his fear to the men manipulating the gun. My finger closed upon the trigger—there was the slight bark of my gun above the roaring motors. I watched for the driver to slip forward and the machine dash wildly off the road and turn over. But no such little amusement took place.

The driver still crouched above the wheel. My finger tightened again—then once more—and a fourth time. It was the fourth shot before I knew the truth, for a tiny crack loomed up in the windshield of the car; a small crescent appeared in the glass just in line with the center of the driver's forehead. But—there was no hole in the man's head, and no hole in the glass.

I understood then why they had been so cocksure. That car was equipped with a bullet-proof windshield. As I realized that, the nose of the machine gun swung more and more around—almost on a line with us now. Once that deadly mouth opened up and spat lead, we were done—nothing could save us. For in the space of a few seconds hundreds of steel-jacketed bullets would be poured into us.

I didn't wait now—hardly more than aimed as I thrust both my arms through that little rear window and started my guns working. Not for the driver this time; not for the occupants of the car; and not for the deadly, threatening machine gun, the mouth of which was almost directly upon us. I spread my lead low, for the right front tire of the car. I didn't rake all across the front, for either tire. One bullet mightn't turn the trick—a tiny hole might only cause a puncture of the inner tube, and that wouldn't help us any. I didn't want any slow leak—I wanted a blowout; and I knew my only chance to get it was to concentrate on one tire.

Did I get it? Man! I should say I did. There was no sound of a bursting tire—my spitting gun and the roaring motors hid that. Also the sudden and deafening spit of the machine gun. The men in the rear seat realized the danger and opened up the gun before it was fairly trained upon us.

One glimpse of a frantic white face, with widely glaring eyes; great knotted hands which clutched at the wheel; straining muscles of thick arms, in a useless effort—and the crunchy grinding creak of suddenly applied brakes. The car swayed madly, lurched to the left of the road, careened suddenly half over on its side, straightened again and dashed wildly for the ditch to the right.

The show was over. Like some snorting, fiery dragon the great car ducked her hood low, dived into the ditch, and turned a complete somersault. Two bodies flew high in the air and—the picture was blotted from view. I was down on the floor with the girl as Richmond took a curve.

"It's all over—they've stopped following us?" the girl asked, as she straightened herself out and climbed to the seat.

"Forever," I told her. "Five of the boys have gone where all bad gunmen go." I wasn't unnerved by the sight. Maybe I'm hard boiled—but truth is truth. I got a real kick out of that turn-over. I had shot it out with death, and won. You'll admit it was a close call.

The girl was not built for somersaulting automobiles and flying bodies. She was whiter than a Ritz-Carlton tablecloth. Besides that, Richmond was handling the wheel of the car like he expected it to come off in his hand. We missed a couple of cars as we shot out of the one-way road, but by the time I quieted him down to twenty miles an hour the boat was running smoothly.

"I'm afraid I'm going to faint." The girl leaned on my shoulder.

"It's all right by me." I looked down at her. Then I pushed her gently over against the far cushion. I'm no parking place for fainting women—especially, women I don't fully understand—and this girl had little playmates who carted machine guns along country roads in midday.

She didn't faint. She bit her lip till the blood came and eyed me out of big, questioning brown eyes. Maybe she wanted to drag in the sex interest—maybe she just wanted a friend—maybe she couldn't understand me. But we were even there. I didn't understand her. And I didn't waste my time trying to. On my twenty-first birthday I gave up all claim to understanding women.

So we pulled into Fort Lauderdale. Two motorcycle cops dashed past us and out toward Miami. I didn't need three guesses to know what was on their minds. A passing motorist had seen the mess and telephoned in. Would we be stopped and questioned? Maybe. Maybe not. But mostly I thought we would.

They wouldn't be likely to find the bullet holes in that tire. But they would be likely to find the machine gun—or what was left of it—in the wreck of the car. A simple thing—hardly worth noticing, that? Maybe—in Chicago. But this was Florida, and I guess the game was a new one. Anyway, I decided to do my best to forestall all investigations of my actions. I'd telephone Gregory Ford, in Miami, and see if he'd be willing to keep my name out of it.

I told the girl to wait while I went into the hotel. It was in her best interest to keep the police out of the thing. She simply nodded, slipping far back in a corner of the seat.

There wasn't much trouble in getting police headquarters. But Gregory Ford wasn't waiting there to hear from me. They thought he was some place else—and "some place else" thought he was at another place. They had said at headquarters that they expected him back any minute. I called headquarters again, to leave a message for him to wait there, if he came in. And this time I got him. He'd just popped up.

"Was Olaf Sankin in that car?" he asked, when I gave him the story.

"No—I got a good look at the late lamented, and none of them was homely enough."

"You know Sankin, then?" he threw in quickly. "You're a fast worker, Race. How come you—?"

111

"Never mind that, Gregory," I cut in. "Will you keep me out of this? I'll deal you in at the end—when we get the big boy—The Hidden Hand."

"Why no investigation?" he questioned—and then "Who was in the car with you?"

"Not a soul." I lied.

"You had a dame with you when you left Miami—a dick spotted you. Who was she?"

I thought quick, and lied again.

"Rosie Sorrelie," I told him. I knew that he wanted Tina Sears. He had tried to get her on the boat, coming down from New York—and tried again in the old warehouse in Miami.

"My Gawd! Olaf Sankin's girl," he gasped. "First, McCleary's woman—now, Sankin's. You sure are rushing some fancy skirts."

"But I think she'll talk, and if—"

"She will talk," he busted in. "All right—go ahead. I don't know your game—but I'll see you out of this. Now—I may pull off a pinch myself. The big boy—Hidden Hand, and all that. Want to sit in?"

"Yes." I gulped. Gregory spoke with a great deal of confidence, and I wondered if he was going to beat me to the pinch.

"Where'll I get in touch with you?"

"West Palm Beach."

"What hotel?"

"Name a good one."

He hesitated a moment, questioned some one—then:

"The Columbus—just off Clamatis Street. I've got to stay here for a message—big message. There was only one way to work this game, Race. It took me to pull it. There's a squeal coming in. The Columbus then—sit tight."

I clapped up the phone and sought the street. Gregory Ford and Old Benevolence Travers wanted to work the same racket—get some of the gang to talk. Now what? If Travers was right, and Gregory took the police into his confidence,

112

and there was a leak—this leader—this Hidden Hand would know, and skip. Well—I shrugged my shoulders. Gregory's squeal was only a promised one. It hadn't come in yet. I'd take Tina to West Palm Beach, ring up Travers, and tell him of the crape that Gregory Ford was trying to hang out.

20

A High-Priced Squeal

When I reached the curb Tina Sears was gone. The space before the hotel was empty. I half turned back to the hotel when a bell boy approached me.

"Mr. Williams?" And when I nodded, "The lady in the big car said to give you this."

I took the hastily scribbled note. Just a line.

> Thank you so much. I can go on alone now.

No signature—nothing. Tina Sears had moved on. And the boy was talking—there was a confidential curve to his mouth and an understanding wink to his right eye.

"And the other lady gave me this." He fed me another note. "I don't know but what they saw each other, sir. I was wise as soon as I—"

I shoved a dollar into his mouth and shut off the gas. In a dazed way I opened the second letter. It, too, read simply enough—and it, too, was unsigned.

> She has gone. It is best. I am inside, in the very dark-est corner of the lobby. I think you should meet me.

So did I. Turning, I sought the lobby, and almost at once spotted the figure in the far corner. My left hand was deep in my jacket pocket as I strolled across the floor. I had my own ideas as to whom I'd meet—and accordingly, I was prepared.

The woman came to her feet, and even in the dimness she was not hard to look at. Black hair, black eyes, and thin red lips. Here was beauty, in a sinister sort of way. Her first words, as she stretched out both her hands and gripped mine, were not exactly the conventional greeting.

"Do you know, Mr. Williams—" she displayed a dental advertisement, "I could have earned fifty thousand dollars while you walked across the floor just now. There's a gun in my bag—a little door behind me—and a high-powered car on the side street."

"And an undertaker's parlor just across the way." I returned her smile. "I'm sorry to see that such a capable woman overlooked that. And you are—" I waited for her to lie. But she didn't.

"I am Rosie Sorrelie—Olaf Sankin's girl." She didn't turn red. "I'm tired of Olaf and I want to make a break. You admit—I could have killed you."

Nice pleasant little party, this. But I knew her breed. She never grew up in Florida. This girl was straight off the Avenue, in New York. I knew her stuff, too. At first I wasn't going to mention the gun that my fingers gripped as I crossed to her. Then I decided that I'd better. She might get playful later, and in fairness to her she had a right to know what to expect.

"But surely—you couldn't—you wouldn't shoot a woman." And she tried to do the baby doll stuff. But her face wasn't built for it and it didn't register.

"I'm a great believer in the equal rights of women. Now— what's on your chest? I'm a busy man."

"I want to blow the works." She shot those sinister black eyes on me. "I'm afraid of Olaf. I'm tired of hanging out in the Everglades. It's only a matter of days before the police will drag me in. And I don't like Olaf's actions lately. He suspects he's not my light-haired boy any more. And I can't fill the part. I've been sent to trap you. Come—look!" She turned to a little window and jerked back a curtain. Just a glimpse I got of a car that stood at the curb—and two men who stared at the window. Then it was gone.

"That curtain was a signal?" I asked.

"Yes—that I failed. I've taken a chance. Even now they may suspect me. But if you got through the trap they laid for you between here and Miami, I decided to go out for myself. I've been sent out to trap you. But I'll doublecross Olaf Sankin for a piece of change and—"

"Police protection?"

"No—I don't need that. They can't hang a thing on me. I've come to you because the regular police won't listen. If you won't play the game I'll blow the show to Gregory Ford. He'll pay for a squeal."

"A piece of change, and what then?"

"Olaf Sankin's life."

"I don't go in for murder."

"Well—his arrest then. But he won't be taken alive."

"How am I to know this isn't part of a trap—hatched by you and the big Swede?"

"You'll have to chance that."

And that simple statement was more convincing to me than if she had given me a complete history of her life and a thousand and one reasons why she should throw Olaf over.

"How much money do you want?"

"Well—" she stroked her chin, "I'd hoped to get ten grand out of it. But I guess that's too much expense money for you to drag down, and I daresay the State don't pay you that much for the pinch. But I'll take a chance on you, Race. I'll split the expense money you get for the squeal. That'll leave something for you on the side—and I expect you'll do the handsome thing by me if—" and she paused now and looked about the deserted lobby, "if The Hidden Hand falls into my trap."

"The Hidden Hand—you know him?" I leaned closer to her now.

"No—not me. But here's Gawd's truth. I do know that The Hidden Hand is to meet Olaf Sankin tonight."

"Where?" Of course I didn't have to swallow it all. But the girl's every action and Old Benevolence's information that she'd sell, lent truth to her words. Besides—well—it was worth listening to.

"I'll tell you where for—five grand." She smiled. "Come— I'm on my way to West Palm Beach. May I drive you there?"

And she could, under the circumstances. The car was a small roadster. Her attention was given to the wheel, and she made no attempt to leave the Dixie Highway. As for me, I wanted to get information, but I didn't intend to hand out any jack for it.

Rosie buzzed it all the way to West Palm Beach. I tried her out on the price—tried to cut it down. But she wouldn't cut. That either showed she was on the level with me or that she was playing a high-class game.

"I'll tell you, Rosie," I finally said. "Here's the lay. You turn Olaf Sankin over to me and I'll get you the money. And here's another offer. If this Hidden Hand turns up in the bag—or if it's through you I put the old mit on his shoulder, I'll double the amount."

"I want the five grand in advance." And she sounded as if she meant it.

Now, you'll admit it was mighty hard to get any place after that. We were as far away as the poles. I'd as soon throw the money in the street as trust her with it. And I told her so flat. She didn't get excited—or mad. She saw my point, and nodded her head.

"What's five thousand in a game as big as this?" she said. "I'd think you'd be willing to toss it in the road even, for the chance of success."

"But, Rosie—it's you I'm doubtful of. Why, only a minute ago you turned white when you mentioned this Hidden Hand. You know the chance you take means death—therefore you—"

"And that's why I want the jack." She flashed black globes on me. "The game's up. I feel the end of it. Suspicion and treachery have undermined the organization. Why did The Hidden Hand offer fifty grand for your death? Because he fears you. And why does he fear you? Because you kill, or pay to get what you want. Don't you think he understands that? Don't you think he fears a squeal? Well—there's a squeal coming. And there's big money for the one who squeals first. If I knew this leader's moniker I'd sell it to you now. I'm not saying the credit for this fear is all yours—there are too many other factors. Discontent; blackmail, in the very gang itself; suspicion; jealousy and hate. I see the end, Big Boy. If there's money to be made, I want to be made, I want it."

"Why not trust me, then—I'll pay you well if—"

"So," she said slowly, "will Gregory Ford. But I want it in advance."

We went over the whole thing again. I tried to convince her that she had the best chance in trusting me. And I wondered, too, if the squeal Gregory Ford was speaking about was to come through her, or if Gregory even knew who it was to come through. And I wondered if the squeal would leak out to the real leader through a police leak, as Old Benevolence Travers hinted. I went over my past record, and the girl listened. She knew the ropes—knew the Avenue up in New York—and she knew that when I got information I paid what I promised. Yet—I couldn't get her to talk.

"Five thousand for Olaf Sankin in my hands, and—" I took her by the arm as I added, "twenty-five thousand dollars if you bag The Hidden Hand for me."

Her eyes shone and she wet her lips. Money! That was it. She hesitated as she drew the car up to the curb near the Municipal park in West Palm Beach.

"I'll think it over, Big Boy," was the best I got as I stepped out of the car. "Let me know where you'll stable yourself."

And when I told her the name of the hotel Gregory Ford had given me, she added, "Stay there—be in your room after dinner." She jerked the car into gear, stepped on the gas, and muttered, "Twenty-five grand—that's a lot of jack." And she was gone.

21

A Woman Scorned

Things were quiet and dead in West Palm Beach. The park was a revelation to me. Nothing like it in the North. Men played horseshoes with the grim determination to win that is seen at the poker tables. Under gayly colored awnings, pinochle, cribbage, chess and checkers games went on. Every inch of space about those tables was crowded. Here were a bunch who made a business out of a pleasure.

I passed between the palms and by the long empty benches before the now vacant band-stand, up a quaint little street, down Narcissus Street—and so to my hotel. I checked in and inquired for any message. My own name I sprawled across the register. I had nothing to hide. I welcomed visitors. There was no word from Gregory Ford.

I did myself a wash, took a stroll down to the lake, stared over at the thick tropical growth of Palm Beach, and after killing a half hour in the park watching the old boys toss the horseshoes, went back to the hotel and did myself a feed. Still no message from Gregory Ford or the girl. Were both going to disappoint me? Finally I took a chance and rang up Old Benevolence Travers. I wasn't South for a rest—this was a business trip and I craved action.

Old Benevolence listened while I spilled my story. I told him that The Hidden Hand and Olaf Sankin were going to meet that night—that the girl had put me wise. I didn't say anything about Gregory Ford. No use to worry him about Gregory's beating us out yet.

"Where?" His question was just a breath over the wire. So he had some emotions after all.

"I don't know where. You're pretty well informed. I thought maybe you'd know."

"Stay at the hotel, then—I'll see what I can learn. Sit by the phone until you hear from me."

That was hot stuff. I didn't tell him that Rosie might blow the works later. I only like to give out facts—not promises nor suspicions. But I pulled out a newspaper and decided to sit it out. There were three calls that might come in, any one of which would bring action. Gregory Ford's, Rosie Sorrelie's and Old Benevolence Travers'. Besides, there might be a chance that I'd hear from the girl, Tina Sears.

It was Tina I was thinking about as I leaned back and stared out the window at the coming night. I was comparing Tina with Rosie, and figuring that after all Tina Sears didn't altogether fit into the picture, as Rosie Sorrelie certainly did. And Tina was in danger of her life—real and immediate danger—yet she wouldn't tell. Whether through fear or a loyalty, I didn't know. And Rosie—well—she was willing to talk for a price. It's funny how the bad win out. Tina would finally fall a victim to this creeping, clutching ring of crime—while Rosie would gather unto herself a bank roll and kick the lid off back in the city. Certainly, when one figures it out, life seems very unfair and— The phone rang.

"It's me—Rosie." And the voice of the dark-eyed girl fairly hissed over the wire. "I've seen Olaf and he's seen me—and him and the—you know who I mean—meet to-night. I'll trust to your honor on the bank roll, Race. They'll be at the old Parks Estate—eight o'clock. Don't come before—don't come after."

121

"Why the sudden change, Rosie?" I was suspicious, of course.

"Never mind—if you don't want to come, I know who will." Then, after a moment's hesitation, "It'll be worth your time besides the money. The—him, the leader has sent out word that Tina Sears is to be shoved over. She's a straight shooter, Race—she don't belong. You'll come?"

I hesitated a moment. I didn't like that final stuff about Tina Sears. They knew my interest in the girl. They might try to trap me through her. But Rosie's voice got me. There was a reckless abandon in it—so different from the determined woman I had left a few hours before.

"Haven't had a spat with Olaf?" I asked, in an indifferent voice—yet, my future actions might hang on her answer, at least the tone of her answer.

"He's beaten me for the last time—the slimy Swede." And there were reasons and reasons—much more convincing than if she had taken an hour to tell her story, or sworn to a dozen affidavits. Yes, somehow all this girl's acts rang with truth. She hadn't told me at first why she changed her mind and gave me information without the pay in advance. She hadn't told me until I asked her. If true, her reason was good and sufficient—that "fury of a woman wronged and scorned" or however it goes, is one of the sure-fire proverbs. She wanted money before. Now she wanted vengeance. She felt she was in a fair way to get both. And so did I.

She didn't go on and paint the glory there would be in the thing for me—the money I would get—how easy it would be to trap this Hidden Hand. With woman's intuition, she stayed away from all that. She played up Tina Sears and her danger. That part I didn't know whether to believe or not. But—

"How many are going to be at this meeting?" I asked.

"Just two—but you better bring Gregory Ford along. You can't handle it alone. It seems impossible to you that this leader should meet Olaf—a wanted man. But he has to. Olaf's broke—he's wanted badly by the police. They know him. He's demanded that the leader meet him—actually threatened this leader. He wants money—wants to make a get-away—and if he don't get money and don't get away clear, he's going to talk. Olaf Sankin—" and now there was strangely a ring of pride in her voice, "is the only one of the crowd that isn't afraid of The Hidden Hand. He isn't afraid of anything—not him—the slimy Swede." And there it was—a strange mixture of hate and pride—the lust for gold and vengeance. Also there was a warning. It was the girl's pride in Olaf's courage and strength and fearlessness that held her to him. Now, at the last moment, might not those bonds be strengthened again? On the level with me now, mightn't she switch again before eight o'clock, and warn Olaf of my coming—confess her double crossing? Perhaps—but I thought not. The Swede had a fiery temper. She wouldn't dare betray him and then tell him about it. No. Yet, women do strange things.

"You'll come—and bring Gregory Ford—and some of his men?"

"I'll know if you're lying to me." I put a confidence in my voice that I did not feel.

"But you'll come and bring—?"

"I'll come—alone!"

I heard her breath draw in sharply over the wire—heard her lips snap closed, as if they killed some words she might have spoken—then came the unmistakable click of the receiver. Our conversation was over.

I took out both my guns, broke each open and spun the barrels. No need to examine them—they're always ready for action. But I'm a careful man, who hopes to die in bed—though I'm not making any bets on it.

Things looked good, you'll admit. Rosie Sorrelie's story was more than plausible. Driven perhaps to desperation by

Olaf Sankin's demands and threats, this leader would meet him to-night. But why think it out? Here was a chance for real action.

If I got The Hidden Hand I got a fortune. If I got Olaf Sankin, and he was willing to talk, as Rosie said—then I'd get the money anyway. Besides that, there was Tina Sears. Where was she?

Now, where was this Parks Estate? I'd give Old Benevolence Travers a ring and let him know what was in the air. I'd need him later on. He was the angel that backed this show. He was entitled to ring down the curtain and take the applause as the author of the play.

I tried his hotel. He was not there. Old Benevolence was out hunting up information for me, maybe? He had told me to sit by the phone. But the necessity for that was over now.

I slipped my guns into my jacket pocket, sought the elevator and descended to the street. I'd have to find out where the Parks Estate was. It sounded big and ought to be easy to locate. I snapped out my watch—it was just seven o'clock. Plenty of time if it was close, and easy to find—not so good, otherwise.

I buzzed the clerk at the desk. He had lots of time, wasn't very busy, and seemed shocked that any one could be interested in real estate. I didn't mention the Parks Estate, but beat all around it. It took the best part of fifteen minutes, and I thought I'd have to come flat out with the name, when he slipped it over himself. The Parks Estate had been empty since the boom—it was along the Ocean boulevard, almost as far down as Lake Worth.

"It's a nice drive if you're interested. Cross to Palm Beach, turn south and follow the Ocean boulevard down as far as The Bath and Tennis Club. Keep left there—don't turn back over the South Borough Bridge or you'll land in West Palm Beach again. Keep along the ocean. Say—if you're interested in Palm Beach, why, I know—"

But I stalled that off.

"Where do I get a car?" I cut in.

"Want to drive one yourself? I do, often. It's cheap. Walk up Datura Street to Olive, and you'll find a place there where they rent them out."

Another five minutes I spent discussing real estate. I wanted to get the Parks Estate off his mind in case he was questioned. By the time I left, he had mentioned every vacant piece of property in Palm Beach—which was plenty. He'd have difficulty in remembering just what started our conversation.

22

The Whole Police Force

I found the "Drive Yourself" stand. "Walk In—Drive Out" decorated the door. So I did that little thing. No questions— no deposit to amount to anything. And I don't blame them. I daresay they wished I'd steal the car they let me have. Again I got my directions to the Parks Estate, and a line from the garage man I might use later.

"If ya get mixed up, ask any one the road to the Lake Worth Casino—that leads your way—and you can't miss the Parks Estate. Not a house a quarter of a mile either side of it—big yellow wall in front—and real estate signs pasted all over it."

And I was off—over the bridge to Palm Beach—down Royal Palm Way, with its towering straight royal palms, the trunks of which looked as if they were made of cement—and so to Ocean Boulevard. It was just seven-thirty. I stepped on the gas—the boat kicked up a fuss, but with careful handling tore off thirty miles an hour.

It was all straight going until I reached South Borough Bridge—but I spotted The Bath and Tennis Club, swung inland and around it to the left, and was on my way.

Two cars passed me, going in the opposite direction—one shot by me, traveling the same way. For a moment it swung to the right and was in the glare of my headlights. It was traveling at a high rate of speed—five men were in the back. Nothing extraordinary in that maybe—but I didn't like it just the same.

A half mile further on I saw the ocean again, just to the left of the road—then the yellow wall to the right—the many signs, and dull background of a large two-story house. Not a light, not a shadow—just blackness as I slipped by, hardly silently—but then, the racket of my engine showed an honesty of purpose.

I was watching now for a side lane, but there wasn't any—plenty of hard sand off the narrow highway, that was all. It wasn't my idea of a good place to park the car, but I finally picked a spot banked high with sand and partly hidden at each end by the thick tropical growth. It was getting late. I slipped in, put out the lights, and climbing from the car started out toward the road—then pulled up sharp.

Three figures had slipped around the bank of sand. I jerked back, and crouching low by the engine jerked out a gun. Then I shoved my gun back into my jacket pocket and my hand with it. A light flashed in the darkness—a light that lit on the blue coat and brass buttons of a police officer.

"What you want, Buddy?" The man with the light spoke, and I noted that the other two figures separated, slipping around so that the car was between them and me.

"A little engine trouble—afraid to stay on the road—too narrow." I forestalled the question as to why I pulled in there.

"Yeh?" The man with the light spat once, walked slowly and hesitantly toward me—and I saw that a gun dangled in his free hand. "Where you bound for, Buddy?"

"Lake Worth. Know anything about engines?"

"Business there—or friends?"

"Just a friend."

"Name of." And I felt his eyes raise and rest on my face with the flash, as he added, "I know every one in Lake Worth."

But I couldn't swallow that—not in the tourist season, anyway.

"Miss Purdy—Agnes Purdy—visiting her aunt—damned if I can think of the aunt's name."

"Where does she live?" He wasn't so cocksure now. Neither was I; that was a sticker and no mistake—and that was where the garage men's line came in.

"Going to meet her at the Lake Worth Casino—don't know her address. Any objection?" I took the offensive.

"No—no." The three of them were all very close to me now, looking at the car and nodding slightly—like they knew where I got it. "But there's been trouble on the road to-night. You're a young man, and evidently a tourist. We take good care of our tourists here. Joe, climb in this man's car—see if you can start it—and if you can, drive him safely to the Lake Worth Casino."

I thought that one over. It would take time—maybe, valuable time. But there wouldn't be much trouble in poking a gun in the cop's ribs, running him out of the car and handcuffing him to a tree a mile or so down the road.

But they weren't as innocent as I thought. A hand rested on my shoulder—the voice of the speaker came, hard and cold.

"We'll have a look at your pockets, friend," he said, and as he spoke, a hand from behind gripped at my right arm.

Here was a pretty mess. The game was up—that is, as far as working the thing alone was concerned. I talked and talked fast. I couldn't kid those boys out of the two guns in my pocket with any yarn about hunting alligators. I gave them the truth.

It took fully ten minutes to get my story over. That I was Race Williams—that if Gregory Ford was about, he could identify me—and that I was supposed to be in the raid with

128

him to-night. That he had called me up from Miami—and that if they got hold of Gregory Ford he would verify my statements and deal me in on the show.

"That's right." One of the men stepped into the light and scratched his head. "Mr. Ford was to bring Race Williams along; pick him up in West Palm Beach. But how come you got here ahead of him?"

"Tipped off that our party might leave. I wanted to be on the job."

"Do you know what's supposed to come off in that house to-night?" The leader jerked a thumb over his shoulder and up the road.

"I know it's something big," I told him. "The biggest thing in Florida." Then I leaned close to him. "Olaf Sankin and the Hidden Hand are at the old Parks Estate."

"Cripes! It's true, then. Sankin, yes—but the other lad! No wonder there's a score of us here. We have orders to arrest any one the least bit suspicious to-night. We'll keep you with us until Mr. Ford shows up—that's the best we can do. No way to identify you?"

And there was. A fourth figure moved through the darkness, spoke to the police captain, flashed a light on my face, and made things jake again.

"It's Race Williams, all right." The newcomer spoke with emphasis. "I tagged him a bit in Miami for Mr. Ford." Then with a smile, "Give him back his hardware, Captain—the boys ain't had much practice and a quick eye and a steady trigger finger may come in handy to-night."

Well—a reputation isn't a bad thing after all. There were a few pats on the back, the return of my guns, and an attempt to wise me up to proceedings.

"We've got the house surrounded and are just waiting for Gregory Ford to show up," the captain explained. "A jack rabbit couldn't get through."

And when I wanted to nose around the house, "Better stick close to us, Mr. Williams," he advised. "All the men are nervous to-night—they mightn't know you—and you mightn't know them. But—" he stroked his chin as we walked up the road, "this is a desperate man—he may make a dash for liberty any minute. There's a window in the rear, close to the jungle gardens behind. I've got two good men there—you might join them. For if this Hidden Hand is in that house, that's the place he'll try to make out."

I tell you it was cagey going after we entered the grounds of the Parks Estate. If the man we wanted was hiding in that big deserted mansion, he'd have to shoot his way out. Men bobbed up about the grounds, some in uniform, some in plain clothes—but all white faces—all hard-set chins—all determined-looking men.

The captain was talking.

"Gregory Ford got his tip a bit late—telephoned me to cover this place and let no one leave until his arrival. I'd like to make a bust in and be over with it—but orders are orders, and Ford's all-powerful with the authorities."

"Where did he get his tip—know?"

"Not me—a squeal, certainly. From the way we found things here it looks like a false scent—but Ford was positive he had it right—at least, that he had Olaf Sankin right."

And maybe he did. But I looked at the darkness of the house and shook my head. Old Benevolence Travers had said there was a police leak—if there was, well—The Hidden Hand would hear of this attempt to trap him. The whole police force must have been there.

23

A Message of Death

The captain brought me to a lad he called Fletcher, who was hidden in thick growth about five yards from high French windows—windows that groaned slightly in the strong, cooling breeze that swept from over the ocean.

"Race Williams—to stay here with you." And magnanimously the captain added, "If anything happens, take orders from him. He's an old hand and a valuable man. I'll drag Frank off." So he spun on his heels, and taking the other man with him, left me alone with Fletcher.

I had a strong desire to get my nose inside that mansion before Gregory Ford showed up. There were several reasons besides just plain curiosity. There was the girl, Tina Sears. Was she a prisoner there, as Rosie Sorrelie had more than hinted? And had Rosie Sorrelie tipped off Gregory Ford as well as me? She hadn't seemed to fancy my idea of going there alone.

Then, again, there was a good chance that The Hidden Hand might have escaped even after the round-up of policemen, or that he might escape while they were still there. If there was a leak in the department, mightn't that leak be some place about the grounds—and wouldn't that man open up a road for this Hidden Hand's freedom?

"Fletcher," I said to my companion, "see that window—it's partly open. I think I'll take a look inside—while you guard outside."

"No—no." He grabbed me by the shoulder. "Orders are to stay here until Mr. Ford arrives."

"You'll have to bust in then. I know Ford—and know the reason for those orders." Which was true. "He wants the glory—wants to shine as the light-haired boy. Now—I have reason to think there's a prisoner in that house—a girl who will be killed when the raid takes place—killed, so she won't give evidence. If I could slip in, take this lad unawares, I might save the girl's life. Come—you have nothing to lose. I'm going anyway—but you can help a little."

He stalled a bit, but he listened to me just the same. There was the glory if we made the capture. The failure to obey orders would rest on my shoulders. He didn't have any order to stop me if I started in, which I certainly would do. I pictured the straps of a sergeant on his arm, his face in all the papers—and told him flat, I'd go anyway. Then I reminded him of the captain's instructions to take orders from me.

"What do you want me to do?"

"Nothing but lay still, and not shoot at the first head that appears in the window after I'm in. Just watch—don't leave, to report. And give me a boost getting in. I don't want to make any noise."

Fletcher agreed, at length. I slipped off my shoes, and lying flat on my stomach snaked across the short grass to the window. It wasn't very high from the ground, but if some one was back there in the darkness they could pot shot me easily as I swung over the sill. The odds were strongly against that for more than one reason. A shot would be heard, and assure the watchers outside that some one was in the house. And the lad or lads inside wouldn't want to take such a chance. They couldn't know how many watched.

As I reasoned it out, I'd be safe until I got within the house. It would be safer to sock me than shoot me. But once inside I had an even break. I never ask for more.

Fletcher gave me the needed boost, so that I could sit on the window sill with both hands free. I made it. It was a wide sill. The windows opened out. They were not locked. I swung one of the French windows wide, and gun in one hand, flash in the other, dropped into the room.

Not a sound—or was there? Did something move there to my right? And Fletcher spoke behind me—hoarsely—but in a whisper that was as loud as a stage one.

"I'll drop back in the bush. Whistle when you're coming out. Whistle 'Annie Laurie'—then I'll know it is you."

I nodded down at his blurred white face, put a finger to my lips, and turning, moved quickly back in the darkness.

Again I thought I heard a movement; this time even more distinct, as if stockinged feet moved there ahead of me. My flash I held, undecided, in my hand. I wouldn't show a glim yet. Softly, I stepped out in the blackness, in the wake of those footsteps—real or imaginary. Then I chanced it. I was sure I heard them straight ahead. I pressed the button and sent out a stab of light. Was there a figure? Was there the outline of a man's shoulders? I couldn't be sure. The light shone now full upon heavy curtains—curtains that waved as if from a draft—yet, I felt no draft. Those curtains were not in line with the soft breeze through the open window.

Releasing the button of the torch I stepped to the curtains, felt of them in the darkness—slipped from the center to the edge, and so through the curtains into deeper blackness beyond. A hall, I thought—then I was sure. There were stairs that led above.

I didn't see the stairs—I didn't have to. I heard them; groan, groan, groan—feet beat noiselessly up. Yep—the feet were noiseless, but the stairs themselves weren't. I could hear each step creak in turn—not slowly, either, but quickly; one creak following rapidly upon the other.

I couldn't be mistaken this time. I haven't got the nerves to imagine such creaks as those. I knew beyond a doubt that some one climbed those stairs. There was a thrill to it. A tingling to my spine. I'm not ashamed of that. If I couldn't still feel the lure of the man-hunt I wouldn't be in the game.

If I'd been dealing with the ordinary criminal I'd of sent a stab of light up those steps, drawn a bead on the figure, and ordered him down or rolled him down. But to-night I hunted big game—shrewd game—not just Olaf Sankin, brute murderer; but the brains behind him and hundreds of others. The leader—this Hidden Hand himself.

Undoubtedly it was known that I entered that window. Undoubtedly shoulders had slipped through that curtain the very split second that my flash lit on them. And the owner of those shoulders had been in the room when I entered by the window. Now—I hunted two men—not one. If I showed a glim and spotted the figure on the stairs, might not another lurk in the darkness? I couldn't chance it. No necessity to chance it with the house so well guarded.

Carefully I slipped a step or two forward, groped around a bit with outstretched hand, at length felt the smoothness of a dust-covered banister and was on the stairs. I couldn't be sure—too light—too imperceptible—but I thought that feet beat above—beat far back in the house, until they were lost in the distance, or deadened entirely on soft carpet or more solid wood.

But there were the stairs. There was some one above—and there was Gregory Ford, to arrive any minute and make a raid. After all, Olaf Sankin might be in the house alone. The Hidden Hand might have had his warning through the police leak Travers spoke of, and if there was any confession coming, I wanted to be in on it. Besides, only the night before I had found Tina Sears a prisoner at the top of such a flight of steps. This time—well—if she was in the hands of this gang, they'd murder her just for vengeance, before the police broke in.

One, two, three steps I took. I tried sticking close to the banister. I tried the center of the steps. I tried pushing my body against the wall. But not much use. Every step gave up its dead—some louder, some weaker than the others—but every one must have registered to listening ears above or below. So I played the game as the lad ahead of me had played it. Forgot the creak and went in for speed.

I made the landing above in safety, listened a moment and hearing nothing took a chance with the flash. In that single second of brilliancy I spotted three doors—two closed and one open. The open door was my lay. I wanted a quick retreat in case of sudden attack—a place to back into that I knew to be empty and safe. Cautiously I approached the door, felt of the opening with one hand and slipped within.

Instinct was working now. No movement—no sound—not even my straining ears or active brain could imagine the slightest breath of life. Yet I felt—yes, knew—that I was not alone in that room. There was another; some place, close to me. It's a strange, eerie, unexplainable feeling—hard to believe, perhaps, but true just the same.

I edged away from the door—got my back against the wall—raised my gun in one hand and my flash in the other—and closed a finger upon the button of the flash. It's moments like those when I feel that I earn my salary.

Snap! The yellow circle split the darkness. No figure! Nothing human! No shot! Quickly I ran the light about that room. It was empty, and still the feeling persisted that I was not alone, and—

The light shot on a closed door—a closet door, no doubt. And the light shone full upon a white square of cardboard, and the black letters upon it. I smiled sort of grimly—the name RACE WILLIAMS stood out plainly. Olaf Sankin's work? And it was. There, a little below my name—was his. OLAF SANKIN stood out in bold letters.

But there was writing between the two names; a rough scrawl that I could not make out at first. A step closer and I read it.

To Race Williams
With the compliments of
Olaf Sankin.

So he knew of my coming. It had been a trap of the Sorrelie woman's then. Olaf Sankin left me emptiness, with his compliments. Childish that—but what one might expect from the mentality of Olaf Sankin. If he had left, who was the other in the house? Who was the owner of the feet that preceded me up the stairs? And if it was a trap, why the police outside? I stepped suddenly to that closet door, tucked the flash beneath my armpit, and grasping the knob jerked the door open, standing back—half behind it.

There was a pressure against my hand upon the knob, a soft swish, a crumpling mass, and a dull thud upon the floor. I half stepped back and clutched at my flash. A body—the body of a woman was crouched there at my feet.

24

I Accept a Challenge

I've always said that nothing is unexpected to me—that I can't be taken by surprise, but if the enemy had planned to trap me then, it would have been child's play for one of them to step through that doorway and put a bullet in my chest or my back—or half a dozen bullets for that matter. For it struck me as I looked at that crumpled heap that had been a woman—that I knew her; that it could be but one woman—Tina Sears.

Fear? No. I don't think you'd call it that. Dread? Repulsion? Nausea? No. Horror best hits it, I guess. A dull clammy sweat crept over me—then a coldness and a numbness, and finally a hope. For perhaps two minutes I was one useless private investigator. At length I pushed myself forward; willed my hands out; grasped that dead body and turned it slightly, then let it slip to the floor. The face now was directly in the splash of light from my flash.

There's no use to go into details. It's not pleasant. I've seen plenty of murdered men—yes, and some women. This was a gruesome job. And—and I half staggered to my feet and came back to life. The dead body on the floor was not that of Tina Sears. It was—Rosie Sorrelie. She had not tried to trap me then, but had played the game straight—and paid for it with her life. This, then, was what I received with the compliments of Olaf Sankin.

I won't try to hide my emotions—make myself out a better man than I actually am. It was a terrible murder—a bloody, brutal affair with a knife. Yet I was relieved. The woman was not Tina Sears. Only a moment did I experience any satisfaction—then I faced again the message on the closet door.

To Race Williams
With the compliments of
Olaf Sankin.

I gripped my gun and my flash the tighter. The dead girl on the floor had played the game with me. Here was her reward—and there was the laughing message from Olaf Sankin, and the brutally murdered woman at my feet to give the message a sinister, grim reality.

Olaf Sankin had killed her. Olaf Sankin wasn't afraid to let the whole world know about it. He had nothing to fear. The police already had enough on him to roast him half a dozen times over. I looked again at the body and again at the message. There was a challenge in it—a challenge which I was willing to accept. And I knew that Old Benevolence Travers was due for another disappointment. Once Olaf Sankin and I met face to face, his talking days were over. Any secret he held, he'd keep. And—upper teeth closed on a lower lip. There was Tina Sears! But where was Tina Sears? Did Olaf—?

My flash dropped to my side. I spun on my heel, and my gun came up. Distinctly from below, inside the house, had come a whistle—a low, soft whistle. Just one of warning? Just one from Fletcher, to call me below, or—? Turning, I dashed madly from the room. I remembered now the figure that had been in the room below when I climbed through the window. I remembered, too, the loud stage whisper in which Fletcher had told me how to warn him of my return. And the whistle that now came from below had a tune to it—and that tune was "Annie Laurie."

The man lurking within the room below had heard Fletcher's whisper, then. The figure on the stairs had slipped back in the house, down the servants' stairs, and was now signaling to Fletcher, who would think it was I. The figure must have been that of Olaf Sankin. He was below then. The man who had murdered the woman, Rosie Sorrelie—murdered her because she had betrayed him to me. Killed her and laughed at me.

I didn't hesitate this time. I simply turned and dashed from the room, down the hall to the stairs. My light splashed out the way ahead of me; the nose of my revolver followed the circle of light. I was mad enough; my heart beat loudly enough, and my blood raced hot through my body. But my hand was steady and my racing feet careful of each step.

I made the hall below—reached the curtains—snapped out the flash and dashed within. The French windows were flung wide; a figure slipped quickly from before them to the deeper blackness of the room. I didn't pause! I didn't wait! I didn't fire! I wanted Olaf Sankin. I wanted to be sure I got him. A stab of flame from my gun now would only direct a sure shot from that figure—a sure shot from the quickest and best gun in Florida. No, when I shot it must be only one shot.

My feet beat the faster. Through the darkness I ran—straight to the window—and straight out through it in one clean jump. My brain, as well as my legs, was working. I landed safely enough, tripped over something, stumbled once and straightened again. But I got one look. I had fallen over a body—the body of a man—dully in the moonless night I recognized that face. It was the cop, Fletcher; called to the window and struck down. But the man who struck him had not escaped. He was still within the house. Lacked time, maybe—or maybe he had waited for me to come below.

"I'll get help, Fletcher," I called hoarsely, and for the benefit of the man in the house, "He must have escaped—we'll search the grounds—warn the others." Then I ran toward the foliage.

A trap, eh? Well—I'd spring a bit of a trap of my own. And I'd spring it so that Olaf Sankin would have to do his stuff with his gun. The quickest shot in Florida? Well—we'd see just how quick that was.

I turned sharply in the denseness of the thick tropical growth. Just in time, too. My friend within the house didn't waste precious moments. There was one chance for him to get through the line of detectives safely—and that was the one unguarded window and the jungle gardens beyond. Fletcher was stretched upon the ground—and I had sought help.

He came—a white, blurred face—a black leg over the sill. A quick turn of his head and he was on the ground. One way only—the way I had come—straight through the thick growth. Bending low now, he ran toward me.

"And that, friend Olaf Sankin, will be enough." I popped from the bush before him. I didn't pound any gun into his chest. My gun dangled in my hand, as did his. I was giving him his chance. If he was half the man they said he was, and he claimed to be, he'd do his stuff.

But his hand never came up. Rather, his head. Slowly it jerked up, and we faced each other. Surprised? You could have knocked me down with a rotten tomato. Even in the dullness of the sky I knew him—the white face—the generous, seemingly smiling lips—and the colorless, vacant eyes. It was Travers—Old Benevolence Travers.

"You—you." And I was so disappointed I had half a mind to stick a bullet in his shoulder for luck. Then, "What the hell are you doing here?"

"Thank God—it's you. The police will never keep my secret, and then—he'd know—he'd know—The Hidden Hand would know. And my information would cease—my purpose be useless."

"But you—here—why?"

"After you telephoned me, I sought information—and found out that your information was true. That The Hidden Hand was to meet Olaf Sankin—but I found out more. That they were to meet here. I tried to get you on the telephone, but despite my—my request, you did not stay at the hotel. And then I learned something else. Rosie Sorrelie had betrayed Olaf Sankin. I was afraid—deadly afraid—but I came just the same, too late to prevent a murder—too late. But it was I who notified Gregory Ford. I had to do that—I couldn't see murder done. But it was too late—too late." He buried his head in his hands, and his shoulders shook.

"But the whistle—you were there then?"

"Yes—I lost my nerve after I had entered the house. I crouched in the darkness. Some one came in the windows. It was you, but I didn't know then. Then you followed some one else above. That some one, I firmly believe, was The Hidden Hand. Olaf Sankin left before the police came. They talked loud—there was a row—and trouble. I think Sankin will now talk."

"Olaf Sankin—won't talk." I set my lips grimly. "Go on. Then what? What happened? You were in the room when I jumped out the window."

"Yes—before that a shadow crept to the window. He whistled a tune. A voice answered—a head came near the window. The man inside struck—there was a falling body. The man jumped from the window and disappeared. I was about to do the same when you dashed down the stairs. But I didn't know it was you. And—I followed. Now—if the police learn that I am mixed up in this thing—information will reach—"

He stopped dead. Voices were calling. And one voice above the others. It was the voice of Gregory Ford.

"Race Williams, eh? Beat me to it. Well—we'll raid the house. If Williams gets in first we'll find a body—not a man. I'm telling you—that lad, Williams, goes in for stiffs."

"I'll meet you at the hotel." Old Benevolence Travers slipped by me—and he was gone. He was a strange old codger. After all, though, despite his trembling lips and shaking legs, I had to give him credit. Imagine him coming there, alone, to prevent murder. He surely got the breaks. He was lucky he didn't turn out a corpse. But—I nodded. The old boy had the guts after all.

I was greeting Gregory Ford just as they found Fletcher beneath the window.

"Don't blame Fletcher," I told Ford, as Fletcher began to come around. "His love of music was his downfall. But I'll take all the blame. I wanted a look-see in that house. I got it—Rosie Sorrelie, Sankin's girl, has been kicked over. Rather a mess—don't let the young hands have a look."

"Rosie Sorrelie—in there—murdered!" Gregory gasped. "She gave me the squeal—and paid for it."

"Right." I let him believe that—and I remembered, too, that Old Benevolence Travers' voice was soft, like a woman's.

"They—the murderer—escaped?" Gregory tucked a thumb into an armhole of his vest and glared at me. "You—messed it!"

"Maybe." I didn't deny it. "But I'll get him for you. Some one smacked Fletcher and beat it." I didn't tell him it was The Hidden Hand. Why give him any more disappointments?

Gregory Ford glared at me disdainfully. But I didn't kick. Why put the blame on Fletcher? I wasn't on the state's pay roll. I heard the sharp, quick orders for the raid, then turned and left the party. Gregory could run his own show.

Ten minutes later I had found my car and was making all speed possible back to West Palm Beach.

25

Olaf Sankin Does His Stuff

It was exactly eight-forty when I walked into my hotel. The clerk stuttered when I asked for my key.

"You've had—had a—a visitor, Mr. Williams."

"Yeh?" I gripped the key and eyed him. "Leave any card?"

"No—no. But I read a good deal—and I've seen your picture—and I know who you are. And I—I can guess why you're down in Florida and—I didn't tell the police the name of the caller yet, nor— He just went out, five minutes ago."

"So, bright boy," I smiled on him, "who was the visitor?"

And I got another surprise—a real shock almost.

"The visitor was," and the clerk leaned far over the desk, "Olaf Sankin. That was the name he gave—and I've seen his picture often enough in the papers to know him."

Involuntarily I looked around the lobby—especially at the thick pillars—and wished maybe they weren't there.

"He said you'd be right back—and you expected him—and if you didn't expect him it didn't matter. I didn't dare cry out. I didn't dare move. The lobby was pretty well filled—but he had a gun under his coat and—" the man's eyes bulged, "I saw his shirt beneath the coat, Mr. Williams—and there was blood on it. And—and—I was scared—too scared to holler, before he was gone—sort of backing away from the desk."

"He—he said nothing else?"

"Except that he'd telephone—and that you'd better wait in the lobby, as time might mean much to you—and that—" He turned suddenly to the girl across the little hall, at the switch-board. "That's the call—cause I told—told her to tell me here, and—"

"Call for Mr. Williams. Call for Mr. Williams." A boy was starting out.

I slipped the clerk twenty, cautioned him to silence, and squelching the boy's bellow, sought the booth. I won't say I wasn't a bit excited. Things for once were moving even fast enough to suit me.

"Olaf Sankin speaking." The guttural voice over the wire didn't waste time. "You saw Rosie to-night, and I left The Hidden Hand for the police to grab off. That evens that score with the dirty welcher. I'm leaving town—got a high-powered car ready—but—I ain't settled with you. You can't buy my gal and step out of the picture. If you want a bullet in the back—all right. I'll stick around and put it there. If you want it in your chest—now's the time to get it there. You've boasted of shooting it out with any gun—any time—any place. I'm your man. What ya say?"

"Where are you?" was the best I could think of.

"I'll tell ya that when you chirp your stuff. I'm close to hand. You saw the mess I made of Rosie. Now—" and he paused just a minute, "I'm giving ya the chance to trade lead with me before I do my stuff on your little skirt—Tina Sears. Well—ain't you got no red blood?"

"Plenty of it, Olaf. But you can't trap me into any lonely house—not like Rosie Sorrelie."

"Hell—I ain't aimin' to. I'll meet you in the open, for all the world to see. I'm within a block and a half of you now. When I hang up, I'll cross to the Park and wait for you there. If you come straight, without seein' or talkin' to no one, I'll wait. If you peep to a soul, a friend'll see it—and I'll blow." For the

144

first time his voice shook slightly, with passion. "I'm gunnin' for ya, Williams. Will ya come down to the Park and take your killin' like a man?"

"All right, Olaf," my voice didn't shake, "I'll come straight down—and I won't talk to a soul." And then, thinking a bit quickly under the circumstances, "How'll I know you?"

"You'll know me all right." He chuckled. "Five minutes— and if I don't run across you, I'll mail you a letter where ya can find the Sears moll—slightly damaged."

"All right, Olaf," I said, quietly enough. "I'll be right down." Call it murder if you will. But truth is truth. I didn't have a bit of doubt that I was going to kill Olaf Sankin within the next ten minutes. Not nice thoughts to contemplate? Well—maybe not. But I was rubbing my hands when I left the booth.

Was this a bluff on Olaf's part? Was this the gunman braggadocio? Did he think I wouldn't come? Did he intend to leave the Park the minute I entered it? No—Olaf would be there. And Olaf expected I would come. And I would. There was no emotion in his voice, except for that brief moment. No curses or cheap threats. Olaf was in the business of killing. In a way, perhaps, so was I. I guess we understood each other.

But with all Olaf's hatred for me; his thirst for vengeance because of the death of his girl, Rosie—for although he murdered her in cold blood, he no doubt blamed me for it—Olaf had been canny, and just a trifle too sure of himself. He knew me—had seen me—had even shot at me down in Miami. But he didn't know that I had seen him—seen his matted hair, his coarse evil face, his thick lips and the scar that ran from his sensuous mouth to one of those narrow, rat-like eyes. Yes— Olaf would know me. But—I would know Olaf—and not, as he thought, trust to garbled and blurred newspaper pictures taken years ago, when Olaf was young and inexperienced and used to make it a habit to be dragged in by the police.

I ignored the clerk's frantic facial contortions, to attract my attention. Hurrying through the lobby, I sought the street—

went rapidly across it, down Narcissus Street, and made fast time to the Park. I didn't watch for a shadow—didn't fear a bullet from some playmate of Olaf. There was no danger of that. This was Olaf's show. This was to take place in the Municipal Park. This was to startle the whole state of Florida and make deeper the fear of Olaf Sankin—and perhaps to make the fear of Olaf Sankin sink deep into the heart of The Hidden Hand—if he had a heart.

There was Tina Sears to think of, if I failed. There was the debt perhaps I owed to Rosie Sorrelie. There was the boyish itch to get even for the shot Olaf had fired at me. But I don't think any one of these reasons was driving me on. Olaf Sankin had said I'd often boasted that I'd shoot it out with any gun—any time—any place. And he was right. I had. I was coming then to the Park for one purpose only. To shoot it out with Olaf Sankin! The Hidden Hand and all the criminals in Florida would know of Olaf's invitation—and they'd know of the result.

It was a warm night. The moon had finally come out and now played about the tops of the giant palms. It was not quite nine o'clock. The band played a march. I knew the piece well—it was the American Patrol. And as the music died almost to a whisper, I caught the dull clamp of iron upon iron as the men tossed the horseshoes against the stakes.

The Park was crowded. The benches before the bandstand filled with people. The narrow walks dotted with strolling, laughing youth. The card tables beneath the colored awnings were a mass of bobbing heads.

Hands sunk deep in jacket pockets, I turned to the walk that led along the street by the Park and down to the horseshoe courts on the extreme west of the grounds.

Three horseshoe courts lay parallel to each other, and were inclosed by a wire fence about waist high. Behind me was the street, and across it the rows of tiny stores now closed for the night. Before me were the courts, fifty feet from fence to fence. Then a ten-foot path and another wire fence and more horseshoe courts.

Bright arc lights shone down upon the iron stakes and the faces of the people who hung over the fence, watching the players. Along each side were benches packed with other watchers. Every court was in play. My eyes ran down the benches, then across the courts to the face that shone out palely in the glare of the arc lights.

There was a good game in progress—the crowd told me that. I edged through the crowd until I leaned upon the wire fence. Indignant citizens closed in behind me. That helped. I didn't want to get shot from behind. But I didn't expect that. Olaf didn't think I knew him. It would be quite a feather in his cap if a bullet was found in my chest.

My position was a good one. Men protected me from behind; every seat on the benches was taken. There was only one real chance of getting a shot at me. And that was from the opposite fence, fifty feet across from me.

My arms were folded across my chest, each hand beneath my coat and up under my armpits. And each hand held a gun. Occasionally I elevated my elbows—to the indignation of the individuals on either side of me. Later, perhaps, they'd thank me for the dig in the ribs. If Olaf Sankin meant business, so did I.

Olaf couldn't miss seeing me. The arc shone full upon my face as I watched the spectators on the opposite fence. I appreciated the warmness of the southern night—few of the men wore hats or caps—those who did, didn't fit in with my picture of Olaf Sankin.

Clink! Clink! Clink! went the thud of iron against iron. An occasional laugh, a shout or two of encouragement, and the soft strains of the distant band.

Then a cap—a dirty, checked affair, behind the bobbing heads of those on the opposite fence. There were broad shoulders and a protruding chin—thick lips and the bluish purple of a vivid scar. Olaf Sankin was getting ready to do his stuff. I smiled grimly. He didn't know that I knew him. And it happened.

He raised his head and our eyes met. Whether he knew, before, that I knew him, or whether he suddenly realized that I knew him, or whether he didn't plan to take chances—I don't know, and never will find out.

But Olaf Sankin didn't wait until he was smack up against the fence. He was quick—like chain lightning the flash of nickel appeared suddenly from nowhere. And my hands flew out. We fired together I think. At least, he got a shot in as he thrust himself forward between two men.

I don't play favorites between my hands. I closed both index fingers at once, and the roar of my guns was as a single shot. The picture before me was clear—the sneering lips, the narrow eyes, and the vivid scar. And the distance was much to my liking.

Glass crashed some place across the street behind me. Both my guns now rested upon the wooden support above the wire fence. Olaf Sankin sort of stretched himself as he stood upon his toes—then the whiteness of his face in the stagelike glare was given color by the two tiny streams of red that came from both sides of his forehead. Not bad shooting that. The coroner's inquest would find that both those chunks of lead met back in what the giant Swede was pleased to call his brain.

He died funny, did Olaf Sankin. Further and further he stretched up on his toes. Then his hands went into the air as if he reached for something. The fingers of his right hand closed about the trigger of his gun. A single shot; a deafening roar in the dead quiet of the Park; a shoot of orange-blue flame toward the distant skies—and Olaf Sankin sank, a huddled, useless mass, on the gravel path.

Like a salute, that final shot was. I think that he was dead before ever his finger closed upon the trigger. But that's only my opinion. I'm not enough of a scientist to argue it out. Now—I gave my attention to the people, and the hands that would soon be grasping at my shoulder.

But the psychology of crowds is hard to understand. There I leaned against the rail, the two smoking guns still in my hands, and no one made a grab for me. Three or four people on the benches stood up, looking dazedly about them. One horseshoe pitcher, with a far-away look in his eyes, tossed a shoe. The man beside me looked vacantly into my face.

"Nice shooting, eh?" I sunk my guns and smiled down at the white face that was streaked with blue lines.

"Fine, sah—very good, sah—and— My God!" he shouted suddenly, "a man's been murdered." Horror, fear, terror—all were in his final words. Then he sank slowly to the ground in a faint. It had taken nearly a full minute for the truth to dawn on him.

People were shouting over by the bandstand. Others were running from the Park. I turned slowly and walked, unmolested, up the street. My lips were dry and my tongue thick. I stopped and did myself a drink at a drug store before the crowd burst in. There was the blowing of whistles, the siren of a police car, and the crack, crack of motorcycles. Then panic as the shouts rang out.

"A man's been murdered in the Park."

Yet we wonder why there are 12,000 murders a year in the United States, and not even one in every hundred convicted of the crime. At least twenty-five people must have looked straight into my face after the shooting—but I'd bet that on the witness stand not any two of them would describe me alike. Yet, I was indifferent to that. I didn't intend to hide my identity with the shooting. Gregory Ford would know— besides, there wouldn't be much of a squawk over the passing of Olaf Sankin.

I was back in my hotel just ahead of the news. The clerk eyed me excitedly. He'd gotten his nerves back somewhat.

"I might have been rich." He shook his head. "If I'd only been slick enough to take Olaf Sankin! There's a price on his head; twenty-five hundred dollars."

"Dead or alive?" I asked.

"Dead or alive," he answered.

I nodded at that. It looked as if I was getting the breaks after all.

"There's a lady in the writing room—came in just after you went out—a Miss Sears."

"Thanks." And the smile I gave him was real. "If I get this Sankin, there'll be five hundred dollars in it for you."

"Think—do you think you—you can shoot as quick as he? There isn't a man in Florida who believes that any one can shoot straighter and quicker than Olaf Sankin."

"People change their opinions." I shrugged my shoulders. "By to-morrow morning every man in Florida will have changed his."

I left him staring after me. Tina Sears was waiting for me. Tina Sears was safe. But I hurried to her. She mustn't be found with me when Gregory Ford came—and the police.

"I had to come. I had to come!" She rushed toward me in the deserted writing room. "I left you in Fort Lauderdale because I thought it would help you. Now—" her hands were on my shoulders, "don't think bad of me—if I live or if I die. Olaf Sankin has sent for me. I have to go to him or he'll tell my secret."

"You don't have to go to him." I lifted her hands from my shoulders and looked down at her. "Olaf Sankin is dead—and he's taken your secret with him."

I sighed slightly. Not that I was sorry I killed him. But he had taken another secret with him—a secret that was worth a fortune. The name of The Hidden Hand. But there was another chance. Beekman was still alive. Beekman knew. I set my lips grimly. And Beekman would talk!

26

Behind the Curtain

The question has often arisen—how does a man feel who has just killed another man? Perhaps this is as good a time as any to wise up lads who ask such questions. I had just killed a man. And I felt the satisfaction of one who has completed a good day's work. I don't know if that's good psychology, but I do know that it's fact.

Olaf Sankin had made his threat. As results proved, he was ill-advised—both ill-advised and dead. Where the old conscience didn't bother me for kicking off The Slimy Swede, the financial end of it did. It had not been good business. Olaf Sankin would have been worth much more to me alive than dead—for if he talked I could have named my own figure to Old Benevolence Travers.

At the present time things looked more difficult than they did in the beginning. Four chances and three of them were gone. Then, again, there was the girl who had plopped right into the picture at the beginning of the case and pulled that stunt which was a new one on me. She had saved my life.

Now I don't like to appear conceited but those who know me know that I don't make a habit of popping out of bad situations through the aid of another. I stand firmly on my own feet. Tina Sears had saved my life. And bear this in mind. She was the first and only one to lay undisputed claim to that distinction. Therefore, I had a debt to pay to her. And what's more, I'd pay it—the best interest of Old Benevolence Travers, the best interest of the state of Florida, or the best interest of myself notwithstanding.

I'm no fool, you understand; no moving picture hero; but I owed my life to this girl and if necessary she could have it—if necessary, mind you. No retrieving a glove from the lion's den; no hanging on a precipice to get my lady a rare flower. I'm not soft-headed, and I wasn't in love with the dame—not me. But—I'd risk my life to save hers if she was in danger.

Believe me, that's no idle boast. She was in danger—real danger, and no mistake. The Hidden Hand and Beekman, the last of the four subordinate leaders of this gang, held a secret over her that would mark her as a member of the gang and lay her open to a charge of murder, innocent though she was in fact.

That was the lay as I looked down at Tina Sears in the writing room of the hotel in West Palm Beach, Florida, and told her that Olaf Sankin was dead and even now the whole town shrieked the news.

"Shriek" was right. They did. As I finished speaking, we both raised our heads. Crowds were running down the street in the direction of the Municipal Park—crowds who were as anxious to get there as the crowds ten minutes before were to get away. That's life! I won't try to explain it.

"He's dead—dead." Tina Sears sort of clasped her hands together in front of her. "But—he's only one—there's still him," her voice lowered to a whisper, "The Hidden Hand—and another who knows my secret."

"Beekman." I nodded. "He won't trouble us long. It may take time for me to hunt him down, but I'll stir him out of his hiding place—make no mistake about that. He—"

"Alexander Beekman." Her eyebrows went up slightly. "Yes, I often thought he was in it. His smiles, his smirks—his assurance, as he watches me."

152

"You know him, then—you see him often?" My hands shot to her shoulders. "You can tell me where he is?"

"Why, that is no secret. Alexander Beekman does not hide. He has his home across the lake, in Palm Beach. Every afternoon he plays golf on the Royal Ponciana Links. He calls himself a New York jeweler, though it is an open secret that he is a pawn-broker."

"And a fence," I cut in. I knew of Beekman back in New York, and knew, too, that although he was a suspected fence, the police never hung anything on him.

"Maybe. But you can learn nothing from him. He is above suspicion—cruel and silent—and I believe the very right hand of this leader, The Hidden Hand. But his acquaintances, his associates, his pastimes, stamp him 'approved' by the winter colony here. And, Mr. Williams, for you own good beware of this man. More I dare not say. His house is guarded day and night. And I know for a fact that one detective who held suspicions, but unfortunately kept those suspicions to himself, entered his house and was never seen again until his body was discovered in the inlet down by the town of Lake Worth."

"He's the lad, all right. Now, Tina, for your own best interests—come clean. I'll see you through—help you—and—"

I stopped suddenly and listened by the curtains. The voice was loud, important, and punctuated by the moving cigar I knew so well. Gregory Ford was entering the lobby of the hotel and passing close to the little curtain by the writing-room door.

"Hell, Captain!" the voice boomed. "No man knows what this Williams is going to do next—but when I saw the corpse of Olaf Sankin, it was as plain to me as if he'd left his card on the stiff's chest. I—"

The loud voice rattled to silence, to boom out distant and inaudible at the hotel desk.

Tina Sears clutched me by the arm.

"It's Ford—the detective," she stammered. "Don't let him

153

see me. Don't let him take me. Hide me away some place."

"It's got to come eventually, Tina, if you stay in this part of the country. He saw you on the boat with Jack McCleary. He suspects you. Why not tell him all that—"

"No—not now. Five minutes' start—two even—and I will be safe. He won't dare arrest me when he—" She peeped through the curtains, then crouched back. "He's coming—I—"

"The curtain—there by the window." I half pushed her toward it. The curtain wavered once, settled, and was still. I turned, to face Gregory Ford and the captain of police I had seen at the deserted house earlier in the evening.

"Gregory Ford knows everything," the detective boomed as he squinted at me from the doorway. "Hello—" he shoved both thumbs into the armpits of his vest, "not in here, surely, to write a letter of confession—or just one of your racy memoirs after that little shooting?"

"So you know all about the shooting." I beamed across at him. I didn't like the way his eyes shot over my shoulder and anchored upon the curtain. "Did you like the killing?"

"First rate." He nodded vigorously. "If I'd been two minutes earlier I'd of heard the shot. Technically, I suppose, you'll have to be brought up and admitted to bail. If you're working for the state, you no doubt can fix that. If it's not convenient," and his cigar did a ring-around-Rosie, "I could fix it for you. Mere legal detail, you know."

"You could hardly take the credit for the shooting." I shook my head. "A score or more of people looked straight into my face."

"Hardly that—but we were working together last night—over on the ocean front. It might help you if—well—you were kind of acting with me to-night. Sort of couple the names, you understand. After all, Captain Rogers here understood we were together. Anyway, it might help you a bit."

How much it would help me Gregory Ford didn't realize. There was, after all, a corpse to account for. Courts are slow and the judiciary ponderous, and I had no backing which I could reveal except my own two guns and the will to use them.

"We'll call it a duet then." I took the extended, pudgy hand. "Sort of acting for you, eh? But independent in the future."

"Exactly. Alone here?"

I turned, too, and looked at the curtain. It was waving slightly. Gregory Ford winked at me and crossed the room. I followed—then stopped. The captain of the police leaned against the wall, his right hand half beneath his coat. He had been warned then. Gregory Ford had not forgotten his last attempt to arrest the girl, and my interference. So I shrugged my shoulders and stood my ground. I'd have to talk him into letting her go.

"No need to feel alarmed, Race." Gregory stood with his hand on the curtain. "The clerk told me of the female who was waiting here for you. She evidently has given you some good advice—and you've acted upon it. You can't fool Gregory Ford." He suddenly jerked back the curtain.

The space behind it was empty. The girl had gone. A long French window swayed slightly in the sudden draft.

27

The Black Sedan

Gregory Ford's unlighted cigar pounded against his upper lip. Leaning forward he peered cautiously out of the window. My grin met his when he turned, but his grin won. Gregory Ford was not a half-bad detective. My smile faded as his grew.

"A young lady of parts, Race. Decidedly a young lady whose acquaintance would be worth cultivating." And then snapping the words, "Well—she's been followed, and if I'm not mistaken here's Fletcher with a bit of information.

Detective Fletcher, the white of a new bandage showing beneath his gray fedora hat, appeared in the doorway. He eyed me, slightly belligerent, slightly shamefaced—but the blow he had received on the head earlier in the evening had not been such a bad one.

"Speak up!" Gregory Ford ordered. "Mr. Williams and I have come to an understanding. It's about the party that just left by the writing-room window?"

"Yes, it is." Fletcher cleared his throat. "We weren't exactly expecting a woman—but Gearson and Brown followed her. She walked toward Clamtis Street and the park. We didn't know if you wanted a pinch."

"You couldn't." Gregory nodded. "For I don't know myself." He eyed me shrewdly. "But we'll be walking toward the park. They won't lose her now."

"No chance." Fletcher smiled. "She saw me, I think, but not them. They slipped into the crowd that are flocking down Narcissus Street, toward the park."

"The park?" Gregory Ford rubbed his chin. "And you, Race—it's an old belief that the criminal is drawn back to the scene of his crime."

"Right." And arm in arm Gregory Ford and I left the hotel.

I didn't fully understand Gregory Ford then. When he blustered and bellowed and puffed, he was as easy to read as an open book. But it wasn't like him to be cagey and evasive. I had a feeling that he knew more than he let out, and that inside of him he was enjoying a certain superiority over me.

"How come you had the window watched—what made you suspect that the girl would be here?"

"This time, Race," he pinched my arm, "the heart ruled the head. My good fortune in having a couple of men outside that window was due entirely to big-heartedness. Olaf Sankin was dead. You had killed him. The law of vengeance is the law of the criminal. I won't say I expected you to be shot dead in the hotel to-night, for I know very well that you can play at that game as well as another. When I entered the hotel I had it watched. That the girl fell into the bag was purely accidental—one of the lucky breaks in the game, of which you have had so many and I so few."

"But the girl, Gregory. She did me a service—a great service. Can't you let her go? The help she gives me will reflect back to you."

"Maybe yes—maybe no. One girl, Rosie Sorrelie, would have talked—and died. Why not this one? Then again—what she has confided to you, I do not know. And damn it all, Race, you can't go on forever. Let us say that it is even money you'll live through the thing—ten to one the girl won't. It's impossible to think that this gang don't know of her meetings with you. No—I can't chance it. She'll talk to me or I'll drag her in."

"And the charge?" I wanted to learn if Gregory Ford, too, knew her secret—the secret that this criminal and his leader held over her head.

"Well—" again the hand caressed his chin, "that depends on who she is and if she has a record. I don't doubt that half a dozen things will pop up after we get her in the line-up. If they don't—there's her presence with McCleary, on the boat."

"She might have just met him on the boat. A passing acquaintance that—"

"Good God!" Gregory Ford stopped dead in the middle of the sidewalk, "you'll be advancing the theory in a minute that she heard of McCleary's past and was trying to reform him. If she's such a sweet, innocent bit of goods, why fear her arrest? She'll undoubtedly put us all to shame and leave the police station with our humble apologies." No—decidedly, I didn't like Gregory Ford's humor this night.

"Just what are your suspicions?" I asked Gregory as we reached the cross-street that led to the park, and waited for the mass of cars to pass.

"Well—there's several. The least of which is not the idea that she gay-cats for this gang; sort of works around in the big houses—spots the lay and maps it for the boys."

"Gregory," I told him, "before this thing's over you'll need me. I'm going to get this Hidden Hand. The girl's done a lot for me—let her go. I'll be responsible for her, and when the showdown comes with The Hidden Hand I'll deal you in."

"Just what has she done for you?" His eyes were narrow as he watched me now.

"She saved my life," I said simply. "I'd do a lot for that girl. You're playing a dangerous game."

The cigar did tricks across his face.

"You went in for a killing this night," he said. "I could cur-tail your activities for some time. And I'm not fool enough to laugh at your bluff. If you tell me that in crossing you I'm playing a dangerous game, I believe it. And I'm willing to believe it. Now—in plain words—is your threat one of indifference to future trouble I may get into, or is your threat one of personal violence?"

We stood on the curb by the thickly packed cars before The Kettler Theater—shoulder to shoulder, face to face, eye to eye. There was no doubt that Gregory Ford was a fearless man.

"There's my position with the State." I played up to his belief that I had been hired by the state of Florida.

"Hell! Forget that. I saw the attorney-general in Miami last night, and the state of Florida has nothing whatever to do with your activities. You see, they think you're working for me."

I guess I smiled rather sheepishly. So Gregory Ford had been carrying me along lately, when I thought that I was carrying him. The line of cars began to move slowly. A big sedan pulled closer to the curb, the door opened and a man leaned out.

"Mr. Ford," he called. "She's in the curtained taxi two cars ahead. Will you or—"

But Gregory Ford was already climbing into the sedan. He paused on the step when I would have followed him.

"For a price." He let the captain of police and Fletcher squeeze by him and enter the car. "The name of the party who hired you, Race. Come—" as the line moved, "the name of your client, for the girl's liberty."

And I—I just stood and looked at him as the door of the sedan closed. There was the hope that the girl might suspect, and get away; the thought that I might run along the line of cars, and popping in on the girl warn her of her danger. But that wouldn't do. As things stood now, Gregory Ford was simply trailing the girl. There was a possibility that she might give him the slip. There was no hope that I could step into her car without the occupants of the sedan seeing me. Such an action would certainly cause her immediate arrest. Surely, this night all the high cards were in the hands of Gregory Ford.

If he had only waited—only given me a chance to get in touch with Old Benevolence Travers. Benevolence, under the circumstances, might allow me to give his name to Gregory Ford. Travers' secrecy in the case was only through his fear of personal violence, I thought—and through his suspicions, which he claimed to be a certainty, that The Hidden Hand had a decoy planted in the very police department itself. But surely he could not for a moment suspect Gregory Ford of being the leak through which information concerning the activities of the police reached this criminal leader.

Of course I owed something to the girl, but that was personal. My ethics have been shot to pieces many times. But under no circumstances could I betray the confidence of my client.

The sedan pulled away, the cars moved more quickly. And I acted. I just hopped aboard a hunk of tin that was three cars behind the police machine. A young lad about nineteen was driving it.

I explained my presence simply enough.

"Detective, Buddy. Follow that sedan. The black one, with the cracked window in the rear."

"Yeh—" the boy's eyes brightened. "About this—this shooting in the park. I wanted to see—"

"Not a word!" I shushed him with a look that Gregory Ford might have envied. "Let me see if you've got the makings of a real flatty in you."

And the boy did. We turned along the lake, onto the road which led to the bridge and Palm Beach. The same bridge that I crossed but a few hours before. A clock somewhere knocked off the half hour.

What was in my mind? Nothing definite at first. A desire to help the girl, of course; perhaps an appeal to Gregory Ford again and, at the worst, when the pinch was made, to stand by her, get her a good mouth-piece and a bondsman.

160

I had to call down the speed of the flivver when we reached the bridge, for we were close to the police car, with only one car between us

"Just hold your distance, son," I told the boy. "I don't want little Mary in the car ahead to suspect she's got a lamb. And never mind asking questions about the shooting in the park," I killed that talk, "keep your mind on the black boat ahead."

Our speed increased as we reached Royal Palm Way, but not to any great extent. Where the black sedan could make monkeys of us, the taxi the girl had probably couldn't. But Gregory Ford was not anxious to overtake the girl yet. He wanted to find out where she was going.

And where was she going? Would her destination strengthen Gregory Ford's suspicions of her or weaken them? From the little playmates the girl seemed to have I thought her destination would rather help Gregory and hurt her. But it might help me, too—that is, as far as the case I was working on was concerned.

A block from the ocean the car between us went straight on but on the police car turned right. Now we were right behind the black sedan. But the speed was not great enough to make Gregory Ford think we followed him. Besides, it didn't matter much what he thought. Common sense told me it would not only be dangerous, but foolhardy, to attempt a rescue. There were at least four, if not five, men in the black sedan beside Gregory.

Faintly I saw the taxi shoot left on a narrow road. Then the rear light on the police car went out—just a black shadow as it, too, made the curve. I leaned forward and switched out the flivver's lights.

"We're playing the game in the dark, too," I told the youth.

"Gee!" and "Gee!" again, was the best he could get out. But there was nothing of fear in his voice—just enthusiasm. That's youth.

161

28

A Single Shot

Dimly, ahead, I made out the tail light of Tina Sears' taxi as it pulled up to the curb by a small house on the left of the road. Directly across the street was the wall of a big estate that seemed to stretch far down to the ocean road. Far back were the lights of a great house—the house itself plainly visible, stretching its Spanish architecture over a considerable bit of ground. But it was the small house before which Tina Sears stopped.

The girl evidently didn't see the shadows of the five men who climbed from the black sedan perhaps a hundred and fifty feet behind her. Dimly, shadowy, she stood by the side of the taxi, paying off the driver. But if she didn't notice the occupants of the sedan, the occupants of the sedan noticed her.

As two of the men started toward the girl, three others hesitated on the sidewalk in the shadows of a tall palm. Would they give their attention to the girl or to the flivver in which I had followed them?

Well—I'd give them a surprise and give the girl a chance. I leaned forward and switched on the headlights. The semi-darkness of the street blazed into light; a circle of brilliant yellow that li...t full upon the five men and reflected clearly the brass...ttons of a policeman's uniform.

...or a split second the moving picture ahead became a ...e girl stood beside the taxi—the four detectives and ...harnessed bull stopped dead, facing the light. I hung ...the step of the flivver. There we...sel for the fraction ...cond, just like a three-sheet po...r advertising a mys-...movie. And the show was on...e toward the girl. Anoth-Two men moved toward me—police, looked out from the er, whom I thought the captai...rtain, the girl stood beside sedan. Silent, motionless and the little house, reached the the taxi. Then she walked...rning suddenly ran frantically gate before the entranc...d out on the road, full into the back across the side...re was no doubt that she unde-glare of the headli...nd there was no doubt of her inter-stood the situati...end. Whether it was panic, fear, or te tion. Diploma...she were caught, didn't matter. She vs not harm...om; running like a common thief from...e certainty...No—there was no doubt that she under...d fleein...was fleeing from. Plainly the glare from...ny law...one upon the brass buttons of a police offic

...had hardly reached the center of the road...ore ...ord's voice called its warning—its order f...r to ...e heard it, of course, but only ran the faster...n the ...broke into life. Gregory's orders were short...effec-

There was nothing panicky about him. H...in no...n. Th... way excited that events had taken such an abr...e har girl had declared herself afraid of the law. Sh... work explaining that later. ...na Se...

Gregory Ford and another went directly...where Two others covered the opposite side of th...rily, ir girl might have sought seclusion, at leas...her. thick jungle growth. Now that retreat w...

To her right was the high wall of the big esta[te]; ahead, the Ocean Boulevard road and the beach; to the jungle growth—but the two officers had made escape way impossible. The girl was caught. There didn't seem chance for her. But I joined the chase, making directly after the girl.

"It's all right.' I recognized the detective who waited, and watched me. "Ra[t]e Wil[liam]s, you know—in on the show, of course." There wa[s] a ring[,] disconfidence in my voice—surely Gregory Ford hadn't di[s]c[onfidence in] my friendship for the girl with this lad.

And Gregory hadn't. The fir[st] of the detective convinced me of that. His name w[as] rotund, garden-growing detective a—a middle-aged, much for him. He ran by my side for a It was all too

"You, eh, Williams? And messed th[e] [g]rumbling.

liht."

With relief I saw him pocket his gun. Th[en] with that hi[m], he gasped, "Who's this dame, anyway— be doing? I wouldn't recognize her if I saw h[er] [an]d on ted[i]er little figure hurrying down the street a[nd in]to [t]axi."

A[nd] that was all from him. He had bad dogs as bein[g] [ov]erweight.

A[nd n]ow the boy driver of the hunk of tin was showing stu[ff] [c]ursed him silently. The flivver had come to life an[d] wa[s] [sh]oting down the road. It wasn't that which bothered me[,] the headlights. He just moved fast enough to flash the [fig]ure of the running girl before the officers.

T[he c]ars was making time—useless time. The detective and [he]rnessed bull across the street were almost abreast of h[er,] [ba]ring prevented her chance of crossing into the heav[y. T]h[roug]h, they cut out into the street, in a fairway to head[,] the b[e]fore she reached the Ocean Boulevard road or thr[o]ugh that would do her precious little good. Gre[g] called once or twice and even threatened to

164

low that lit full upon the five men and reflected clearly the brass buttons of a policeman's uniform.

Just for a split second the moving picture ahead became a still. The girl stood beside the taxi—the four detectives and the one harnessed bull stopped dead, facing the light. I hung half on the step of the flivver. There we posed for the fraction of a second, just like a three-sheet poster advertising a mystery movie. And the show was on.

Two men moved toward me—three toward the girl. Another, whom I thought the captain of police, looked out from the sedan. Silent, motionless and uncertain, the girl stood beside the taxi. Then she walked toward the little house, reached the gate before the entrance, and turning suddenly ran frantically back across the sidewalk and out on the road, full into the glare of the headlights. There was no doubt that she understood the situation now. And there was no doubt of her intention. Diplomacy, bluff, or her own assurance that they could not harm her was at an end. Whether it was panic, fear, or the certainty of disaster if she were caught, didn't matter. She was fleeing for her freedom; running like a common thief from the law. It wasn't the fear that some of this Hidden Hand gang were after her. No—there was no doubt that she understood just what she was fleeing from. Plainly the glare from my headlights shone upon the brass buttons of a police officer.

The girl had hardly reached the center of the road before Gregory Ford's voice called its warning—its order for her to halt. She heard it, of course, but only ran the faster. Then the police broke into life. Gregory's orders were short and effective. There was nothing panicky about him. He was in no way excited that events had taken such an abrupt turn. The girl had declared herself afraid of the law. She'd have hard work explaining that later.

Gregory Ford and another went directly after Tina Sears. Two others covered the opposite side of the street where the girl might have sought seclusion, at least temporarily, in the thick jungle growth. Now that retreat was cut off to her.

To her right was the high wall of the big estate; directly ahead, the Ocean Boulevard road and the beach; to her left the jungle growth—but the two officers had made escape that way impossible. The girl was caught. There didn't seem a chance for her. But I joined the chase, making directly after the girl.

"It's all right." I recognized the detective who waited, and watched me. "Race Williams, you know—in on the show, of course." There was a ring of confidence in my voice—surely Gregory Ford hadn't discussed my friendship for the girl with this lad.

And Gregory hadn't. The first words of the detective convinced me of that. His name was Brown—a middle-aged, rotund, garden-growing detective of fiction. It was all too much for him. He ran by my side for a moment, grumbling.

"You, eh, Williams? And messed things again with that light."

With relief I saw him pocket his gun. Then, as I gained on him, he gasped, "Who's this dame, anyway—and what's she been doing? I wouldn't recognize her if I saw her—just spotted her little figure hurrying down the street and slipping into a taxi."

And that was all from him. He had bad dogs as well as being overweight.

And now the boy driver of the hunk of tin was showing his stuff. I cursed him silently. The flivver had come to life and was shooting down the road. It wasn't that which bothered me. But the headlights. He just moved fast enough to flash the picture of the running girl before the officers.

Tina Sears was making time—useless time. The detective and the harnessed bull across the street were almost abreast of her. Having prevented her chance of crossing into the heavy growth, they cut out into the street, in a fairway to head her off before she reached the Ocean Boulevard road or the beach—though that would do her precious little good.

Gregory Ford called once or twice and even threatened to

fire, I think. But the dick with him was an athletic fellow; didn't waste his breath, and was eating up the distance between himself and the girl—making feet out of yards, and then inches out of feet.

Tina Sears lost her head completely. At least she seemed to, for she ducked suddenly and dashed madly toward the stone wall. Even if she could have jumped up, grasped the top and swung over, the opportunity was lost. The man was right on top of her.

I saw her reach the wall, turn suddenly in the brilliancy of the headlights, and face her pursuer. Gregory Ford shouted something; the two men crossing the street called out hoarsely; the young fellow driving the flivver shouted, too, and swerved the car as, for the first time in the excitement of the pursuit, he saw the two officers directly in his path.

I guess they had a close call but I couldn't be sure. The swerving of the car blotted out the picture of the detective in the very act of pouncing upon the girl. The shadow of the wall, a banyan tree that hung over it from inside the grounds, and the sudden disappearance of the headlights all helped make the semi-darkness of the southern night seemingly black.

There was a stab of yellow, the roar of a gun—and silence. Then a curse from Gregory Ford, the answering shout of men, and a voice above the others.

"It's Gearson—and the dame has killed him."

Then came the voice of Gregory Ford, in breathless, hoarse jerks.

"But the girl—where is she, you fool. I—damn it, man, she's gone."

The next instant I was on the scene. Flashlights were out. Detective Gearson lay upon the coarse grass close to the wall, a huddled silent mass.

Shocked? Yes, I was considerably shocked. I knew that the girl carried a gun. I knew, too, that in that last few seconds she had a chance to use it. I knew, too, that she feared capture.

But—well—a shot in the arm, the leg, or even the shoulder would have served her purpose to escape. And Detective Gearson had been shot through the neck. But he wasn't dead. The tiny trickle of blood told me that the bullet must have missed his jugular vein.

Gregory Ford took one look at the inert body, rolled Gearson over on his back, cursed out the taxi driver and the lad who had driven the flivver, and was a man of action again.

"There—" he thrust out a pudgy finger. "A gate—come on. We'll get this she-devil. Hatton," he turned to the harnessed bull, "stay by Gearson until Captain Rogers comes up. Chase that taxi for an ambulance, and the other bloat that drove Williams, for the nearest doctor. As for you—" he turned to me, "come along, if you want to be in at the end of it. I've got a charge now—and it's 'Murder.'"

"But—Gearson may pull—"

"Not him." Gregory Ford nodded vigorously, and I saw the gun he held in his hand.

Gregory, the two detectives, and myself passed through the little gate and found ourselves in spacious, well-kept grounds. Distantly, the lights in the house stood out. A fountain, great clusters of unfamiliar bush, an occasional giant palm, and just behind us the great banyan tree which overhung the wall.

But across that vast stretch of open, well-kept lawn no figure ran. No windows were open at the big house, no heads peered out. Not odd that, for it was hardly possible that the shot had been heard, or if it had at that distance it might easily be taken for the backfire of a car, a blowout, or just the roar of the ocean as it pounded softly on the beach.

I think that I saw the girl first; her lithe figure dashed suddenly from behind a marble fountain and sped straight across the open, toward the house. That she saw us was certain, but again just one thing was in her mind. Speed! What she hoped to accomplish by speed now, I don't know. Certainly there was no place to hide close to the house. Certainly she was clearly outlined in the moonlight. Certainly she couldn't hope to get around the house.

And certainly she didn't intend to try to get around it. The house was broad; she ran straight toward the side of it; straight toward a little side porch before two lighted windows.

"Don't be a fool, Gregory," I called hoarsely as I knocked up his gun hand. "My God! you wouldn't shoot down a woman like that. Not give her a chance."

"A chance!" And the words that followed sort of stuck in his throat as he ran. "What chance did she give Gearson? There'll be a wife and two kiddies there." And when I ran ahead and got between him and the girl, he said, "You're right, Race. She can't escape me now. I'll sweat her for this night's work—by God, fry her, too, if Gearson dies."

I left Gregory Ford far behind in my dash toward the house. He didn't order me to stop. There was nothing I could do now to help the girl, and I knew it. My speed was accentuated by the speed of one of the other detectives, and I saw, too, that in his hand there flashed the silver of metal. It was Fletcher.

What would the girl do? She was almost slap up against the big house. She couldn't hope to avoid her pursuers even if she did have access to the house—some millionaire's estate. Certainly she wouldn't turn and try to shoot it out with all of us. And—I couldn't picture the girl in the rôle of a killer—a common, ordinary moll of the underworld. Yet—what was I to believe? I knew that she had a gun—and there was Gearson, a living—or perhaps now, a dead example of her will to use it.

She reached the porch, dashed up it, struggled a moment before the door—and was gone. Disappeared within the house. Fletcher and I stood silently waiting for Gregory Ford and the rotund Brown to come up. The door was now locked from the inside.

"Cover the grounds," Gregory told Fletcher and Brown. "I'm going in. Now—who belongs to this palace?"

"Andrew Gordon King." And there was awe in Brown's voice.

"Not—not the New York banker." And Gregory's voice showed that he, too, had respect for great wealth.

"Exactly." Brown nodded. "He's in Palm Beach now, too—and from the lights, I'd say he was at home. He's got a bad temper."

"What do I care for his temper?" Gregory swaggered slightly.

"Well—you better had, if you don't want your activities in Florida stamped on." Captain Rogers came suddenly upon the scene. "If he's made men, he's broke men, too. I—"

"You don't need to come in. This dame killed a man and I—"

"Gearson ain't so bad," Captain Rogers went on. "I had a look at him before I followed. This girl may work here as a blind—may even be gay-catting for The Hidden Hand. But handle Mr. King with kid gloves, and I wouldn't mention any shooting on his lawn. He don't favor notoriety."

"Yeh—" Gregory Ford went to stroking his chin. He wasn't so cocksure of himself. And he was right. Great wealth must be respected, and the name of Andrew Gordon King was mentioned with the names of the mighty.

Captain Rogers went on.

"We'll watch the grounds. Perhaps she'll try an out on the other side. I don't know what she looks like but we'll arrest any dame who looks suspicious. We'll all be needed out here."

"Right. I've handled bigger things than this." Gregory Ford puffed a little. "My name will mean something even to Andrew Gordon King." Then to me, "You better come along with me. I want to keep an eye on you."

29

A Real Shock

I laughed a bit, I guess, as I followed Gregory Ford to the front door. I was glad Gearson wasn't so badly hurt, and I noticed, too, how quickly the police left the little porch and scattered over the grounds. It may have been southern efficiency—and again, it may have been a desire to steer clear of the millionaire. As for me, I shrugged my shoulders. I had no political job to lose.

Gregory Ford was a good diplomat. Andrew Gordon King proved affable enough, if a little impatient. It appeared he was ready to go to some social affair or benefit at the Beach Club.

He spoke with quiet dignity.

"Of course I shall not leave the house until you have convinced yourself that all my servants are honest and respectable. There may be one or two new ones, whom my butler will point out. You say the woman actually ran in the side door. Gracious me—she may be hiding in the house now, though that seems impossible."

"No one has come in or gone out." The butler was quite emphatic. "The side door is always locked. A common thief, sir? Surely, not a desperate character?"

"No cause for alarm," Gregory Ford assured the old retainer. Not to ease his fears personally, but because he thought that the butler would be more willing to point out places where one might hide—if that one was harmless.

Then more delay. The lady of the house pounded down the great stairway and wanted to know what was what. We had to go through the thing again, while Mrs. King pulled "oh" and "ah" and "impossible" and her husband assured her that "these men are but doing their duty to the city and the state—and are no doubt mistaken."

I'll give Gregory Ford credit for sticking doggedly to it. He didn't tell Mr. King outright that he thought the girl was part of the household. But strange crooks don't wander into a house like that and conceal themselves; especially, after being driven out to that house and having made a bee-line for it. Gregory believed, and so did I, that this girl would turn out to be a maid, a secretary, or a domestic of some sort. The butler left us, to line up the servants.

"All—mind you," Gregory said severely. "If there's a suddenly sick one, we'll visit the room."

The butler's look of dignified disdain that one under his domain would practice such deceit would have been a credit to the stage.

Gregory paced nervously about. Mrs. King toyed with a tiny statue upon the mantel, and Mr. King spent his time between watching that I didn't lift any of the knickknacks and pretending to peruse a book of poems. As for me—I hung out against the mantel, in the most approved detective style and wondered what the ponderous, dignified banker would actually think if he knew the type of young lady who was somewhere within his house. Mrs. King, I got a kick out of. She seemed a motherly sort of soul under the thick coat of veneer. Wealth and position sure stick out all over people, like molasses.

There was Mrs. King, going out no doubt to guzzle champagne and choke over a cigarette, when a handful of coffee and doughnuts would of had more appeal. It's a life that—

Damn it, I hadn't more than seen the legs on the stairs when Gregory Ford smothered a curse and reached for his gun. Not only reached for it, but actually jerked it into his hand. Yep, it got a rise out of me, too. I jumped erect—arm off the mantel.

Beautiful? Sure. Low cut gown, delicate neck, flesh-colored stockings and silver slippers. Little jewelry—nothing, in fact, but a single string of beads. I'm not going to hide the truth. I was stumped. For the girl who stood silently now on the last step was Tina Sears, who less than fifteen minutes before had shot down a policeman at the little gate.

Gregory stepped forward with the gun still in his hand. His eyes bulged and his mouth hung open. He bent a bit and peered at her as if he were looking through a telescope. Then he gulped, tried to speak—swallowed a couple of times and looked at me.

And the girl spoke.

"I couldn't help but hear." There was just the faintest tremor in her voice, that neither the banker nor his wife seemed to catch. "Some one in the house—and wanted by the law. How thrilling! And these gentlemen are detectives?"

She came down the last step, and with an easy, graceful, and perhaps somewhat definite swing of her body, crossed directly to Gregory Ford.

"How thrilling." And she beamed on Ford as she held out a little white hand—a hand that should have been stained with blood. "A real detective—" she turned to Mr. King. "You must present me—really."

"Mr. Ford, my dear." And the "dear" held a note of protest. "This, Mr. Ford, is my daughter, Miss Tina King."

His daughter—the daughter of Andrew Gordon King!

Ford stared at the girl. I don't know what was in his mind. I guess it was a certain gladness that Gearson hadn't been killed—not gladness for Gearson, nor his wife and children—but a gladness for Gregory Ford himself. No one would envy him the job of laying his hand on the shoulder of Andrew Gordon King's daughter and saying, "I want you for murder."

And what's more, Gregory didn't. He let her take his hand and let her put it back at his side again, and then with a stern look he pocketed his gun. He knew her and knew that he knew her, and yet he was telling himself that he never saw her before in his life.

"And this gentleman?" The girl turned to me. "He, too, is—"

And I stopped her. She wouldn't make any monkeys out of me—millionaire or no millionaire. She could high-hat and pound down Gregory Ford with the weight of gold, but not Race Williams.

"No need of an introduction to me, Miss King, surely." My words wiped the smile off her face like you'd rubbed a mop across it. "Surely you remember me—on the boat, coming down from New York. I shall never forget how pleasant you made my trip, nor how you gave me air when I was—" and I hung over the word until she went white and wobbled on her feet—"was seasick," I finished.

Her smile now was a sickly one. She turned her back and walked to the window. It was then that the butler came in with the information that the servants were all gathered in the servants' hall.

Gregory Ford looked over the servants like a man in a dream. They all looked thick enough to be honest.

What Gregory told Andrew Gordon King, I don't know— nor do I think that Gregory himself knew.

Andrew Gordon King saw us to the door and watched the butler lock it behind us, before he went down the steps to the big Rolls Royce that waited for him. I managed to get in a word with Mrs. King.

"You have a son, Mrs. King?" And I watched her face. Tina had said that the boy who was killed was her brother. There had been nothing like that in the papers. I wondered if Mrs. King knew of his death—or his activities before his death—or if as far as the family was concerned he had been dead for years.

"Son!" She looked straight into my face without emotion. "I have no son."

"He—died then." There was just the right touch of sympathetic apology in my voice.

"Died?" And the woman was certainly hiding nothing. She had one of these western faces—the great wide open spaces. "I never had a son."

There was no secret, no worry, no lines of sorrow in Mrs. King's face. She had not lied to me. If Mrs. King had no son, her daughter had no brother. Tina, then, had lied to me.

30

I Say My Say

Andrew Gordon King and his wife drove away. The watchers joined us as we reached the gate. Gregory Ford was strangely silent after he ordered the man to get the car. But he stayed by the gate with me. Finally he produced half a cigar from a vest pocket and spoke.

"What do you make of that—and what the devil are you laughing at? What's funny in seeing a man shot down and then—"

"Why not make the pinch? This bowing to wealth doesn't fit you, Gregory."

"It's not that." He shot his jaw out at me. "That's a damn lie, and you know it. I played safe. I had to. Suppose I took her in. Who's to believe my story? My men only know that they followed a girl. If I get a judge to hold her, how will I get a jury to convict her? If she were poor or unknown, or even a crook— But the daughter of Andrew Gordon King; a leader of the younger set—I can't get a motive. I'd be laughed at—or driven out of court by money."

He paused a minute, then jabbed me in the chest. "She's a cool one and no mistake. It can't be money she wants; it can't be— By God! it's blackmail and fear. See the girl, Race—tell her I'll give her twenty-four hours to come clean with me. Then—I'll either ride with her, or I'll wind the web so tightly about her that all her father's millions won't pull her through the mesh. But to shoot a man—" Again his hand went to his chin, but he didn't finish the last sentence.

"You've got to be with Gregory Ford or against him." He turned to me before he climbed into the sedan that drew up. "Tell her that. And think it over yourself. You've both got to come clean with me. I want to know who she fears—and I want to know who hired you; and both your ropes will be considerably shortened if you don't come clean."

I turned back to the house as Gregory Ford drove away. He wasn't such a dumb-bell after all. It was better to play with wealth than against it. The state of Florida couldn't pay the half of what Andrew Gordon King could pay. And I wanted to talk to the girl myself.

The butler threw his eyes up near his forehead when he saw me, but I pushed right by him and swung toward the room to the right, across from the living room. I had seen those curtains moving when I started back toward the house. I wanted to surprise the girl. Was she telephoning some one? Was she laughing at the way she had put it over, or—and I stopped dead in that room. The girl was sitting by the window, and though her eyes were dry there was agony written plainly on that fine young face.

"All right," I told Butts, when he followed me in. The girl nodded and finally found words to dismiss him. He didn't like it—but he sniffed once, and left.

"What do you want?" The girl I knew as Tina Sears turned and faced me, one hand gripping the arm of the couch.

She didn't know what was in my mind until too late. For I stepped across the room, flung back a pillow and picked up the revolver I had seen her slip there when she heard my feet.

"I want this." I smelled it—broke it open and snapped it

175

closed again. It was fully loaded—and had not lately been discharged. Then I looked at her face again and threw my bomb.

"The detective won't live." I lied. "How does it feel to add murder to the list?"

"Murder! Detective!" If it was acting, it was great stuff.

"Come, Tina." I shook her by the shoulder.

She stopped me—made me tell her what I meant by "murder" and was so insistent that I finally went through with the thing—just as if she didn't know all about it.

"So that was the shot I heard." She nodded. "I thought they were shooting—to frighten me."

"You're not going to tell me you didn't—"

Again she stopped me. Great brown, frightened eyes looked into mine—a white face was close—perfect lips trembled—but her voice, though low, never broke.

"You don't believe I fired that shot?" And when I would have laid the whole thing before her again she cut me short. "You don't believe I fired that shot? Yes or no."

And, damn it all, I answered, "No." What's more, it was the truth—not thought of before that moment. I was a fool maybe. But it wasn't the eyes; the soft, beautiful face; the delicate lips. It was something deeper than that—something that came from inside me, not the girl. There was no reasoning to it—just instinct. I didn't believe she fired that shot.

I didn't go into the thing with her then. I took advantage of her mood; her fear and agony; the reaction of her desperate acting a few minutes before. I even forgot the lie about her brother. I just gave her Gregory Ford's message and followed it up with one of my own. Somehow I felt that I knew why the gun was beneath the pillow, and what she contemplated doing with it. And I kept it.

"Come clean, Tina. Trust me." I gripped her arms and pulled her to her feet. "You saved my life on the boat—again in Miami. You can't carry your burden alone. I'll see you through. Why did you save my life, if—"

"I don't know. I don't know. Something snapped within me. It wasn't reason; it wasn't the will to do good. I deserve no credit for it." And then suddenly putting both hands on my shoulders, "Don't ever trust me, Race Williams—don't ever believe me. I'm weak and bad—that time on the boat probably some inherited good swayed me against my will. I don't want to be bad; I don't want to die. But I don't want others to know my sorrow—my shame. I saved you then, yes—and I may pay for it—may even die for it—may face disgrace for it. There's suspicion and doubt and uncertainty among these vile criminals—even up to the power himself— this Hidden Hand."

"When crooks fall out, honest men get—" I started.

"Honest men, yes—but not me—not me. I saved you once; perhaps twice. I might betray you tomorrow. Maybe—" And suddenly her arms went around my neck. She was clinging to me, crying softly, and talking as she pulled my head down close to hers. "I didn't know then. I don't know now. But you're brave and strong, and I thought that you could— For they fear you as well as hate you. It's not the law, nor the electric chair, nor the mass meetings in the parks and the rumbling threats of the outraged citizens who demand that this Hidden Hand be dragged from his hiding—it's you they fear. And—oh, Race—that time when I stepped before you and was shot in Miami, I'd of gladly died then that you—you—"

And I didn't push her away. I could see her eyes swim, and knew the truth. She wasn't acting now.

"Listen, Tina." I held her by the shoulders and straightened her up. "I'm in the game and I'm going to run down the leader. And get this: You saved my life. You're the only one to lay claim to that distinction. Somehow, when the show-down comes, I'll see you through. If you ever need me, I'll come to you—or for you."

"No—no," she cried over and over. "Never trust me— never. I'd sacrifice my life that my mother shall never know—but don't ever trust me. If I send for you, ask for your help—don't come to me, not even if they kill me. For I'd trap you as I did before, in Miami. And the next time—but don't come—never come." And her head went down again on my chest.

I used my hand to push her chin up this time. I looked straight into her eyes and I took my time before I said my say. "Tina," I told her, slowly—making every word count, "I've always paid my debts. There's no one can say Race Williams ever laid down on a friend. You saved my life. If you ever need me or if you ever want me, I'll come to you—trap or no trap." I stopped her when she would have started in again. "It's no use. I'll pay my debt—whether it's the good or bad in you that calls when you send for me."

Melodramatic? Maybe. Stage heroic? Perhaps. Just plain dumbness or cheap conceit? More than likely. I shan't make excuses. I hadn't fallen for a slender bit of dress goods. But one thing was certain. I meant exactly what I said. If Beekman or this Hidden Hand himself, or any other member of the gang hoped to trap me through the girl—why—they'd better be ready for the fireworks. For I'd come—walk right into the trap with my eyes open—my guns, too, as far as that was concerned.

There was the whir of a motor, the thud of a closing door, footsteps on the porch, and the ring of a bell far back in the house.

"This way—" the girl led me to a window. "It's father—forgotten something—he always leaves his notes behind when he's to speak. I'm—I'm not just fitted to explain your presence away now."

I left her, spotted the car before the house, hopped the wall and sought the ocean road. I reached Gus' Baths before I found a taxi and was driven back to my hotel in West Palm Beach.

31

A New Racket

I wasn't getting any credit yet for that bit of shooting in the park. The story was out that it was police business. There was a letter in my box. Not a word or a line from Old Benevolence Travers—just a check for ten thousand iron men. Well—he couldn't have said more if he wrote volumes. Somehow, then, he knew that I pulled off that little bit of gun play. Why not? He didn't need three guesses.

But I knew his hotel and where he'd be, and I knew, too, that my job was to get hold of Beekman. That shouldn't be very hard, if he wasn't in hiding. Just to get him alone, where we wouldn't be disturbed and Travers could lay his evidence against Beekman before him and offer him his liberty for a squeal on The Hidden Hand.

This time I didn't intend Beekman to turn out a corpse. It was my last chance. From the way I understood it, there wasn't another living soul who knew who The Hidden Hand was. No, sir—Beekman must be delivered up to Travers in a glass case. Well—there wasn't any special hurry. It was possible that Beekman had not heard of Olaf Sankin's death—it might be to my advantage to wait until the morning papers were out. Maybe it would strike some fear into Beekman.

Besides, I had twenty-four hours anyway before Gregory Ford would take a crack at the girl or myself. It wasn't much after eleven when I hit my room, and lazied off in the chair to smoke—not to think. Just smoke.

I was just about ready to turn in, when the phone rang.

"That'll be Old Benevolence Travers," I thought. And it wasn't. There was nothing disguised about the voice over the wire; no attempt at being dramatic. Just like an ordinary business call.

"Mr. Alexander Beekman—wishing to speak to Race Williams. Ah—I expected I'd find you in."

"Right!" I said, trying to make my voice as indifferent as his, and going flat on it, I guess.

"You rather ran out on me to-night." He laughed musically. "Just got a glimpse of you as you jumped the wall over at Andrew Gordon King's place. You gay young Lothario—but I'm not married myself and certainly Miss Tina King—or Tina Sears—is a most charming girl. Especially appealing—lady in distress, and that sort of thing."

"Yes," was the best I could get off. I was talking to a high-class lad this time—and I knew it.

"I was talking to Miss King just a moment ago and I was pleased to know that you were interested in me. May we have a talk at some place I suggest?"

"I would prefer to suggest the place myself." I gave him the answer he might have expected.

"I know. I know." I could hear him chuckle. "But I have with me now a mutual friend. A lady you made a promise to—a rather reckless promise, I gather. I think the young lady would appreciate it if you came to see me—at the place I suggest. I am almost sure, too, that it would be for the best interest of her peace of mind. But—I am positive, Mr. Williams, that it would be best for her physical well-being."

"If the young lady is there," I tried to keep my voice calm, "I might speak to her." And when he hesitated, "I would like simply to assure myself of her presence there with you."

180

"Very well." There was a moment's silence—then the shrill voice of a girl—the girl—Tina.

"Don't come, Race—don't come. They—he—" A muffled scream, distant like—and the voice of Beekman again.

"Women are so temperamental," he said, without emotion. "But it is enough, Mr. Williams, to let you know that she is here with me. She has very obligingly told me some interesting facts. She wouldn't at first, of course—but under persuasion—I have most persuasive ways—she spoke of falling glass and much-needed air to a friend. You understand—your presence, then, against the girl's—freedom." And in that final word lay the whole story—the whole threat.

"Let me assure you that nothing will happen to you. I—"

But I cut in on him.

"I'll come," I said. "Give me the place and the time."

"The place and the time." I heard his chuckle grate along the wire. "You see, I'm careless in business matters. I don't really know the place yet—but the time; say, now—to-night. A friend will call for you with a car. You will listen to his suggestions—understand that they are imperative and follow them to the letter. I won't threaten you, Mr. Williams—and not being a doctor, perhaps I shouldn't speak with too much knowledge. But I'd say that the little lady's life is in danger—a stimulant such as your presence, might—indeed, would—But, there—she's young and strong, also rather a dainty bit of beauty, and—"

A dull click—and silence. I sat there, the receiver in my hand. I didn't have a bit of doubt that Beekman would torture information from the girl. I didn't have a bit of doubt that he would kill her. And I didn't have a bit of doubt that he was planning to lead me to my death. But I was going. I'd keep my promise to the girl. And she was plucky, at that. No matter what they had done to her—no matter how they had threatened her, she told me not to come. She knew then—knew they planned to kill me, and her too. Yet, with the opportunity I had given her, she might have saved herself much pain by calling me herself and trapping me some place. I clenched my hands at my sides. I'd come for her all right— I'd come.

And I wouldn't come as Beekman expected me to come. I'd come in a way that would surprise him. Oh, if I had to— and thought the girl would go free— But time was passing. Beekman's "friend" would call. I took to cleaning my guns— with special attention to my tiny twenty-five caliber automatic. Then I dressed again.

I took several clippings from my wallet and went carefully over them. They were well done—about half a dozen of them—looked exactly as if they'd been cut carelessly from the New York newspapers. I placed them on the little desk, just under the telephone. The one on top began pleasantly enough.

NOTORIOUS DETECTIVE SUSPECTED OF BEING UNKNOWN TORTURER

Criminal Dies in Hospital After Hours of Indescribable Agony

There was more, of course—well written, by a lad with a morbid imagination and a gift of expression. They were good stuff, with a ring of truth in the writing. It even got me mad just to read them over. Now, for the first time in my career, I intended to make use of them. Would the man who was sent for me come alone? Much depended on that. As I placed the phone down on the clippings, it rang. I had a visitor.

I knew him, too. It was the ugly, lead-pipe face that had been shoved against the window outside Stinnes' office in Miami. He was nervous and ill at ease. It may have been the new blue suit, the stiff collar, and the straw hat that was on his head as if nailed there. Surely, he'd looked better in a sweater and cap and dirty trousers. He was a tough-looking baby; a lad they wouldn't miss if I knocked him over. At that,

I like him. He was just the type I needed to complete the plan I'd made.

"No tricks, Bozo." He closed the door and started wandering about the room—searching the closet, looking under the bed, and sticking his big head into the bathroom. "I know ya and know ya record. I ain't aimin' to cross guns with ya. I'm here to search ya an' take ya with me."

"I'm to go without guns, then—that's it?"

"That's it—right enough."

"And if I won't go, which of course I won't—what then?"

"There's the woman." He twisted his lips. "She'll be a pretty mess if you ain't there by midnight. But—"

The phone rang.

"That'll be Beekman." He jerked a dirty thumb toward the telephone instrument. "Lis'en ta him. The party's yours an' his."

"On time?" Beekman's voice came to me as I lifted the receiver. "My man is there? Good—now, we'll have no firearms—nice peaceful affair. I'll call back in ten minutes— my man can tell me then if you're agreeable to come, and— But listen."

Shrill, piercing—a scream of agony came over the phone. And then a voice—her voice—Tina Sears'.

"No more—no more. I can tell you no more. I—" And then, louder—and shrill with horror and perhaps pain, "Don't come, Race—don't come—to—"

We banged down the receiver together, I guess. The flat-faced man was looking at me—sneering at me—grinning evilly.

"That'll be my job if you don't come, and I get—"

"I'll come. A drink first—in the bathroom—sit there."

With an unsteady hand I lifted the phone so that the clippings came to view. Then I half pushed him into the chair by the table. Unsteadily I walked toward the bathroom.

In the doorway I swung about and watched him. His eyes

were glued on those clippings. He bent forward, lifted one—two—three of them, and scanned the headings quickly. Then he dropped back to the first one and read the whole business. I heard his lips smack, saw him look toward me and reach slowly back to his hip pocket.

He never reached the gun. I'd laid the foundation for what was to follow. He saw me coming—came to his feet, jerking at his pocket. And I had him. One hand at his throat, as my right fist pounded down on the flat nose.

He was all soft face and hard heart. No guts. It was his fear as well as my strength that beat him to his knees there on the floor.

"Not me—not me," he choked. It was a cinch that his mind was on those clippings. "Don't—don't!" He tried to scream as my fingers closed tightly about his throat and my gun thrust forward suddenly into his quivering lips and between his chattering teeth.

I gave him a chance to spit a tooth out—then spoke what was on my mind.

"Where's the girl—where's Beekman?" I asked him.

"I don't know." He shook his head and whimpered there on the floor. And I believed him—believed that he didn't know. Beekman was too cagey a lad to be caught like this—yet; well—I hadn't expected too much.

But I put the fear of Race Williams into his miserable soul.

"You know me. You read those clippings. You understand. Two can play at the same game, Mr. Flat-Face. We won't speak of retribution. We won't speak of jail. I won't make empty threats of having anything on you. But you're going to do as I wish to-night—and if you don't, I'll come through alive—as I always come through—then there'll be another clipping from a Florida paper, that you won't be alive to read."

He was thoroughly cowed when I got through with him. He cursed Beekman for sending him to me—and the girl—

and The Hidden Hand. But he didn't curse me—was rather polite in that respect.

Beekman did well not to trust such a messenger. I got information from Flat-Face that rang with truth—at least, I had to accept it as truth. I had played successfully upon the man's fear—now I tried his greed.

"If we save the girl and get Beekman, there will be a pile of jack in it for you. Death, if you fail—and I'll watch you every minute. Now, tell me again—how does Beekman work this racket with me to-night?" And I made him repeat what he had just told me.

"There's a car below. It's to drive you to Beekman. Where, I ain't been told. I'm to go with ya. Before God, that's all I know. I'm to search ya—be sure ya ain't got no hardware."

"And the driver of the car below—does he know?"

"I guess, yes. But you can't stick no gat on him. He's watched. If he leaves his seat or acts queer, Beekman will know."

Very readily—too readily—Flat-Face agreed to everything I suggested.

The phone rang. It was Beekman. I let Flat-Face talk to him. Flat-Face did his part well—followed my instructions to the letter, telling Beekman that things were fixed and that I had been searched, and was unarmed. I frisked Flat-Face, chucked a gun and a knife under the pillow on the bed—and we were ready to start.

32

Flat-Face Shows His Breed

Arm in arm Flat-Face and I left the hotel. No words were spoken as we stepped into the car at the curb. The driver sat stiff and straight behind the wheel. If eyes watched us I did not spot the owner of the eyes. We were off—and I was armed.

"What are your instructions when we reach our destination?" I stuck a forty-four playfully in Flat-Face's ribs.

"I put the gun in your back and lead ya to Beekman," he growled. And then, "It'd be better if ya never come. How you goin' ta overcome that part of the program?"

"How many'll be there to—to receive us? If you lie I'll shoot you as soon as we arrive."

He hesitated a moment, looked at me shrewdly and wet his lips before he answered.

"There'll be four. They'll search ya agin. Beekman don't take chances. If there's a shot, he'll get from under—but the girl will be a body. I tell ya, Mister—trust to me—pay me well an' I'll see ya through."

I did have some idea of making a quick stick-up; a few shots and a dash for Beekman. But with four to receive me and Beekman not among the four there didn't seem much chance of rescuing the girl.

"We'll be there soon." Flat-Face cut in on my thoughts. "You're goin' to ya death sure—and me, too. Lis'en, Mister—slip me your rods; turn up without hardware—once with Beekman I'll double-cross him, stick a gun in his back, turn him over to you an' fade from the picture. All I want is a load of jack afterwards and a free ride from the state. Whada ya say? Quick!" he whispered, his shrewd, ratlike eyes fastened on the back of the driver's neck through the glass.

And I decided to play a desperate hand. If four men were to search me again, they'd surely find my two big guns. I couldn't watch them and Flat-Face. He only had to wink, to give them the up and up on the real situation. Intently, Flat-Face watched the driver while I did some thinking.

"Hurry, Bozo." Flat-Face was whispering excitedly. "Once in the house it'll be just you, me, and Beekman. I'll stick; give me the artillery."

And I did—suddenly slapped both my guns into his hands.

"It's your one chance of freedom," I told him. "If the girl dies, or I die—you're equally guilty with Beekman. And—Gregory Ford already suspects Beekman." I lied.

"Yeh—I know that." He nodded, which surprised me a bit. But he clutched the guns in either hand, and even in the darkness I could see the color begin to come back to his face. He was prepared to double-cross me, I thought—and I was prepared for him to double-cross me. Innocent me? Maybe. Under other circumstances I wouldn't be there, of course. I owed my life to Tina Sears—maybe I'd pay to-night. Maybe I wouldn't. But you know me. I'm no fool. I always have a trick up my sleeve. But one thing I did know—call it instinct; call it a sixth sense; or maybe, under the circumstances, call it just plain common sense. But I did know that sudden and violent death was in the air.

The car stopped on a little road. The driver got out and opened the door. Just darkness, the outline of a house, thick growth, and no figures. There was no attempt to blindfold me; no attempt to keep me ignorant of where I was. It was a cinch that, once I entered the blackness of the house, the show was over. The curtain would be rung down and I wouldn't walk out again.

The driver of the car was a slow, methodical fellow. He produced a gun most leisurely and placed it against my back. Then, and then only, did two men step from the bushes and confront me. This was a well-laid plan. They even expected that I might flim-flam Flat-Face, and start shooting the minute I arrived.

It was evident, too, that they weren't satisfied with Flat-Face's search. I stood there with my arms at my sides while one man went through my pockets and another patted my clothes. Then came the orders for my hands up—but I never got them up.

I think I saw the flashing shadow. Anyway, I half ducked as the arm came through the air and the thud of metal pounded on my head. I staggered under the first blow—and gave with the second. I didn't need to be told what was happening. I half turned as the second blow fell. Beady of eye, twisted of lips, cursing vile epithets, Flat-Face struck again.

It wasn't the force of the blow that sent me to the ground. It was reason. As I sunk to the roadway it was in my mind to kill this lad, Flat-Face. I have my own temper, you know. But reason conquered. The girl was still in danger; so far I had accomplished nothing. Besides, now that I was helpless in Beekman's hands he would want to talk with me.

I looked up at the cursing, snarling beast who stood above me. In his hands were both my own guns, covering me. The man was in a passion.

"You'd manhandle me, would you? You'd knock out my teeth, would you? You'd—"

"Don't—you fool." Two men rushed forward, grabbing at Flat-Face's arms. "Beekman'll want to—"

The men were not quick enough to knock away the two guns which the infuriated Flat-Face pointed down at me.

Once—twice—three times his fingers closed upon the triggers. But there was no report—no shoot of flame. Just a curse from Flat-Face as he broke open the guns and discovered that the bullets had been removed. I didn't need to tell him I had dropped them on the road before giving him the guns.

It was simply that I wasn't getting the breaks. It wasn't Flat-Face's intelligence or cleverness that rained on my parade—but his passion—that passion which is most men's undoing had served him well. And there's your psychology busted again by fact.

The two men held Flat-Face now, while he pleaded with them to let him do me in. But he finally contented himself by throwing an empty gun in my face and telling them the trick I'd put over on him.

"You dirty, lousy double-crosser," he bellowed down at me as he kicked me in the chest. "You'll pay for this. You can't beat my face in an' get away with it. No one can." And then, turning to the others, "I'm all right now, boys. I'll see the thing through. Don't wise up Beekman—I want ta be in on this lad's death. If ya tell Beekman I lost my head, one of you'll go in with this yeller bum. Leave him ta me—if trouble ever starts you'll be away an' have an alibi. Come boys—Race Williams has put us all that much nearer to fryin'. Leave me finish it. I'll cut his—"

There was a sudden silence. I was jerked erect. Crunching feet were beating over gravel.

"What's this—what's this?" The voice was soft and low and I knew it for the voice on the phone—the voice of Beekman. "Not putting up a row. Surely, after coming all this way, Mr. Williams, you don't want to turn back."

In the blurred darkness I saw the broad, squat figure, the little round eyes, the long hooked nose, and the two or three chins that left the idea of a collar in doubt.

"Everything is fit and as it should be?" the soft voice went on. "Mr. Williams has come in peace and carried nothing that would mark him as any but a law-abiding citizen? That is good—come." Alexander Beekman whispered something to one of the men. Flat-Face stepped forward and shoved a rod in my back. A loaded one this time, which he received from one of the boys—and with Beekman taking my arm, we walked along the gravel toward the house.

A single light shone in the hall—not visible until we were mounting the porch.

We were in the hall before I saw the gun in Beekman's hand. He smiled and nodded as I looked at it.

"Between us, Mr. Williams, threats would be idle things indeed. I hope you will not discourse on future retribution. I assure you that I attend services each Sunday morning and have heard the last word on retribution. Beautiful thoughts for McCleary, Stinnes, and our late overzealous, and as events proved, over-confident friend, Olaf Sankin.

"But do not think that these deeds of violence have aroused in me a hatred toward you—nor even a fear. Apprehension is the word perhaps. The passing of these three men simply means greater responsibility for me—and with that greater responsibility; greater—let us not say, pecuniary gain—rather, a remuneration adequate to my efforts. McCleary, Stinnes, Sankin, and now—" He paused a moment and frowned. "And now one called Alexander Beekman."

33

A Question and an Answer

Up a flight of stairs we went. Beekman crowded close to me; Flat-Face came along behind and the hard surface of a gun was ever against my spine. Beekman didn't speak again until we reached the landing above, passed down a long hall and stood before a door. There he hesitated.

"We must all practice self-control." Beekman laid his hand upon the door knob. "Be prepared, then, to show that fortitude for which you are—notorious. I would be very sorry if at this time you should meet with an accident. But I wish you to know that the young lady is—at present—quite well." Beekman swung open the door with the final caution, "The man behind you is nervous and anxious, and if I do not mistake his facial expression, hardly as interested in your immediate future as I."

My head jerked up and my shoulders shot back as Beekman held me from dashing forward. There was Tina—upright in a chair, her feet securely bound, her hands behind her back, her little black bobbed head held erect by a strap, and a white cloth across her mouth.

"As you see, she is quite well," Beekman went on softly. "Warm and comfortable, for there is a fire in the grate."

I looked toward the grate, noted the burning coals, and saw, too, the two irons, the ends of which were a vivid yellowish red. I sucked in a breath and clenched my hands at my sides as I saw that the girl's feet were bare and rested upon a tiny footstool.

"My friend behind you, in his duller days, was an expert with rivets—red hot rivets—but no more. It is unpleasant to speak of and I am sure, unnecessary to contemplate." He left my side and walked to the girl and slightly jerked upon her loose blouse—there, just below her throat, were three tiny scratches—evidently made by the point of a sharp knife. "Shall we go below and talk, Mr. Williams?"

"May I have a word with—with the girl?" And despite my efforts, the words stuck in my throat.

Beekman smiled—yet, he didn't know that he was never nearer death than he was at the moment when he touched the girl. There was terror—horror—in those fearful brown eyes that stared at me.

Beekman hesitated for a second or two, and finally nodded. Then, as if he read my thoughts:

"She will assure you that she has not been, as yet, mistreated."

Alexander Beekman removed the gag from the girl's mouth; motioned me to approach.

"Tina—Tina," I said. "They have not harmed you?"

She sort of swallowed.

"No—no—not yet. But don't believe them—don't tell them anything. No matter what happens, they will kill you and me, and—"

My fingers bit into my palms as Beekman's hand went across her mouth and Flat-Face's gun dug deeper into my back. With a gentle, almost fatherly warning, Beekman removed his hand.

"Mr. Williams is here to save your life, my child. He owes much to you, and will—I am sure—be a gentleman and repay it. You must believe in him and encourage him."

192

"Yes, Tina. You must believe in me." And I put everything I could into those words. If the girl didn't get it, Beekman did—for he looked at me shrewdly. But he read my words wrong and only nodded.

The girl's face softened slightly as she looked at me. The worn, deep lines seemed to recede, and I bent forward as her lips barely moved. But I caught the words.

"Race, to betray your trust will perhaps make my death easier—but none the less sure. Race—" Hopelessly, fearfully, her eyes shot to Beekman.

He stepped back, lowering his head. I barely caught her words.

"It's the end." Tina's lips framed the words which I read but did not fairly hear. "I love you."

I leaned forward, my lips close to her ear.

"Buck up, Kid," I barely breathed. "We'll dance on this lad's grave yet."

She heard the words all right, but I don't know if she understood then. Her head turned slightly and her lips brushed my cheek as a gun dug the deeper into my back.

What sensation did I get? One of a great, burning love? Hardly that. I won't go into it. Other things were on my mind. I'll simply say that Tina wasn't a bad kid.

But I did get a chance to nod and wink at the girl as Beekman replaced the gag and Flat-Face forced me to the door at the point of his gun. Her eyes still followed me with fear—and yet, a puzzled sort of fear. After all, was the thing registering with her that Race Williams wasn't exactly a child in arms? But the situation was a delicate and a desperate one. I didn't dare tell her more.

Again the three of us paraded down the stairs, passed through the hall and entered a long library. The shades were drawn, the lights soft, but illuminated the room sufficiently for me to see that no one else lurked in the corners.

Beekman flopped into a chair before a long flat desk, motioned me to the seat opposite, and waved Flat-Face back a few feet where he could have a good shot at my back.

I took one look at Flat-Face, then leaned back in my chair. Beekman was at it again.

"A pretty sentiment, above—Mr. Williams. I envy you your youth and opportunity. The little lady is indeed a cute bag of tricks. And her beauty is young and fresh—nothing to mar it but for the scar or two upon her pretty—There, there—" He jerked his chair back, almost knocking the phone from the table as I half shot forward.

But I looked at Flat-Face and leaned back again in my seat. Beekman went on.

"Let us not be melodramatic, Mr. Williams—or if we must be, let us sugar it with common sense. In plain words, you would kill me. Why should I not kill you now that I have you here with me?"

"Because your activities are known—your connection with a certain party suspected. If anything happens to me, Gregory Ford will know."

"Of course—of course. It is a grand gesture, Mr. Williams. You come here in silly sentiment and with an idea that you can bluff me by your stupid suggestion that Gregory Ford knows of your whereabouts. That Gregory Ford may suspect me is possible—that you have told him or any one else of your venture to-night, impossible. Yet, you have come. I wonder why."

"For Miss King." I looked him straight in the eye.

"Somehow, I believe you—and with that belief goes my respect for you. After all, then, you are simply the common type of thug; a bragging, swaggering gunman." Then sharply, as a pudgy hand fell upon the table, "Come—we waste time. Your freedom and the girl's freedom for the name of the man who has hired you to run me down." He didn't wait for me to answer him. He went right on talking. I listened. He wouldn't be the first man who talked himself into an early grave.

"Certainly," he snapped—the softness out of his voice and a steely hardness taking its place, "I shall not threaten you with physical violence. I know you are a courageous brute. You owe your life to this girl—now her life rests in your hands. It is she who must pay, if you will not talk—and it is you who must watch her pay. Look at me. You know I do not bluff."

And I did know it. I didn't mince words with him.

"Just what do I get in return for giving you the name of my client? And just what assurance do I get—that I get it?"

"You get your freedom and the girl's freedom. So much for the name of the man. And you get the assurance that the girl's secret will be kept. You must take my word. It is useless to discuss it—you have no alternative. And I suspect enough to know if you lie."

"Very well." I looked over at Flat-Face. "Is the boy friend in on the show?"

Alexander Beekman hesitated a moment, then waved Flat-Face to a far corner of the room. But he raised his own gun and placed it against my heart as I leaned over the desk and put my mouth close to his ear.

"The name of the man is Howard Quincy Travers," I whispered steadily.

"God!" he shouted, and sprang to his feet. His face went white, his little round eyes opened and rolled, the chair he had been sitting in crashed to the floor.

34

Flat-Face Tries His Hand at Murder

If I had half suspected, I could have had him by the throat and the gun from his hand while his body was between me and Flat-Face. But the next instant the opportunity was gone. Flat-Face called out hoarsely and jumped forward, covering me again; Alexander Beekman half staggered back against the wall. He may have suspected the name—certainly he believed me. But it was a great shock all the same.

As for me—had I betrayed my client? I didn't think so—events would tell. Maybe I'm overconfident, maybe I'm too cocksure—but I thought I had the situation well in hand. Only time could tell.

"Well—" I said, "anything else you want to know? And why the surprise? You know this man?"

"Yes, yes—I know him." He came back to the desk, but the hand that held the gun trembled. "He is my friend, wormed his way into my confidence, advised me and admonished me in my—money lending. And now—he would betray me into the hands of the law. I thought that he dealt only in the spiritual—not the physical or legal. I am afraid that he can greatly harm me if it is his wish."

"Now, Mr. Beekman," I began to play a few of the cards in my own hand, "if you want facts I'll give them to you. When I'm through, you'll understand that I did not put my life in your hands when I came here—but that I hold your life in my hands. Dismiss that hyena behind you and I'll talk turkey to you."

The color was beginning to come back to Beekman's face. He looked at me, looked at his gun, and looked toward Flat-Face. Then he motioned him still further away. But a nod of understanding passed between them. Beekman rose, crossed the room and handed his gun to Flat-Face. If he had another he didn't produce it. But he was forestalling all possibilities of getting another shock and having me take the gun from him. As if he had read my mind, he spoke.

"We can talk low, now, Mr. Williams. Any attempt on your part to overpower me will bring you instant death." Pulling his chair around close to me and putting me between him and Flat-Face, he said simply—"Proceed. You interest me."

"It's this way." I kept my voice down. "Travers won't betray you to the law unless something happens to me to-night. The hour I disappear, the evidence that will burn you goes to the state."

"Just what evidence?" He was very calm.

"That I don't know."

"You wouldn't." He nodded emphatically.

"But Travers has the evidence. We have been unfortunate in our dealings. With you, Beekman, we hope for better things. This evidence will never appear against you if you divulge the name of The Hidden Hand."

His eyes widened again.

"To you?" he asked.

"No—to Travers. Give him the name of your leader. Give him the opportunity to rid the state of this monster—and he will help you to freedom."

"Generous—most generous. 'Monster,' eh?" He laughed but his laugh was rather a grating one, and for the moment I wondered if it was possible that, after all, Beekman himself was this Hidden Hand—this unknown leader. But, no—Old Benevolence Travers did not believe that.

For perhaps two or three minutes Beekman drummed his fingers on the desk.

"You hold the cards," he said at length. "I understand better now why you came here to-night. Your client's offer is most generous—and I accept it. And since the police already suspect me, let us go through with the thing to-night. Your client wishes to speak with me. You may send for him now— to come here. If his offer is good and sincere—and knowing the man I most certainly believe in his sincerity—I will blow the show."

"Why—" I hesitated, "I can't run my client into danger."

"But surely he protects his evidence against me with papers which will be delivered to the law if he should— should meet with an accident."

"Of course." I nodded my agreement. "I'll go bring him here."

"No—no, Mr. Williams. I am a man of impulses. You will telephone him now—the phone there—and you will simply tell him that you have the man—and that the man will talk. You will tell him nothing more—except that you and I are alone."

"And the place?" I said.

"And the place!" He screwed up his face. "Simply say that you await his arrival—at the man's home. You and the girl, of course, will be hostages for his good faith."

"Good." I fell for his smooth tongue like a débutante for a new swear word.

One minute later the voice of Old Benevolence Travers came to me over the wire. I spoke my piece.

"I am with the man, and he will talk. Come quickly to the man's home—and carefully," I added, before Beekman's hand stretched out and jerked down the connection. That last crack was because I didn't know if the boys outside had gone.

"And now, Mr. Williams," Beekman chuckled while I stood

there with the phone still in my hand, "you meet the end, the girl meets the end—and this friend of society meets his end. You have called him to his death. If there are papers, they will be searched out and destroyed—but there will be no papers. First, then, you—" He half turned to Flat-Face.

That was the cue I had been waiting for all the time I was there. I didn't hesitate. The stage was set. I brought my left hand over and down. The heavy telephone crashed upon Beekman's head. He just slunk deeper into the chair, his chins folding up on his chest.

Flat-Face fired as I dropped behind the desk. I heard the glass crash in the heavily curtained window behind me.

"None of that, ya lousy, yeller bum." Flat-Face wasn't overoriginal. He believed in getting one good line and sticking to it. "Come out from behind that desk or I'll plug ya." As innocent as a lamb being led to slaughter, Flat-Face came on. His feet pounded toward me. The curtain was about to go down on the last act. I did my stuff and pulled down the house. I just popped straight up from behind that desk.

We fired together. But my gun was up and Flat-Face's gun never got any higher than his knees. His bullet crashed against the desk—and mine? Well—there was a tiny hole that was growing and growing right in the center of Flat-Face's forehead. Once he seemed to try to raise his hand—once his mouth opened, but he didn't speak. He sort of sucked at his lips—then slid to the floor like a wet rag.

Under ordinary circumstances I might have played the thing with the sympathetic understanding of a stock company hero, and shot him in the shoulder. But my bullet came out of a twenty-five caliber automatic, which is more or less of a toy if not handled expertly.

Sure! That was the trick I had up my sleeve—literally, not figuratively—a little twenty-five caliber automatic. After all, Flat-Face's passion had been his undoing. His boy friends outside the house were just about ready for me to put my arms up in the air when Flat-Face lost his temper and struck

199

me. You can't hide a rod up your sleeve if your arms are patted while being held in the air. But why bother about that? Certainly, I had done anything but betray my client.

I turned Flat-Face over on his back. He wouldn't worry me any more. He only needed a bit of ground and a shovel. I listened by the door and peered out the window. Then I turned to Alexander Beekman. Old Benevolence Travers would be along in a few minutes—and Beekman and I would have to be ready to receive him.

The girl was safe enough above. I'd release her just as soon as Travers showed up. I didn't have any handcuffs, or rope with which to tie up Beekman. Besides, it was only a matter of minutes before Beekman would talk.

I lit myself a butt and waited. Five—ten—fifteen minutes, at the most, and the name of The Hidden Hand would no longer be a secret, and I—well—this time I had played the game—and there was a fortune in it for me. Beekman was alive and Beekman would talk. He was that kind of a bird. There was nothing to do but wait. I sent a curl of smoke toward the ceiling. Now—just who would The Hidden Hand turn out to be?

35

The Closing Door

The house was deadly silent; the surroundings what you might call weird if you were disposed to be fussy. Flat-Face lay upon the floor, a tiny hole in his forehead. Alexander Beekman slumped unconscious in the chair. I watched the clock upon the mantel as it slowly beat off the seconds. This was the end. Old Benevolence had my telephone message and would be coming any minute now to question Beekman. Then—what would I charge?

I thought of Gregory Ford. It looked as if I'd beat him to the pinch. Not a bad guy, Gregory, as private detectives run. A wise bird, too. I smiled. It would be a feather in my cap if I put it over on Gregory.

And Old Benevolence Travers—what of him? What was behind his effort and his money in running down this Hidden Hand? Certainly not just the good of the community. Probably a secret wrong to him or his. But I shrugged my shoulders. That was his business, not mine. I was paid to act—not to think.

Yet, one thought was dominant now as I looked at the dead gunman on the floor and the unconscious, huddled mass of flesh in the chair. Tina King was above in the deserted room—and Tina King was bound to a chair—and Tina King had saved my life. What horror must be running through her mind since she heard those two shots! She would wonder if I were dead—and she would be expecting her own death. I shook my head. I had been thinking only of her physical discomfiture, and now there was the mental—much worse—far worse.

I glared at the clock upon the mantel. Twelve-thirty—all my glaring couldn't make the hands move faster. Five minutes more—ten—fifteen—maybe less—maybe more. And the girl was above.

I looked again at Alexander Beekman. His breathing was loud and jerky, but good. A snootful of brandy or a faceful of water might do the trick sooner—but I'd say that, let alone, he was good for another twenty minutes anyway. That slap on the head with the phone hadn't been exactly a love tap.

I stepped into the hall, left the library door open behind me, and peered out the front window. There were no lights of the car that had brought me there; no figures of the men who had been waiting for my arrival—nothing in the brightness of the Palm Beach sky to alarm me.

I went back into the room, put my own little twenty-five caliber automatic that had been in my sleeve in my jacket pocket and picked up both of Flat-Face's guns. Nice, heavy, serviceable artillery they were. I went through Flat-Face for a knife, but found none. Then I thought of the three tiny scratches on the neck of Tina King. There'd be a knife, above.

It wouldn't take a minute to run up those stairs, cut the ropes that bound the girl, tell her everything was jake, and let her lie down while I awaited the coming of Travers.

But something held me to that room; I hated to leave it. Tina King was a good Kid. Tina King had saved my life. Tina King, in the fearful moment when she saw no chance of life, had told me that she loved me. Tina King was—and I cursed inwardly—not the girl, you understand—but the events that brought her into the thing. I was playing a game where only the slightest movement of a trigger finger stood between life and death. The sex interest had no place in my scheme of things. But bound, gagged and suffering untold mental agonies was the woman—the girl who had saved my life.

I raised my gun and stepped toward Alexander Beekman. Then I swung back to the hall door. It was in my mind to tap him again. Hardly a laudable idea—and certainly not a noble thought that restrained me. To be perfectly frank about it, I was afraid I might put him out for an inconveniently long time, and that Travers wouldn't be able to get a squawk out of him when he arrived. Why lie about it?

One more look at Beekman; one more look at the curtains by the window, and I slipped into the hall and passed quickly to the front stairs. The light was still burning, there were some shadows—but no sound. There were the stairs—and darkness above. I shrugged my shoulders and tackled the stairs.

It didn't seem possible that any one was above except the girl. Surely, those two shots would have attracted attention. Halfway up in the darkness, I paused. Unmistakably, I had heard a sound. Whether it came from above or below, I couldn't be sure. It sounded, too, like the tread of feet—or the tap of feet. That was it—the girl's feet. She had heard the guns, and in fear, was trying to free herself. Common sense told me the noise came from above—but my hearing told me that it came from below.

I waited fully five minutes in the darkness of the stairs, Flat-Face's gun ready in my hand. But the sound was not repeated. Then, as I stepped upward, it was. At least there was a sound—softer this time—perhaps a bit louder. I knew—unmistakably it came from above. But had the first sound come from above? Still I hesitated which way to go— up or down. When I hesitate, things get mixed up. I'm a man of action—not a man of deductions and thoughts and reasonings.

For the benefit of the girl I should go up. For the benefit of my client I should go back down to the library and make sure that Beekman hadn't recovered. But he couldn't have; just the restless unconscious movements of his body in the chair. Well—I'd go down anyway and have a look.

But I didn't go down. I turned suddenly and dashed hurriedly up the stairs. The girl was in real danger—physical danger. From the back of the house, on the second floor, had come a crash and a muffled scream. I knew where the girl was—knew it was the door at the end of the hall. Now, as I ran, I could even see the thin sliver of light beneath it.

A quick turn of the knob told me that the door was locked. I listened a single moment. There was a shuffling movement within the room—a struggle was taking place. Somehow, the girl had freed herself and was even now fighting with an unknown enemy—perhaps battling hopelessly with The Hidden Hand himself.

Once—twice—my shoulders pounded against the door. There was the splitting of wood, the creak of iron, and a sudden snap. The lock crunched through the wood and the door burst open. I didn't land in that room on my face—not me. Years ago, perhaps. For this wasn't the first time I'd hurled myself through a locked door—and what's more, I didn't intend it to be the last.

My gun was in my hand. This was action. This was the game; the man-hunt as I understood it. I expected a shower of lead from within that room and was ready to meet it—even anticipate it.

But there was no flying lead to greet me. No shouted order to "stand back"—no menacing gun in the hand of a killer. The room was small; the fireplace burned brightly; the dull brilliancy from the shaded light covered the whole room. Not a place to hide in but a little closet.

The situation was not hard to explain. There was the overturned chair, with the girl still strapped in it. She had struggled to free herself, probably frantic with fear, and so overturned the chair—or maybe she had heard the shot, thought the police were there, and tried to attract attention.

I jerked the chair erect, stepped across to the closet door and threw it open. It was a small washroom—and empty. I returned to the girl. Wide, frightened brown eyes stared at me. I smiled cheerily as I spotted a knife on the mantel above the fire, cut the cords that held her and jerked off the gag. She couldn't speak at first—sort of gulped, and a dry tongue licked at drier lips. Once she tried to rise from the chair, and fell back again. Despite my smile of assurance, she stared at me questioningly. Then her eyes fell to the gun in my hand.

Her face flushed a quick red and turned again to an ashen gray sort of white. She looked at her bare feet and the two long bits of iron that glowed a vivid red on the burning coals.

"You're just as safe as if you were in your own bed at home," I told her. "Safer—I guess." I followed the question in her eyes. "The lad that used to do fancy tricks with red-hot rivets is working at his trade where it's appreciated—dead," I explained, when she didn't seem to get it. "Beekman's taking a nap, and—"

She swayed in the chair. Her lips framed the word, "water." I hustled to the little washroom, found a glass and brought her a drink. She gulped it down. It stuck in her throat. She coughed once, gagged, drew in a deep breath, and began to take an interest in things. The life came back into the dull eyes, the color that rushed to her cheeks wasn't such a vivid red. I nodded in satisfaction.

"Take me away." She came to her feet, took a step forward and tumbled into my arms. "The Hidden Hand is to come here—Beekman told me—told me I was to see him, and—"

I held her for a moment, close to me, before she came unsteadily to her feet again. A young, beautiful, and very wealthy heiress—and she had told me that she loved me. What emotions did I feel—what thoughts shot through my mind—what words sprang to my lips? Well—simply these:

"Yes, Tina—what did Beekman tell you about The Hidden Hand?"

"That he would be here with me. Beekman laughed then, and I could not understand his next words or did not fully grasp them in my horror. He said, 'The Hidden Hand and you shall be here together—and The Hidden Hand and you will go away together.' At least that's what I thought he said."

"Then he's coming here to-night!" I sure got a kick out of that. "Now, what else—" I stooped and caught her as she fell. Her hands just reached for my shoulders, missed, and she slid toward the floor.

I lifted her in my arms. Her face was white and the black circles beneath her eyes stood out vividly; not deep lines—just those tell-tale rings of sleepless nights and days of fear.

I hesitated between taking her down the stairs and placing her on the couch to the right of the fireplace. I'd be a fine specimen of action with the unconscious girl in my arms and my guns in my pockets if any one got into the house. Especially, the one Beekman expected, from what the girl had said. The leading man of this drama; the cruel, unscrupulous, intelligent murderer behind this organization—The Hidden Hand himself. No—I'd leave her on the couch. Heavy, steel shutters guarded the window.

I stepped to the couch, leaned over it with my frail burden, when her two arms went suddenly about my neck.

"Don't leave me here, Race—don't. I—don't you see—don't you understand—I'm afraid. And what I told you to-night—was true—was true. I—"

She hesitated. We were deadly quiet for a moment.

This time she didn't finish. Nor did I get started on my opinion of her for pretending to faint at a time like this. Plainly, from below came footsteps—distinctly I heard the tread of feet across wood; hurrying feet that beat onto carpet and were deadened to a dullness that was partly imaginary. But the tread of those feet across wood was not imaginary. It was as if the walker tripped, caught himself again and ran for a few steps.

My first thought was, Alexander Beekman. My second thought was, The Hidden Hand. My third thought, Old

206

Benevolence Travers. Certainly, my third thought was the most reasonable. Travers was expected, and Travers was about due—and Travers evidently knew his way about the house.

"There's the key, in the washroom door," I told Tina as I placed her on the couch. "If anything happens, simply cry out—run to the washroom and lock yourself in. I'll be here before you can be hurt."

"Who is it?" She tried to hold me but I pulled her arms from about my neck and ran lightly across the floor. Then I was out in the hall, my rubber-soled shoes making little noise as I sought the stairs and gripped the banister.

I had no more than started down when I heard the click of a latch; the sound of metal against metal. I didn't need three guesses, nor did I need to see the outline of the library door when I was halfway down the stairs. But the library door, which I had left open, was now closed.

How long it took me to finish the stairs or cross that hall, I don't know. Not so long—not fast enough, either, to make a sound. I put silence ahead of speed. If it was possible for Alexander Beekman to close that door, I didn't know—now. A few minutes before I'd say it was impossible. Certainly, though, he was not trying to escape. Voices—or at least one voice—came from within that room.

36

The Hidden Hand Strikes

I reached the door and listened. But I couldn't understand the low, sharp, imperative whispers that reached my ears. I put my hand on the knob, turned it slowly—noiselessly. The hum went on from inside the room, the latch slipped back without a sound and I pushed gently. The door was locked.

Now what? This door was strong and heavy, but so am I. I daresay, if it came to a show-down, I could bust in. And I certainly would, before I let Beekman—who was actually worth his weight in gold—escape. But to what purpose would I bust in? If some one was bent on rescuing Beekman, that some one had only to take him through the window. If The Hidden Hand had come and locked the door, then I'd be playing his game by busting in and taking a chestful of lead. I tried to figure out the time. How long was it since I had telephoned Old Benevolence Travers? Certainly he could be here by now. The house wasn't far away from his hotel. Hardly fifteen minutes' drive as I came—and when they brought me they had twisted and turned considerably. My guess was, we were right in Palm Beach itself.

Surely this must be Travers. But could Beekman talk? Was I wrong about how hard I had hit him? If it was Travers and I interrupted the conversation, mightn't Beekman decide to shut his face? In other words— But two were talking. I strained against that keyhole, listening. Certainly Beekman was talking. I could tell his voice—but his words? No—just a "damn his soul" occasionally, and again "you'll do the right thing by me—I was but putty in his hands."

So Travers had gotten his confession and the money was mine. I raised my hand and tapped slightly on the door. A dead silence—heavy feet and a key turning in the lock. I stepped back as the door was flung violently open. And I gasped—the man who faced me in the doorway was Gregory Ford.

"You. You!" I gasped, as I tried to step by him.

"Me—sure." He shoved me back, closing the door behind him. Then he laughed. "You set the stage, Race—but I took the final bow."

"He—he told you something?"

"Something! I should say he did. He told me the name of The Hidden Hand—nothing left now but the pinch. Hold on, there, you stay out of that room. There's the girl—right room, back—upstairs. And don't gape at me like that. I hung around the King estate and saw him leave with the girl. They went out like old friends. I had my suspicions of Beekman and followed him here, with the boys. Nice and friendly, they seemed—not my business. And when I'd about decided to go home and call it a night, you flopped out of a car. I knew they handled you rough but didn't see the details.

"We pinched the lads outside. It took time to do it, quiet. Then came the shot, the broken window, and my chance to slip in, douse Beekman with water from the kitchen, and get an earful. He was ready and anxious to blow the works. After I heard him I didn't wonder. It's a most remarkable story—a most remarkable story." A great hand fell upon my shoulder, a generous mouth cracked into that superior smile he was pulling lately.

"And you know—who The Hidden Hand is?" I just

couldn't think of anything else to say. My promised bank roll was taking wings.

"Gregory Ford knows everything." His gun went into his pocket and his cigar ran across his mouth. "You're a fine detective you are. But there's the girl." And he pushed me back into the hall.

"But—him," I jerked a thumb toward the library, "you want to—watch him." I looked into the dining room and saw the light through the other door to the library.

"He's handcuffed to a chair." Gregory laughed. Surely, he was in a jovial mood. "The house is surrounded. That is, as much as it can be surrounded—there're four men outside. That's why I came in alone. I'd like a dozen. Do you know who's coming here to-night?"

"Who?" I thought at once of what Tina had told me.

"The Hidden Hand—himself—in person. Beekman told me. You can stay and see the show, Race. After all, you're not such a bad lad. You helped—yes, decidedly you helped. But a gun and a finger and a clear eye aren't enough always. You need brains, my boy—brains."

"How did you get in the house?"

"Through the window behind the curtain. That was a close call, too. I was right at the window when the shot came—and I reached a hand through the hole, and parting the curtains saw you leave. Fletcher's out there now."

"The Hidden Hand may be able to enter the house."

"He will—he will." Gregory nodded, paused, and smiled. "Mr. Hidden Hand is welcome to come in. There'll be no one to hinder him. But going out again—that's the thing, my boy. Now for this girl—"

"Well—" I turned a bit sulky, "what of the girl?"

"Safe, as far as I am concerned. She's an innocent victim of The Hidden Hand—drawn into the net for the purpose of future blackmail—and, perhaps, also for information of the rich. The price of their jewelry—the—"

"She never helped them," I cut in.

"No—no." He waved a hand. "Your faith in the girl was justified. Beekman has been very obliging—very talkative. When they wanted the girl they had only to send for her—just the threat of giving her secret away. Her secret was, that she trapped a police sergeant to his death. And she did. But not knowingly. Still, the fact that she kept silent would have been strong against her. It would even go hard on her now if I did not have the facts from Beekman. But—" he frowned, "where I may be able to give evidence that will save her a prison term, the hurt to her family will still be there. If Beekman don't talk, The Hidden Hand will. They'll attempt to use the Andrew Gordon King millions to protect themselves. It'll be an ugly story—hard to believe in her innocence. Great meat for the papers. But there's her brother, whom she—"

"But she has no brother. Her mother, Mrs. King, told me that."

"Were those her exact words?" Gregory Ford smiled.

I thought a moment.

"Mrs. King told me she never had a son. If she didn't have a son, then Tina couldn't have had a—"

"She might have also told you she didn't have a daughter," Gregory Ford shot in. "The police have not been idle since that shooting in New York. You recall the youth who was killed in your arms. Good! His widow received a large sum of money—and that money came from the daughter of Andrew Gordon King. I knew that this morning—and when I met the daughter to-night—well—she's an adopted daughter and she's never seen her brother. She was taken from an orphanage when a baby. Lately, her brother was discovered, sick—dying—and a criminal.

"It was the call of the blood, I guess. No one knew. No one must know. But she saw in him only a product of environment—somewhat as she might have been had not her brown eyes and beautiful face attracted the attention of Mrs. King so

211

many years ago. I doubt if the girl, herself, actually knew she was adopted until this scheme formed in the mind of The Hidden Hand."

"And your information came from—"

"Partly police work—partly Alexander Beekman."

Mostly, Beekman—I thought, as I asked:

"And to-night—the shooting by the gate?"

"Beekman himself, I think—though he blames it on the dead man there in the library."

"Poor Kid," I said, "she's gotten some tough breaks."

"Yes." He nodded. "And King's a powerful man. I won't talk unless it's necessary to get a conviction. But Beekman's a rat—he'll squeal to save his miserable hide. I promised to do what I could for him, if he talked. But—the girl—come!"

We mounted the stairs and went down the long hall, to the rear room directly above the library.

"It's all right, Tina." I raised my hand to tap on the closed door. "Gregory Ford and I have come to—"

I stopped and turned sharply. Gregory Ford's voice came hoarsely in my ear.

"What was that?" He fairly screeched the words, swung suddenly and dashed down the stairs. Wildly, eerie, that scream—more a gurgle of terror—came again.

I was right on Gregory Ford's heels when he reached the library door and flung it open. Gregory jarred so suddenly to a stop that I crashed against him, knocking him forward. Then I, too, drew up sharply.

I'm used to all kinds of violent death—but this was rather a hideous affair. Alexander Beekman still sat in the chair, the handcuffs plainly upon his wrists—but he wasn't a pretty sight. A knife had been pulled across his throat from ear to ear. I half turned my head away. Then I thought of the girl; of the tiny knife scratches on her throat, her bare feet, and the red hot irons on the grate. No—it was hard to get up sympathy for Alexander Beekman. He had intended to torture the girl before my eyes, to get knowledge from me.

Gregory gulped once or twice, stepped forward—and hung back. Not me—I took in the position of the dead Beekman, the open dining-room door, through which the murderer must have entered, and the swaying curtains by the window. And Gregory Ford, too, saw the curtains. His gun jerked up—his voice shook as he spoke.

"Come from behind those curtains or I'll shoot."

There was no response; the curtains still waved. I slipped back into the shadows, covering the window and giving the dining room door a wide berth.

"He can't have escaped," Gregory whispered loudly. "Fletcher's just outside the window. The murderer's still in the house, or behind that curtain, and—and it's The Hidden Hand."

Raising his gun Gregory Ford slowly advanced toward that curtain. Back against the wall I waited and watched. Was the man there? Was the man all Florida searched for and feared, within a few feet of us? Or was he back some place in the house—in the shadows of the dining room?

37

Gregory Ford Explains

There was a hoarse call behind me in the hall, and the bang of a door. Nerves keyed to a high pitch, Gregory Ford fired at the waving curtains. I swung about and raised my gun. Fletcher, the young police detective, was in the hall, running toward me. Gregory Ford was at the curtains, had flung them back and was staring at the open window.

"You—you, Fletcher." Gregory Ford swung around and walked across the room. His face was red with anger, his eyes blazed, and his words caught in his throat. "You had your orders—'stay by that window.' What the devil do you mean by—"

"The cry—the death rattle in a man's throat." Fletcher was breathing heavily, his face ashen as he looked at the mess that had been Beekman. "I thought it was you, sir—or—I didn't dare come by the window, and—"

With disgust Gregory Ford turned to the open window. His broad shoulders rose and fell with his heavy breathing. At length he turned his back to us, spreading his arms far apart.

"It was this leader—The Hidden Hand—and he has escaped us. Now—" and then coming toward Fletcher.

"Maybe it isn't so bad. I know who he is—if he don't know that I know, we'll get him. If he does know, if Beekman told him, or—" He wasn't a bad fellow, was Gregory Ford. He walked to Fletcher and dropped an arm on his shoulder. "Always obey orders—let neither fear nor courage, nor the thoughts of condemnation sway you. We had the man in our grasp—the most feared and most dangerous criminal in history in our hands—and you—"

"It was you I thought of, sir. You had gone in. Then quiet, and I could see nothing through the curtains. I was watching for the coming of the man, not the going of him. It was terrible—that cry—that death cry. I—I felt it my duty to—to come."

There were other footsteps now—other voices. Captain Rogers, of the police, was in the room—also Brown, and back in the hall another detective. Gregory Ford grinned sickly.

"I know. I know." He shook his head as they explained their coming. The cry of agony brought one; the shot that Gregory fired brought the others. But all came to face danger, not to shirk it.

"There's the house." Captain Rogers coughed slightly. "He may be here now. It's Beekman, ain't it?" He blinked at the body. "I never really believed he was in it. He's paid now. But this murderer—why couldn't he be hiding in—?" He stepped back suddenly from the door which led to the dining room. "He might be in there. I had a feeling that a figure slunk through the bushes less than—"

"Sure you did," Gregory shot sarcastically. "And if you take a look at Beekman, you'll know he didn't carve himself up like that. But there's no use to search the house. There's the window—"

"But Fletcher was there, and—"

"Fletcher left, just as you left your posts."

"But this murderer couldn't know that. As far as he knew, he might jump right into Fletcher's arms. He couldn't have guessed that Fletcher'd come to the front door and—"

"Don't be a fool," Gregory snapped. "The man's a mile away by now. He didn't know, in the first place, that Fletcher was there at all—Fletcher was back in the bushes. There's no doubt it was The Hidden Hand. There's no doubt he killed Beekman. Then he jumped out the window and escaped."

That sounded reasonable, of course—not only reasonable but logical. I began to worry and wonder a bit about my client, Old Benevolence Travers. He was about due—even past due. Had he recognized the situation—guessed that the police were there? Or had he heard the shot; even the last death cry of Beekman, and slipped back out of the picture?

And I stopped thinking. Gregory Ford was playing the stage detective. He had done a good night's work and he didn't care who knew it. He threw out his chest and bit into his cigar as he talked.

"Beekman spilt the works, boys, before he died. It is just possible that this Hidden Hand, whose name I now know, guessed that he gave the show away. But what this Hidden Hand did know was, that Beekman would squeal to save his own skin. Beekman was that kind, as proven by the fact that he did squeal to me. Yes, gentlemen, I know the name of The Hidden Hand."

Gregory Ford strutted a bit about the room as he gave that line a chance to sink in.

"And if he don't know that I know his identity, I'll have him in irons before the sun is up. And here the possibility arises that he may know the truth—that I know him. I can't think of myself then. I can't think of the personal glory. I shall think of the citizens of Florida, and the state that employs me. I shall tell to you men—and even to my dear colleague, Race Williams, the name of this man. That it will surprise you is certain. But picture the situation—" Gregory Ford paused with the name on his lips; he couldn't help playing to the gallery.

"We have, then, Beekman handcuffed here in a chair, and in his mind the betrayal of his master—the master whom he

216

feared. He had not only that betrayal in his mind, but he had it on his lips—he tells me that name. He don't dicker for his freedom. He knows that the game is up. He takes my word that I shall present his case in the best possible light, and save him from the chair. But, gentlemen, he has another reason for talking—one that is even stronger than his love of life. His hate; his vengeance; his—"

Gregory Ford stopped again, and stepped to the dining room.

"So we see this master—this criminal—this murderer, who is called by his associates The Hidden Hand, advance upon the prostrate Beekman, handcuffed there in the chair. He comes from the dining room—so—and stands behind Beekman." Gregory advanced and stood behind the hideous sight in the chair. "Does Beekman hear him? I think so, for he raises his head—and there in the mirror across the room their eyes meet. Does The Hidden Hand see in the eyes of Beekman, hope—the hope that now that his master has come he, Beekman, will be saved? No. The Hidden Hand sees fear in the eyes of Beekman—fear that is caused by Beekman's guilty knowledge that he has betrayed his master. There is little more. Beekman cried out once before the knife crossed his throat—and that is all. The second cry was simply a gurgle—a death rattle.

"And then what? Does The Hidden Hand slink back in the house, to hide? No. He hears footsteps above. Williams and I are running down the stairs. He doesn't hesitate. With the bloody knife still clutched in his hand he grips the curtains by the window. See—" Gregory walked briskly to the window and held up a section of the curtain. Plainly there was blood upon it. We all leaned forward as Gregory continued.

"He is out in the night and away—but there is just the possibility that he guesses that he has left his name behind him, with me. The possibility that he read that betrayal in Beekman's eyes. If that is true, he will not dare to face it out, but will leave the—"

"But—who is he?" Captain Rogers couldn't hold his curiosity a moment longer.

"All in good time." Gregory smiled. "When the state of Florida hired me they expected results. When the state of Florida hires Gregory Ford they get results. Now Williams came into the thing. A contest there—a friendly one, of course—but we are old rivals in the game of man-hunting. Williams has worsted me on small cases. I have taken it good-naturedly." Which was a lie. He had never taken it good-naturedly. He certainly loved the footlights. He certainly was dragging out the name of The Hidden Hand. And what had he done to get it? Nothing but listen to the babbling of a ter-ror-stricken squealer whom I had ripened for the big bust. So, the detective posed by the window, the blood-stained curtain in his hand.

"Now," Gregory Ford ran on, "that the catch is made, let us welcome Williams among us. After all, a quick eye may—may—"

I saw the flash of orange-blue flame before I heard the shot. I saw, too, Gregory Ford sort of lurch forward in a convulsive jump, as if he had been violently pushed from behind. I saw his mouth twitch and his hands clench spasmodically as he crashed to the floor, dragging the curtain and pole down on top of him.

38

Through the Jungle

The others may have stood paralyzed with fear, horror, or shocked surprise—according to how a man's emotions work. But not me.

I was over the prostrate form and at the window almost the moment Gregory hit the ground. And what's more, I didn't stop at the window—a dark figure in a lighted window is a tempting target. I kept on going—was out that window and crouched in the darkness below. No shot greeted me—no figure was running across the lawn. Which way would I turn? Which way would I go?

Things were clear enough. Gregory Ford's love of self-glorification had been his downfall—perhaps his death. The Hidden Hand had jumped from the window, as Gregory ha said—but he had stayed there beneath the window. Perha he listened. Perhaps he even peered into the room—bu I don't think that was possible, with the curtains. But he ha a good look when Gregory Ford raised the curtain and sod squarely in the light of the window. And now— If I wat to the front, the man might go to the back. If I went b the back— But I decided to stay just where I was a bit and listen

It was useless to hunt a man in that mass of jungle growth all about me.

And I saw him—at least, a figure; a shadow that moved close to the garage by the back of the house, almost around the edge of the building. In the moonlight I saw the heavy growth beyond the garage.

Was the figure The Hidden Hand? Was it the man who shot Gregory Ford and murdered Beekman? If I called out to the figure to halt, it had only to slip around the garage and into the thick growth.

Well—life is full of chances. Surprises are great things. I might fire and cop off a detective, or even a watchman for some estate who, hearing the shooting, was investigating. I have yet to see the man I won't meet halfway. I raised my gun—dashed from the house and shouted my warning.

The figure didn't stop and shout out his name. The figure didn't turn and take a shot at me. It just slipped around the corner of the garage as I fired. No—I didn't expect to hit it; that was impossible then—but if it were an honest man the warning should be enough. As it was, I clipped the stucco off the corner of the low building as my bullet sped into the night.

Ten seconds later I was around that building and into the jungle growth that the millionaires claim, and keep as the natural beauty of Palm Beach. The moon was bright enough overhead, but it couldn't do its stuff in that foliage. My eyes didn't help me any, but my ears did. I could hear my man crashing along ahead.

I was faster than my fleeing friend; but my fleeing friend had the advantage of knowing the ground. That sort of evened things up. There was a path through that labyrinth of heavy bush and thickly entwined, queer-shaped trees. There were turns, too, and every time we made one I bumped off the path into the bush and thick, heavy grass. On the path the ground was hard; in the bush it was soft. But I stumbled along through the night.

Each time I missed the path, I got my bearings so to speak.

For in that pause I clearly heard the running feet ahead, the breaking branches, the crunching twigs—and saw, too, in the moonlight the waving of small palms and giant foliage.

It was a great game. Never a chance to shoot; never an object to shoot at—just the creaking and cracking and smashing ahead that let me know I was holding my own. Deeper and deeper we seemed to get into the jungle, and harder and harder became the path to follow. But the tougher the going on the path the better chance I had—there was more noise ahead. If I could hear the fleeing figure, certainly the fleeing figure could hear me. I began to lose respect for The Hidden Hand. Where was his nerve? To turn and shoot it out gave him better than an even break. There were stretches of generous width in the path—curves that he might stop beyond and open fire as I made the turn.

Almost with that thought I threw myself flat on the ground, off the path and into the tropical growth. There had been no roar of a gun; no stab of yellow—but something just as significant. There had been a sudden silence ahead of me; feet no longer beat over loose twigs; a body no longer crashed through the heavy growth. There was only one conclusion. The fleeing figure ahead had stopped suddenly.

Cautiously I lay still and waited, then I raised my head and looked to the right—snaked a bit over the grass and found that I was looking out over a stretch of open. Huge palms, but no more jungle. There before me was a narrow, rough road, and as I strained my eyes across the stretch of moonlight and down that road I saw—yes, it was a car, parked between thick pines—but a car nevertheless. No lights, no moving figures— just a long affair whose nickel trimmings gave it away.

I nodded in understanding, and waited. Here was the get-away car. Here was the car which had brought The Hidden Hand to the house. And here was the car that was to take him away. He hoped that I would crash through the bush, miss him, return or get lost—and he would slip out of the jungle, climb aboard and disappear into the night.

Silently I recovered my breath. Things were looking up. Gregory Ford, the only one who knew the name of The Hidden Hand, lay wounded, or perhaps dead, in the house. And I—well—there I was, some feet away from the man for whom all Florida searched. Here was my chance to drag him in; disclose his identity and claim the reward—the unlimited amount which Old Benevolence Travers was to pay.

Not a bad outlook that. I spun the cylinder on my revolver and waited. If I saw him and he didn't see me, a bullet in the leg would do the trick. If he saw me and—well—you can't make applesauce without busting up a few apples. Either way it went was all right with me. Tina King had saved my life. All who knew her secret were dead, except The Hidden Hand. Surely, if he got messy and I laid a bit of lead in his chest there would be some satisfaction. If he didn't—but there's no use crying over spilt gin.

I smacked my lips and got my gun set. Scarcely fifteen feet from me the bush cracked. A long period of silence and another crack. Five minutes more and again the crack of heavy growth. This time I moved slightly, with the crack. I had only to come to my feet, step forward and be in the open—the open that my murdering friend was now seeking.

The movement now was more pronounced. The figure had certainly come to its feet. Good enough! I slid to one knee, tuning my movement with the movement of the one in the bush. Then I waited. After all, it was I who was to be in on the kill—action had won over "brains." One minute—two maybe—and the mystery of The Hidden Hand—the identity of the great criminal—would be a mystery no longer.

A shadow, an outline in the moonlight—and I raised my gun. We stepped out of the bush together. The harsh words of command died on my lips. The figure heard me and turned in the moonlight.

"Tina—Tina!" I gasped. If there wasn't a welcome in my voice, do you blame me?

"Race—Race." She half staggered toward me and started

in to cry. There's no understanding women. Was she going to faint again? And if she did, this time would it be real, or fake—like the last?

"What are you doing here?" I asked, as I half held her. Then remembering the car I dragged her back into the bush.

"There were you—and that detective at the door. Then the horrible cry; the shot from below; the calling men and stamping feet. I didn't want to be found there by the police. There were the rear stairs. I stole down them, opened the back door and went out. Then a shot—a running figure—and I thought of the path and that my car would be there with Richmond, my ever faithful chauffeur and friend.

"There was another shot, and I grew frantic and ran. I didn't want the police to find me—I didn't want The Hidden Hand to find me. For if I saw him and knew him—even suspected him—it would mean death. Don't you see—don't you understand that all who knew him—are dead? They—" And she started in to pull the Nigara Falls all over me.

"I'll see you home," I told her.

"No." She shook her head. "The car is there, and Richmond. And, Race—" two little hands sought my shoulders; tear-dimmed brown eyes searched mine. "Is there any—chance for me?"

"Yes," I told her, "a good one. If The Hidden Hand is caught, and squawks, Gregory Ford will stand behind you. A newspaper scandal may—"

"I don't mean that," she said softly. "I mean—what I told you to-night. I'm sorry—I was frantic—I thought that I faced death. But—but—don't you see I mean it. I love you, Race. You—"

"There—there." I patted her head a bit. Things sure were complicated enough as they now stood.

"Oh—I'm not a silly, love-sick girl." She threw the words quickly at me. "I have a purpose in—well—anyway, you said I saved your life—you would do anything for me in return. You did to-night. You came, facing death—for me. Now—

what of me?"

"You need not worry about that, Tina. I'll do it again—any time you need me, I'll come."

And she took it wrong—all wrong. Her lips were warm and soft—but after all she was only a kid and didn't fit in with my scheme of things. Here was pampered youth and wealth and romance and sordid reality—all mixed in together, and in a way she couldn't distinguish the one from the other.

She cried a bit and laughed a bit and clung to me, and told me that she didn't care for herself and now that she "knew the truth" it was of me that she thought—and that they'd kill me.

And I stood there and took it all in, and tried to listen for a movement in the jungle and watch over her head for a figure by the car—and all the time Gregory Ford lay back in that house and The Hidden Hand put miles between himself and me.

She wouldn't let me take her to the car. And in a way she was right. Richmond, the faithful chauffeur, would be waiting behind the wheel for her. There was a chance that The Hidden Hand might still be in the bush—and besides, I'd be needed back at the house. If Gregory Ford talked, I wanted to get an earful.

So I stood and watched her as she ran across the open, turning once to wave to me—for all the world as if she were just leaving me after an ordinary love tryst. I watched her and nodded for a bit, and wondered—and then I shook my head, for there had been another girl not so long ago. The radio and the smoking jacket and slippers are nice to think of—but somehow they didn't fit in with gun play and murderers and the man-hunter who stalks his prey in the night.

I heard the hum of the high-priced engine and saw the man climb from the car almost as she reached it. Tina was running, but stopping she turned once as if to wave to me again. But it was a jerky sort of a stop—and the man reached her. Two hands shot out for her, and I heard her scream and saw her struggle, and saw the whiteness of a hand that was raised above her head and the blackness of an object that swung downward in the moonlight.

39

Captain Rogers Needs Help

Tina's scream died, her struggle ceased—and I dashed from the bush and ran across the open toward the trees and the car.

The man saw me, of course, but he never turned—just backed quickly toward the car, losing precious moments but saving his life, for he held the girl in his arms and I couldn't fire without hitting her.

It was impossible to get to them in time. Several quick steps the man took backward—and reached the car. I slowed down—almost stopped—watching for him to turn and enter the car. I'd get him then—but I wanted to be sure of my shot.

He didn't turn—he stepped back and up onto the running board of the car. Nothing for him to do then but deposit his helpless burden upon the seat, and shoving the car into gear, drive off.

One chance—one long chance—and I took it. He raised the girl high in his arms, protecting his body, as his left foot sought the step behind. For a second, then, his right foot was on the ground—a dark, distant object. I stopped dead, drew a bead and fired. Got him, too—for he staggered slightly, swayed forward, and—damn the luck—he backed into the car with the girl still in his arms.

The cards were against me. No sudden jerk forward and stalling of the car. It roared off in a single bound, made a bend and disappeared from view. The girl was in the hands of the enemy—what enemy? The Hidden Hand, without a doubt. But what was there to fear in that? Hadn't she been at all times under his control—subject to his beck and call, since he knew her secret? Now—but I gulped. She had seen him— seen his face—knew him—and to know him would mean what? Just one thing—that thing which had happened to Gregory Ford—a shot in the back—death.

I had been a fool not to go with her. But had I? No—there was just as much chance that the master criminal was hiding in the foliage. Besides, if I had gone with the girl, expecting to find Richmond, the chauffeur, in the car—I might have been shot down. Was that it? Was that why The Hidden Hand had waited in the car? To get me—not the girl? But what had he to fear from me? For that matter, what had he to fear from the girl? I gulped. I thought I knew the answer to the second question. The Hidden Hand had been outside the house when the girl left it by the back door. She had seen his running figure. What was more likely than that he had seen hers—perhaps even recognized her and thought that she recognized him.

There was a sudden noise behind me—a cough and a grunt. I swung sharply and saw the man sitting on the grass. It was Richmond, the chauffeur. I had to listen to his story. There wasn't much to it. He had stuck his head out of the car a few minutes before, to find out who was coming—and he never did find out. The time between that look-see, and the moment he sat up on the grass was a blank.

I wasn't in a panic. I wasn't in a funk. There was fear, of course, for the girl. One thing I was sure of. If harm came to her, I'd find this Hidden Hand and lay him so cold you could skate on his chest. Vengeance, that? Maybe. Call it by whatever name you please, but it was gospel just the same. Somehow I was beginning to think that Tina King wasn't such a bad kid.

I didn't try to advise Richmond. I didn't tell him what had happened to the girl. He had his instructions what to say at home if she didn't show up. She often absented herself for days at a time. There were many girl friends who served as alibis—besides, that's modern youth, whether you think well of it or not.

And I couldn't find my way back to that house. But that didn't bother me—after all, the show was over. I gave Richmond a hand and we started off toward town—along the country road, to the main highway. Richmond was full of conversation, and if I had visions of terrible things happening to Tina King, they were nothing to what was in that morbid mind of Richmond's.

He was for telling the police one minute and for telling Mr. King about the girl's strange visits the next. Altogether, he wasn't a very encouraging companion. When he asked for my advice, I gave it to him flat. Hold his tongue for a bit and see how things broke—that was Miss King's advice to him at all times.

We didn't go very far before there was a yip out of Richmond. There, less than three-quarters of a mile away, was Tina's big car. And Richmond pounced on it. He cooed over it like a mother over a baby. It was in good shape. The Hidden Hand had evidently changed to his own car. A couple of seconds later we were off. Richmond could leave me at the hotel of my client. Old Benevolence Travers was entitled to some information—besides, I was just a bit worried as to what had become of him. He was long past due at Beekman's. Had he been met and knocked over on the way? Had he arrived, and seeing the police, beat it? Or had—?

We were close to the bridge when Richmond jerked on the brakes. Captain Rogers, of the police, had been on the job. A blue-coated figure held us up, and when he talked he held a gun in his hand. So did I, for that matter—but he couldn't see it. This Hidden Hand wouldn't be above impersonating an officer, and uniforms are cheap. I had been taken in by such a little masquerade once before. I didn't know this cop.

But the cop was stupid enough and earnest enough to be the real thing. We didn't get any more than started on our questions and answers when a carful of men pulled up. Captain Rogers was in it. Another shot by—a closed car—and I caught the flash of a white coat. It was an ambulance. I spotted Rogers and answered his excited questions.

"Didn't find him; this lad's been driving me about. Drives for Miss King." I explained Richmond. "Now—what about Gregory Ford—doctor been? What does he say?"

"He'll die on the table if—if he ever gets there." And there was real emotion in Rogers' voice. "The dog—to shoot a man in the back," he muttered. "But I've telephoned for Dr. Carey, of New York—he's stopping here in Palm Beach now. Coming along?"

"Not just yet." I shook my head. "But I'll want to learn about Gregory—at once. Where are you taking him?"

"Jones' Private Hospital—best in the country. Better stick with me. I've had every road covered, and called out every man. We'll hunt this killer down."

"Did Gregory Ford—talk?"

"He never opened his face after he fell—and never will, I guess. You're a good man, Race—Gregory and you worked the same game in different ways. You won't—you'll work for him now?"

"I'll work for him." I nodded. "Get along. I'd go with you, only I'm expecting a bit of information at my hotel." I lied. And then, "Don't stick any flatty on me, Rogers. It'll spoil the game."

He didn't apologize—didn't even grin sickly. He just nodded, and turned to a man beside him. It was a cinch that he had already given orders to have me followed.

"Don't shadow Race Williams, here. He saw Gregory Ford shot down. He will stick with us now. He's that kind of a guy—is Race Williams."

"I'll be that kind of a guy, Rogers." I took the moist hand he shot into mine.

"That's right." His head jerked, like it worked on a wire.

"Gregory Ford was big enough for this game. It has swamped me. Ford may have been out to beat you—but he spoke the best of you to me. We'll appreciate a hand from you now— we'll need it. It's all too much for me."

Maybe I didn't feel much better than Rogers. Maybe I was nearly as much at sea. But my nature isn't built to be weighted down with discouragement. I sort of absorb it and turn it out again in new energy. I hit Rogers a clap on the back and tried to brace him up.

"Stick to it, Captain," I told him. "We'll pat this lad that got Gregory in the face with a spade yet. Tell the boys to give me a hand when I need it."

"Aye—all of that." But his voice lacked enthusiasm. Rogers was completely crushed by events. Then, just before he drove away, he leaned out and whispered, "Ford thought a lot of you. He criticized your methods and roasted you for a killer. But when we looked down at the dead body of Olaf Sankin, in the park—and thought of those he'd brutally murdered— and his last victim, Rosie Sorellie, Gregory said to me, 'Rogers, I'd give my right hand to have been the man who killed this filthy carrion.' And he meant it. I wouldn't a told you—only—he's booked over."

"Right." And the words I wanted stuck in my throat. "Gregory's a good guy," was all I said as Rogers drove away.

Funny, wasn't it? Gregory Ford was the only one who knew the name of The Hidden Hand—and neither one of us had made the suggestion that the doctor try to jazz him up— even for only a few seconds—so he could speak. No—it wasn't The Hidden Hand we were thinking of; it was Gregory Ford, big, blustering, confident. I watched the car drive away—then I climbed back with Richmond and was driven straight to the hotel where Old Benevolence Travers stopped.

40

"He Must Live"

Hours are never respected at Palm Beach. It was nearly one-thirty when I sought the room of Howard Quincy Travers, and the clerk was not surprised. It took time to get Travers on the phone and took more time to get in to see him. Finally I opened his unlocked door, and walking through the narrow hall, entered his living room. Travers' expensive quarters did him proud.

I stopped short when I first saw him. His face was white and colorless—like his eyes. Vacantly, those peculiar eyes stared at me; then his mouth smiled and he stretched forth a hand. Again I felt the moist palm and the thick, dry fingers. He didn't rise from the chair where he sat with a rug over his legs and his dressing jacket tight about his throat. Nor was he surprised or excited by my visit. It seemed as if he rather expected me. It was he who spoke first.

"I'm glad you came—sit down there." Then lowering his voice, "It's Beekman—you have him—can it wait—can you keep him until morning?"

"Then you didn't go to the house at all?"

"No—no. I couldn't go. I tried to tell you—tried to hold the wire—but you hung up on me. I was afraid, too. I heard a voice behind you and I thought—but no matter—I couldn't come. It's my heart again—very bad this time." He clutched at his side. "If you please, Mr. Williams—the Digitalis, there in the bathroom."

I brought him the dope and fed it to him from a dropper. His hand didn't shake so bad and his voice seemed a little better. For five minutes, I guess, he sat and stared at me, his hand half raised for silence. This was a new Travers; the drawn, haggard face didn't fit the moniker of "Old Benevolence" I had wished on him.

At length he spoke, slowly and distinctly, and with a visible effort.

"The heart must last until the end of this. I must see it through. Will Beekman talk? You must take his message for me. I cannot go. You must get the name of this—"

"Beekman is dead," I cut in.

The whiteness of his face never changed. If he felt any emotion it was shown only in the sudden tightening of those long fingers upon the arm of his chair.

"You killed him?" he asked.

"No." And I broke into my story, leaving out nothing but the real name of the girl. When I finished, he leaned forward.

"Gregory Ford—he— You think he will—will not live?"

"That is the opinion of the doctor—that he'll die on the operating table, if he even reaches the table. But a noted specialist will be on the case—at once."

"He must live. He must live!" His strength seemed to return somewhat as he repeated the words. "These police surgeons know nothing—money mustn't matter. Gregory Ford alone knows the name of this monster. Everything rests upon his life. Gregory Ford must live. He told you nothing—absolutely nothing?"

"Nothing," I said. "Absolutely nothing."

He shook his head sadly and laid a hand upon my arm. "You must go to Gregory Ford, watch his condition—a change for the worse or the better. At a moment's notice complications may set in; his life may hang on the advice of a single man—and we must have that man. Do not divulge my connection—but if medical authority is sought, you can act as if for yourself and I will pay any figure."

"About yourself—" I tried to show an interest in his health, "you have no one here with you?"

"Do not worry about me." His smile was about as cheerful as a politician at a prohibition banquet. "I have my man in the next room. This heart comes and goes—until the day when it comes but does not go. If I feel up to it I shall seek seclusion in my little bungalow up the Lake Trail. You will watch this Gregory Ford and then let me know. And if I want you—he is at the hospital?"

"Jones' Sanitarium. I'll be there or at my hotel." I turned toward the door.

"And, Mr. Williams—" he stopped me. "This girl—I think I understand."

"I'll find her," I clenched my hands, "above anything else."

"Of course. I would not push my desire to end the career of this Hidden Hand before the personal good of this girl. We must forget the dead and pray now for the safe return of the living. I— But it is not so many years since I felt as you feel now."

"It's not—" I started. And then, "She saved my life. If anything happens to her, I'm in the hunt now for both money and—vengeance."

"And vengeance will prove the stronger passion." He looked at me long and steadily. "There was a girl in my life— whirled into this maelstrom of crime and horror. Her flesh has long since turned to clay, but her spirit lives. Bear with me, then, if I do not think first of humanity—and understand me when I say that my will to live will overcome what is but physical in my body. There are times when I fear—physically fear—that this Hidden Hand suspects my activities, as you tell me Beekman did. So—the physical man in me bids me hide away, but the mental man in me still urges me on. Go. Gregory Ford must live."

And I went. Strange bird, Old Benevolence. But then, I had never fully swallowed his story that he simply thought of the good of humanity. No—I always thought that in a way he wanted vengeance for some past wrong. Well—I wanted a little vengeance of my own. And, like Old Benevolence Travers, I knew on whom I wanted this vengeance; but I didn't know who the man was or where to find him. Still—I shrugged my shoulders. Somehow I felt that it was in the cards that we should meet.

I had a new insight on Old Benevolence Travers, too. I hadn't known that he sported a bad heart. But if he did, I could understand it suddenly taking a twist on him. It wasn't so many hours ago that he was in the deserted mansion with The Hidden Hand himself—where Rosie Sorellie was murdered.

Also here was a new version of his generosity—his offer to pay me whatever figure I named, once I disclosed the identity of The Hidden Hand. He had said, "even if I took his all." He didn't expect to live long, and wanted this man brought to justice or to death before that heart of his kicked up a fuss and knocked him over. Food for thought there. Great stuff, if I brought The Hidden Hand in and the very shock of the joy killed Travers—before he paid me.

Rather low-down thought, that? Perhaps. But it was what I was thinking when I went to the hospital. Of course, I wouldn't act on the thought—but it was there just the same. I laughed sort of mirthlessly—thought of the girl and pulled in the laugh.

Jones' Private Hospital was an old place, set far back from the road. It was big and roomy and had more wings than a flock of birds. There was a hearse backed up to the side door and my heart did a jump that would have knocked Old Benevolence out of the picture. Was Gregory Ford—? I gulped, mounted the steps and went in the open door.

There were Captain Rogers and Fletcher and Brown, standing around. Funny that. They should have been out and doing—but, so should I. Of course we all wanted to hear the name that Gregory Ford would mutter as soon as he could speak—if he ever could speak. But I don't think it was that. The faces were hard and grim and determined. All of these men would have gladly gone out and tackled The Hidden Hand, even if he had a machine gun and they were unarmed. Me, too. It was hard to understand how Gregory Ford could suddenly get under your skin like that. But I'm no psychologist—fact is fact.

"Doctor Carey came at once," Captain Rogers whispered to me, although there was no one to listen and certainly no one to disturb. "Gregory can't live with that bullet in him— and it's a hundred to one he won't live if they try to take it out. What's the answer?" He tried to shrug his shoulders indifferently, but it didn't fit in with the film over his eyes.

"Operate," I guessed.

"He's on the table now." Rogers nodded. "I don't like to wait, because I know the news'll be bad—could tell that from Dr. Carey. Hardly a hope. But—if Gregory gives me that name, I'll—" he stopped suddenly and jerked himself to attention. Fletcher and Brown did the same. You'd think they were on inspection. And—damn it all—when you come right down to it, I felt my heels click and had half involuntarily raised my hand in a military salute I hadn't pulled since the Big Fuss over the Pond. But Gregory Ford was, to say the least, a courageous man and—the man in white who descended the broad stairs before us was Doctor Carey, the famous New York surgeon.

Carey's smile was all mixed up between a politician's, a clergyman's and an undertaker's. He had one of those faces that are supposed to be open—but lie. You couldn't hazard a guess if he brought good news or bad news—or even no news. But he took his entrance like a stage celebrity, coming slowly across the room to Captain Rogers. When he did finally open up and talk, there was no pussy-woggling about it. He snapped out his words and came to the point.

"The operation has been a success. Mr. Ford's chances of life are most excellent. But remember—" and sharp, gray eyes flashed around us as a slender finger went into the air, "to me Mr. Ford is a patient—not a witness. If he talks at all before the next twenty-four hours, he will never talk again. I will see him in the morning." He swung on his heel and walked to the front door.

Doctor Carey may have been some surgeon but he certainly wasn't a "good fellow well met." But I changed that opinion before I had fairly formed it. For as he reached the door I saw that beneath the white trousers there were no socks, and that the yellow stripes of a pajama leg showed plainly. Not a bad skate, then, for, after all, from his point of view, he was a very famous doctor and Gregory Ford only a common dick.

Fletcher followed, to drive him home—but at the door Doctor Carey turned and beckoned to me.

"Mr. Williams," he kept those gray eyes on me, "I've seen your picture and I know your reputation just as well as you know mine. I know, too, that nothing I could say or do would keep you from getting a word out of Mr. Ford if you made up your mind to get it. You've killed men in your day—but in this case, at least in my opinion, it would be your first—murder."

He stood there eyeing me a minute, as I grinned at him. Doctor Carey couldn't tell from my face that he was as near getting a slap in the mouth as he'd ever be in his life.

41

Ten Thousand Dollars—Cash

We stalled a bit after the doctor went; made a few guesses as to where The Hidden Hand could be and how to get at him. But above all we nodded, that Gregory Ford would live. Twenty-four hours, then, and the name of The Hidden Hand would be a secret no longer.

Captain Rogers was just as friendly as ever but the enthusiasm of an hour before, when he met me on the lonely road, was gone. His dazed expression and helpless, hopeless attitude to cope with the situation was wiped away with Doctor Carey's announcement that Gregory Ford would live. He was kindly; still interested in me, but more in a superior fashion than a helpless one.

"You better get a sleep, Williams," he told me. "You're a brute of a man, without fear and used to the reckless life of New York's underworld. I don't doubt for a minute, when the end comes—when we must hunt down The Hidden Hand, that you will be a rather useful ally. Come—run along and turn in—every necessary step to guard against the flight of this great criminal will be attended to. There—" he gripped my hand as he squared his shoulders. "There's no denying that you've been a help to us."

Magnanimous? Sure! He was grand. Gregory Ford would live. Gregory Ford would talk. Gregory Ford would tell him the name of The Hidden Hand, and Captain Rogers would gather unto himself the glory of the capture. It would be great stuff. I had half a mind to let him wallow in his own mud—but I didn't entirely. I gave him a bit of advice, that would help both of us.

"You won't be able to keep things from the papers," I told him. "And the moment the news leaks out that Gregory will live, The Hidden Hand will be gone. He shot the man because that man knew his secret. That man still knows his secret and still lives. Better give out the word that Gregory Ford cannot live—and that he is still unconscious, and has been since the moment he was shot—and that it is not expected that he will recover consciousness. Lay emphasis on the fact that Gregory Ford will never talk again. It's the only way to keep The Hidden Hand in Florida."

"I thought of that—I thought of that." Captain Rogers stroked his chin. "I'll have to telephone Doctor Carey, and—"

"You needn't worry about Carey," I cut in. "He won't discuss his—patient. It's the boys; the young doctor in the hospital; a nurse or two; gossip that gets from room to room. Or better still, take the newspapers into your confidence."

"I've handled them before." He puffed out his chest. "Have no fear—what is best to be done will be done. I've held this job of Captain for fifteen years."

"Fine." I nodded. But I didn't tell him he'd probably hold it for fifteen more before any one thought of pushing him up a peg. He was that kind; faithful and sober, steady and honest—and did no doubt prove a big hit at tracing lost milk bottles and rolls from the doorsteps of residences.

Things weren't so bad, if I got in to see Gregory Ford the first time he was able to talk. He'd recognize the merits of turning the man-hunt over to me. Besides, even though Gregory was acting in the public interest now—he was, after all, a private detective paid by the state of Florida. Surely we could reach some agreement where the interests of both of us would be best protected by forming an alliance. I could sort of be working for Gregory—and still, by bringing The Hidden Hand to justice, collect my fee from Old Benevolence Travers.

I'd have to be at the hospital at the right moment and get in to see Gregory Ford as soon as Doctor Carey gave the word. Doctor Carey wouldn't let the gang in and surely Captain Rogers would reserve that right for himself. I'd have to think up some plan to keep from being frozen out.

Things were quiet around the hospital—the dead wagon had moved away. I slipped around the grounds; wide, well-kept lawns, thick growth, and to my nostrils the sweet smell of the night-blooming jasmine.

In the back of the hospital was a little terrace; a balcony effect, and a window with a light that occasionally flashed upon the lawn as the black shade waved slightly in the east breeze from the ocean. I was trying to piece things together— remember what Gregory Ford's final words had been, and wondering what familiar name that of The Hidden Hand could be. Of suspected criminals who might head such a gang, I could think of many. But it would be months and months before they could be traced down, their whereabouts ascertained and their alibis investigated. And then—perhaps a blank wall. No—somehow I had the idea that this criminal's finger-prints would be unknown; his face missing from the police gallery of artistic portraits.

Back and forth by that lighted window, a figure moved— pacing slowly up and down the room. Once I caught the flash of a white coat. A young medical man, thinking over his problems? Maybe. But most young medical men that I know— But we'll let that slide. I slipped nearer to the window. This might be the doctor who brought Gregory Ford to the hospital. If he was, he'd no doubt like to talk—and if he'd like to talk I'd like to listen. A delirious thought—or even a word from Gregory Ford as he came out of the ether might give me the key to The Hidden Hand. A name that might be familiar to the doctor might pass unnoticed. Here, perhaps, was a chance to steal a march on Captain Rogers and the boys.

The window was of the long French variety. It was partly open. I wanted to be sure that the doctor was alone. I bent down and looked under the curtain. A white-coated figure paced the room—noiselessly going back and forth. He was alone. I was about to tap lightly on the glass when he turned suddenly and sought the door, tried it to see if it was locked, and went to the desk in the corner. His eyes bulged as he laid what he lifted out, on the desk; so did mine. It was money—tightly bound stacks—one, two, three, he laid on the desk before he thought of the window. I saw the flash of century notes. I don't need spectacles for that. I know money when I see it.

Over his shoulder he spotted the window. He had a young face, and his thoughts were stamped upon it—like a movie actor's. Hastily he dumped the money into the drawer and came toward the window. That was my cue—I jerked the shade slightly and let it snap up. He fell back as if I had struck him, but he didn't seek the door to escape. It was as if he looked frantically about the room for a weapon.

Almost paralyzed with fear he stood leaning against the table as I forced in the window, and stepping over the sill stood in the room. His hands were empty—mine in my pocket—and both of them clutched a gun.

"Good evening," I said, as I closed the window and pulled down the shade. "I'm a detective investigating the shooting of Gregory Ford—and you—"

"A—an—house doctor—here." Furtively his eyes still sought the open drawer. If ever guilt and fear were written on a man's face, they were stamped on this boy's. It was a cinch that he was new at the game—whatever that game was.

"And you, I suppose, were counting your savings." I jerked the drawer wider and pointed at the money.

240

"Yes—yes—" he stammered. And then suddenly, "No—no—the money is not mine."

I looked down at the bills. There were several more stacks of them; thousands of dollars. And there on the top of the stack was a slip of paper. I divided my attention between the young doctor and the typewritten line. As I finished reading it I whistled softly. Certainly the note was simplicity itself—and right to the point. It read:

If Gregory Ford never speaks again you may expect ten times this amount.

"How much is it—all told?" I looked over at the young doctor.

"Ten thousand dollars," he stammered—and then suddenly coming forward and clutching me by the arm, "You don't think I'd—I'd do that—that I ever meant to do that! I—"

"What did you intend to do?" I put hard eyes on him. Here was a first offender, and easy meat for the experienced detective.

"I was—just going to turn it over to the authorities."

"How did it get there? When?"

"How, I don't know. Just a few minutes ago, when I came into the room after the—the operation, it was lying there in the open drawer."

"After the operation—how fortunate not before."

And I had him. He denied it all in fear and trembling—and horror, too. But I got the story, and believed him. He intended no harm to Gregory Ford—he intended to turn the money over to the police. Then he got thinking. He could keep it. No one would ever suspect—no one would know he had it. He had to do nothing. He was young—wanted to get married and was hard up. Why give it to the police? They would only suspect him.

Yes, he admitted having heard Captain Rogers speaking to Doctor Carey. He knew that on the life of Gregory Ford depended the capture of the south's greatest menace—The Hidden Hand. And he suspected, too, that the money came from him—in some mysterious way—probably through the open window.

His logic that he should keep it, say nothing and do nothing, wasn't bad. It wasn't his honesty that made him pace the room in doubt. It was the possibility that, after all, Gregory Ford might die, his secret of the money be discovered and suspicion be placed on him—for he knew that his hand would tremble when he dressed the wound. And he was crying like a girl before I got through with him. He would take the money to the police now—to Captain Rogers.

But I stopped that happy thought. Rogers would question him and wonder why he didn't come with it directly. Then—well—if they didn't suspect him, they'd draw him off the case, anyway, to be on the safe side. No—I thought that little transaction would be best kept between the two of us. In fact, I didn't see any reason why the police should get the money, if things broke right. Let the young doctor have it—if he could earn it on the side of justice—not against it. It would be great stuff if The Hidden Hand paid the price of his own downfall. Not good ethics, maybe—but good, sound common sense.

"Keep the money in the drawer," I told him, "and say nothing. We may turn it over later—but I'll take the responsibility of keeping it secret. The police might misunderstand your hesitancy in handing it over. You'd have to tell the truth, you know—the police have a way of getting at that."

He listened now as I talked, and the shaking of his head soon changed to a nod as I laid down the law to him. I wanted him to do me a little favor.

"You'll only be defeating the ends of justice by refusing my request," I told him finally, "besides putting yourself in a devil of a hole. As far as Mr. Ford is concerned, it won't matter which one he talks to first as long as he's able to talk. Confidentially, he'll prefer me. But if he's too weak to put up a kick, these toy man-hunters will gum the works. Anyway, I'll pass my word to you not to open my mouth until you say the word—or Doctor Carey says the word. And I won't even disclose myself, if I can hear."

"I'll do it," the young doctor finally agreed. "And you won't have to speak. The room's built for it. You can be behind the curtain—there's room for a chair between the curtain and the wall, and it's right smack against the head of the bed. You can hear every word, Mr. Williams—if these policemen try to freeze you out."

"They'll do that all right." I shook his hand. "There'll be a bit of change in it for you if I'm the one to nail this Hidden Hand—we'll discuss that ten thousand dollars later, when we see how things break. Good-night!" I turned toward the window—then gave him a parting shot. Not that I didn't trust him, but I like to play safe. "You'll keep an eye on Mr. Ford at all times—if he took a bad turn now, I might even have my own suspicions."

"He won't." The young doctor nodded. "Doctor Carey's a wizard with the knife, and between you and me I think Mr. Ford is a great deal better than Doctor Carey says. By this time to-morrow he'll be able to talk—to any one. His constitution is like a bull's."

His conversation, too, I thought—but I didn't say it. Somehow, since Gregory Ford got shot down like he did, I was seeing only the good points in the man—and they were many more than I ever suspected.

So much for that. I turned toward the window, but changed my mind once I got a look out in the moonlight. A man in uniform paraded slowly up and down. I shrugged my shoulders, left by the door and sought the entrance.

Brown was there and watched me pass out. He eyed me sharply but said nothing. I wondered, and got to stroking my chin.

42

A Wildly Excited Visitor

My taxi driver was asleep in his cab, but I stirred him up and drove directly to Old Benevolence Travers, reaching his hotel just as the dawn popped up. He was entitled to some information. This news that Gregory Ford would live should strengthen his heart.

Old Benevolence looked haggard and worn. He still sat in the same chair, as if he expected my return. He rubbed his hands, and his lips made an effort at appreciation in a thin smile. The room seemed hot and stuffy, yet he clung to the rug. He certainly didn't look like a well man.

"What are your plans?" he asked, after I told him that Gregory would live and that Gregory would talk.

"First, to get a good sleep; second, to try and be in on the show-down when Gregory Ford springs the name of this Hidden Hand."

"You think—that The Hidden Hand has left the state?"

"No—I don't. He tried to bribe someone at the hospital."

"It didn't work?" His colorless eyes flashed into life.

"It didn't." But I didn't tell him about the young doctor, the money, or my scheme to be in the room behind the curtain when Gregory Ford spilled his stuff. And I didn't tell him the real hope that was in my mind—that Gregory Ford might talk sooner, either rationally or in the delirious mutterings of a sick man. I didn't want to give Old Benevolence false hopes, for one thing—but most of all I didn't want him dragging that sick heart of his to the hospital and squeezing in beside me. I recalled too vividly his visit to the lonely house when Rosie Sorellie was murdered—and how he was paying for it now. No—I couldn't chance the possibility of his insistence—and the probability that he'd kick out trying to pull off the trip.

"And the girl?" He looked straight at me.

"Well—Gregory won't talk until to-morrow morning, when Doctor Carey comes. I'll snatch a few hours sleep—spend the afternoon and evening looking for the girl—and turn up at the hospital and try to talk Captain Rogers into letting me in on the show."

Old Benevolence clutched at my hand before I left.

"This girl," he said unsteadily. "I understand. I want you to put her welfare first—before my interests—ahead of the name of The Hidden Hand. If you learn anything—hear anything—see the slightest chance of saving her, don't hesitate. If I don't know the identity of The Hidden Hand, I do know the character of his associates. Any one of them would slit her throat for a few dollars. So—think of her first."

"I will," I told him grimly. "And I'll slit the throat of any one of this gang for half the price."

"I believe you would." He looked at me queerly, and as I left the room I heard him mutter, "Remember, Race Williams—above all, the girl comes first."

Strange—he had never taken an interest in her before—except perhaps to warn me against the wiles of women. Now—well—when we are sick, when the end of the road appears in sight, our views on life are different—more tolerant—more human. Poor Old Benevolence Travers—he wasn't such a bad skate. However he mixed himself into a thing like this I couldn't understand. His hobby should have been something to do with a school for young girls.

But I got to wondering just the same. This sudden interest in Tina King! She was, after all, an orphan—of unknown parentage perhaps—of— And Old Benevolence! Was her brother, who was murdered in my arms, something to him—was it he that Old Benevolence was trying to avenge; and had he found out lately that the girl was this boy's sister? Was Old Benevolence, after all, the—? I shook such thoughts. Still— But I needed sleep—one thing kept crowding out other thoughts. Funny, that dominating thing now. What was the color of Old Benevolence Travers' eyes?

It was well along in the afternoon when I popped out of bed. An easy conscience that. I'd slept like a baby. By the time I had dressed I had made my plans. Old Benevolence Travers had told me to think of the girl first. I would.

There was no use of me going out hunting up clues. I wouldn't recognize one if I met it face to face. But I had a plan to save the girl that made monkeys of these intellectual, scientific detectives who catch their man with a microscope and a dust pan.

First off, I went out and hired the fastest thing on wheels that West Palm Beach could afford. Then I went to the airport and engaged the use of a plane for the next twenty-four hours. No—I didn't expect to use it—but then, I'd have it just the same. My plan was simple and included, as usual, violence and perhaps sudden death—for those are part of the game that all criminals understand.

I'd be by the bedside of Gregory Ford and get the name of The Hidden Hand—then I'd call up Travers and see if the name helped him fix The Hidden Hand's whereabouts. That is, if Gregory Ford didn't know his hangout. If it was near, I'd use the fast car at the hospital door. If far, I'd play the plane. But I'd reach The Hidden Hand before the police. Then I'd get from The Hidden Hand the place where Tina King was kept prisoner.

Maybe he wouldn't tell? No—that didn't enter into it at all. He'd tell, or those imaginary newspaper clippings with which I'd frightened the dead, Flat-Face, would be mere nursery rhymes to what I'd do to The Hidden Hand. He'd play the game of murder and torture. Now—what's the use to lie about it? Why make himself a better man than I am? Fact is fact. He'd tell me where the girl was, or any horrible recollection of "police brutalities" would become pleasant memories to him. Not nice things for an upright young man to contemplate? Maybe not. But I was going to save that girl.

I arrived at the hospital after dinner. Half a dozen gardeners puttered around the well-kept grounds. I whistled softly. Every one of these men were of the police. Brown, I recognized—the only lad who seemed to know what the dirt was for.

Captain Rogers met me in the hall. He was pompous and on his official dignity; a good sleep had swelled him up considerably.

"Mr. Ford does well," he told me. "It's Doctor Carey who's tying up the thing. He sticks to the twenty-four hours, though the nurse tells me that Gregory is quite strong and spoke to her twice to-day. He seems clear and rational. But Carey holds out for another night's rest."

"I'll be around." I looked at him in child-like innocence.

"It isn't necessary." Rogers puffed out like a poutered pigeon. "If we need you we'll get hold of you." And then, self-contentedly, "I've never needed outside help yet, and—"

"Why the crowd outside?" I interrupted him.

"So you noticed that." He seemed annoyed. "Well—it's possible that The Hidden Hand might try to strike—here."

I nodded. The same thought had hit me, but in a different way. If The Hidden Hand was desperate enough to try murder in the hospital itself, my idea would be to encourage his coming. A common ordinary second-class New York pickpocket could spot that gang outside as flatties a half mile away. But I let that slide.

"I'll stick around," I told Rogers. "You can't tell what may turn up. I'll leave—probably, in an hour."

247

"See that you do," was the best threat he could think of.

He rubbed his chin and blew his nose and scratched his head, but he didn't have the guts to come right out and order me off. So I nosed around a bit, found a book, and when Rogers went for a walk about the grounds I cornered the doctor.

"I'll leave around twelve," I gave it to the doctor right, "and be back at your window shortly after. Arrange to call off the cops on that side—and do it when only one cop is there. Go out and call his attention to something in the rear. Leave your light out and I'll slip in."

"I hope it goes all right." He was nervous.

"You better hope it does," was all I said. Then I returned to the library and nailed my book before Rogers came back.

Captain Rogers watched me when the hour passed. I never looked up from my book, but I could feel Rogers' eyes upon me. Things were mighty quiet. It was getting close to twelve; then it struck twelve—crept to five after. And Rogers spoke his piece.

"Mr. Williams—" he played the heavy sleuth, much as he had seen Gregory Ford do it, "it is decided that you shall not in any way play a—"

Catain Rogers broke off suddenly and swung toward the hall and the front door. A policeman in uniform was backing up before a wildly excited man, but losing ground just the same. And the man was Andrew Gordon King, New York millionaire and adopted father of Tina King.

43

Tina Speaks

"It's the criminal—the murderer." Mr. King advanced threateningly on Captain Rogers. "This Hidden Hand, that through your incompetency, still—and now I'm refused admittance."

Rogers and I had to help him to a seat and get him water, but despite our cautions, to get his breath—he kept talking.

"My child—Tina—her mother distressed. Tina—this Hidden Hand has taken her—this criminal—he will kill her—tonight—within the next couple of hours—by two o'clock—unless—"

"You pay money," Rogers filled in.

"Money—money—money. No!" The excited man raced on. "Why—I'd of paid that—any amount. It's not that. She discovered a secret—a murder—and this man will kill her. Come—hurry—all the men you can gather—there are half a dozen there—desperate criminals."

"Where did you get this information, Mr. King?" I horned in.

"From her—from Tina herself. On the phone—less than an hour ago. She's in fear—terror. But it's true—I questioned Richmond, her chauffeur—he confessed to keeping her secret, that she—"

It took careful questioning but we got his story. Less than

twenty minutes ago he was called to the phone. His daughter spoke to him; told him she was imprisoned in a house out by the orange groves, twenty-five miles away. She knew the house—Richmond would know it. She had been tied—freed herself—reached the phone and called her father. Half a dozen men were in the next room—she heard one say she was to die at two o'clock.

"You're sure it was your daughter's voice?" I asked.

"Absolutely—" and jumping to his feet, "Come!"

This new event sent Rogers higher than a kite. He hadn't heard of the disappearance of Tina King.

"Twelve—two," Rogers muttered. "We'll be back before Doctor Carey lets Ford talk." And he started out after his men, while I buzzed Richmond, who stood by the door. Yes— he knew the house in the orange groves. Tina had gone there a few months before, to see her brother.

The insistence of Andrew Gordon King and the money that stood behind his name threw Captain Rogers into instant action. Yet, he gave his orders to his men before they hurried down to the police car and the big Rolls-Royce of Mr. King. I was not invited to join the party—but I had my own car at the door.

The detective gardeners were drawn in, but two officers were left outside, to watch the hospital.

If Captain Rogers saw me climb into my own hired car and take the trail after the police car and the Rolls-Royce, he made no attempt to stop me. We were out to rescue Tina King and I wanted to be in on the death—for there would be death. Half a dozen detectives—half a dozen desperate men—and the young girl between the fire.

I wanted to reach her as soon as the others; wanted to until we had made about a mile. Then I tapped the driver of my car on the back.

"Turn around," I said, "and go back to the hospital." Was I deserting the girl? Maybe? I didn't know. My old think-box was working. Indeed, the thought had come to me with a sudden clap.

Tina King was a prisoner, whom six men guarded. Yet, she was able to free herself and use a telephone. Funny that— very funny! If true, Captain Rogers and his men could no doubt make a rescue. If not true, had Tina King rung up herself? But her father had said that he recognized her voice. Even so. What was on my mind? Simply this: The Hidden Hand had seen that Tina King got to the phone. Why? So that the police and I would be pulled away from the hospital. Why again? I shrugged my shoulders. Maybe, so that he could visit that hospital and silence forever the words that Gregory Ford would so shortly speak.

A quarter of a mile from the hospital, and I got out and hoofed it.

"Stay here," I told my driver. "Don't come for me unless I send for you, or the police car returns—then draw up before the hospital."

I reached the hospital, and when the cop passed around the back, shot through the open French windows and into the young doctor's room. It was easier than planned—the heavy guard had left with Rogers.

Ten minutes later the doctor came in. We were set for action. I had a feeling that things were going to break.

"It's harder than I thought." He was visibly nervous. "A policeman sits before the door of Mr. Ford's room and a nurse sits in the room, by the window."

"You must send the nurse downstairs for some purpose— and you must draw off the policeman for the few seconds it takes me to get in the room. Can I find the curtained closet or do I use my flash?"

"There's a small light over the head of Mr. Ford's bed. It's enough for you to see the curtains. What will I tell the policeman?"

"Call him to a window down the hall and point out one of

the policemen who's on guard—act as though you thought it was some one else. Ask him what the man is there for—you seem nervous, anyway."

"I am," he said. "Come!"

There was no trouble about the nurse. The doctor sent her to the kitchen for something. I passed up the stairs and crouched low in the darkness of the top steps. In the dim hall light I saw the outline of the cop, his chair tilted back against the wall. Rogers wasn't doing things so bad—so good either. I'd of encouraged trouble.

What the cop thought when the doctor called him, I don't know. But he was glad of the excuse to stretch his legs. Peering around the hall, I saw his back by the window. I stepped quickly across the hall, noiselessly pushed open the door that was partly ajar since the nurse left, and entered the room.

The light above the bed was very dim. But clearly enough I saw the face of Gregory Ford. It was white and bloodless and the puffiness of his cheeks was gone, and the redness of his full thick lips was now a pasty yellow. He was breathing through his nose in quick, sharp, uneven jerks—but there was strength to it. Occasionally his head rolled upon the pillow, as if he fought to pull himself awake but couldn't. And twice before I reached the dark curtains on the other side of the bed I saw his tongue come out and lick at dry lips.

Then I slipped behind the curtains, found the straight-back chair, held the curtains so that they would be steady when the nurse came back—and waited. I hadn't expected to have a policeman and a nurse on guard. The policeman, of course, didn't count now that I was in. But the nurse—would she be of a nervous temperament—but most of them aren't.

I was right by the edge of the bed and close enough to Gregory to stretch out a hand and touch him. But I was in the blackness, for the shaded lamp over the bed gave little more light than a candle.

Five minutes later the door closed and the nurse came in. She was a stoutish girl. I heard her squat herself near the open window at the farther end of the room. She rocked a bit and the chair squeaked, which made things easier for me.

I couldn't see her without fiddling with the curtains, and I wasn't sure if she could see the curtains move—so I kept still. Once she crossed the room and stood looking down at Gregory, while she took his pulse, pawed around, and wrote something on the chart which she held beneath the light. I could see Gregory and half the bed between the two curtains by bending forward slightly.

Then just the squeak of the chair and the sharp spasmodic breathing of Gregory Ford. My thoughts were of Tina King and if, after all, I should have gone with the rescue party. This game of brains didn't fit me maybe. Had I guessed wrong? And if The Hidden Hand was desperate enough to try to murder Gregory Ford, wouldn't he send one of his assistants? I thought not. The men through whom The Hidden Hand directed his acts were all dead. Of course, he may have had means of communicating with his gang—yet, this was a big thing to trust to a subordinate. On the life of Gregory Ford depended the life of The Hidden Hand. He knew that—had risked his life outside Beekman's house when he shot Gregory. Now—

I bent forward and listened. There was a new sound in the room. And I sat back again. The nurse had joined Gregory Ford in slumber, and she wasn't any too quiet about it either. Not loud snores, you understand—more a muffled sort of gasping noise. I didn't condemn her for that, and I wouldn't tell on her afterward. Dear old girl—she made things easier for me. I didn't have to be so stiff and tense about my own breathing. I half dozed myself—but always kept enough awake not to breathe too loud.

It seemed like hours, and I was expecting the dawn to come up when I heard the distant clock strike the half hour after one. The nurse heard it, too, for there was a sudden jar— as if she had rocked suddenly back against the wall—and she sucked in one of those loud, quick snores you hear just before a person wakes up. In fact, she pulled two or three grunts, as if her dreams weren't so good.

Then she didn't snore any more. I heard her chair squeak lightly, as if she got up. Time for another chart, I thought. She didn't like being disturbed, for she moved slowly and heavily—but softly, if you get what I mean. This time she brought with her the smell of medicine; no doubt, something for Gregory I whiffed it in as she came, one foot scraping behind the other in a queer sort of way.

It would be tough if she discovered me now and let out a squawk, and I wished I wasn't there but with the rescue party that went for Tina King. After all, The Hidden Hand couldn't come, even if his life did depend upon the life of Gregory Ford. The Hidden Hand would be lucky if he was able to walk about at all with that bullet of mine in his leg. Why—he'd have to scrape the leg along like—like—And my eyes shot wide open—like the nurse who was crossing the room and bringing with her the sweet smell of chloroform. And I knew the truth—the nurse had been by the open window—her sucking breath was not a snore.

I sat straight and stiff and wide awake. The nurse had been chloroformed and THE HIDDEN HAND was in the room.

44

The Hidden Hand

I bent forward quickly so that I could see the bed and the face of Gregory Ford. I did see the bed and I did see the face of Gregory Ford—but I saw something else. A flash of steel, the whiteness of a hand, and the blackness of a sleeve.

There was no time to cry out a warning—there was no time to shoot, for I could not see the man who held the knife—just the arm and the—the knife—poised above the unconscious detective.

I shot forward, propelled by my will more than the muscles of my body, I guess. My fingers tightened upon the wrist that held the knife. I stood in the open room now—with The Hidden Hand.

I swung him around and we both jerked erect. Man to man—face to face—The Hidden Hand and I.

My brain is usually keyed to razor edge on such occasions. But something fogged it here—something that took only the fraction of a second away—something that made me cry out instead of acting.

"You—you—The Hidden Hand?" My tongue cried out involuntarily, not believing the truth even as my brain recognized that truth. For the face before me in the dim light was a face I knew well.

He jerked up a hand and fired once. Red-hot fire seared my side as I shot from the hip. He didn't fire again—he didn't cry out. He smiled once, with his lips only—then folded up and slipped to the floor. He wasn't dead, if he got any consolation out of that—for as I kicked the gun out of his hand he looked up at me with those colorless eyes and spoke.

"So—after all my plans, it was fated to be you."

"It was in the cards—Howard Quincy Travers," was all I could get off as the door crashed open and the harnessed bull rushed in, waving a gun about.

"The Hidden Hand—The Hidden Hand!" was the best I could explain to the cop and the others who now crushed into the room. But I guess, at that, I was the only one who held my head as they carried the wounded man to a chair.

Gregory Ford was half sitting up in bed. And his words were clear and rational.

"Got him, eh?" he said weakly. "And as usual—no finesse." Then with a twinkle in those usually hard eyes, "I tell you, gentlemen, this man Williams goes entirely in for stiffs."

There was no Doctor Carey to give orders now—no Captain Rogers to mess things up. My side hurt like blazes, but I didn't need the young doctor to tell me that The Hidden Hand—alias, Howard Quincy Travers—alias, Old Benevolence Travers was slipping over.

As for myself—well—I didn't know how bad I was. But one thing was certain. If I cashed in from that shot I'd meet Old Benevolence in the next world on even ground. He'd have no secret from me. He must talk. He—my client—The Hidden Hand! It seemed a sad jumble.

And he was willing to talk. It was jerky in spots—but clear enough, pieced together. Yes—he was The Hidden Hand who, over the years, formed and headed this great crime ring.

He went on talking.

"I built for myself a Frankenstein monster—something that

in the end threatened to engulf me and swallow me up in its mire. I had enough money—millions—but the four leaders whom I had made powerful kept me at it. If I deserted them they would sell me to the highest bidder, or betray me to save themselves from the electric chair. I was through—satisfied—and I wanted to quit. But this octopus of crime which I had created stretched out four of its arms toward me—McCleary, Olaf Sankin, Stinnes, Beekman. I dared not leave them. They drove me on, fearing me, yet threatening me in unspoken words. I would have killed them all—but there would be three others to suspect the death of one, and then exposure. If all were dead my secret would be safe—if all were dead.

"Then the state of Florida acted and hired Gregory Ford. He in turn sought you, Race Williams. You—the man I feared most, for you meet death with death and gun-fire with gun-fire. Then the great plan came to me. To hire you to rid me of these four men. If you did, I was free of them—and my secret safe. If you failed, I would be free of you. It was a great plan. Death, following your coming into the case, would cause little suspicion. It was your way—you were notorious as a gunman and a killer. I could pretend to you that I sought vengeance for a wrong to one dear to me. I could pretend to you that there was a police leak, so I dared not seek their help.

"First came McCleary, and you killed him protecting yourself. The second—Stinnes; I put poison in the glass of water he drank. Oh—he knew me, but he never suspected. He thought I had doped you and was there to save him—but he realized the truth before he died. Olaf Sankin was easy—he shot it out with you in the park. But I feared him most in the physical sense. Instinctively, he distrusted me and even threatened me, and demanded a great sum of money."

"This girl, Rosie Sorellie—what of her—when you were in that lonely, deserted house?" I asked.

"Sankin killed her." His lips curled. "Cut her squealer's throat, as I cut the throat of Beekman. Sankin talked to her. It was she who sent word to you and the police." And there was the snarl of an animal on his lips. "But Sankin had left before you came. He had threatened to kill me that night—and I lingered behind, fearing he lurked outside the house."

He paused a moment and took the drink the young doctor offered.

"It was a great game." Those colorless eyes sparkled for a moment. "The greatest game that man ever played, against the law. And I nearly won—nearly won. To-night I failed—for I read wrongly in your face the love of a woman. I planned that—let this Tina King reach a phone. But you—you suspected me, and were here. Did you suspect that my weakness and pallor was not from the heart, but the foot that bled beneath the rug?"

I didn't say anything. Maybe I even nodded, for the admiring eyes of the young doctor, the harnessed bull, and even Gregory Ford who was leaning far over, listening, told me that they thought I was a pretty "wise bird" after all. And I didn't question him about the ten grand the young doctor found in his room. I knew that he must have followed me to the hospital, placed the money, and returned to the hotel before me.

"And Tina King—" I jerked up his hanging chin—I didn't like his breathing. "What of her—where is she?" Imagine my thinking for a moment that she might be related to this human hyena.

"Safe," he said. "I had no use to kill her. She didn't know me. I wore a mask there in the car. I simply took her when the opportunity offered, thinking that in the future I might hold her to again trap you. I turned her over to some of the boys before I sought my hotel. They never suspected I was the real leader."

There was the shouting of men, the stamping of feet, and little respect for other patients in the hospital. Captain Rogers and his men were returning. They were excited—all speaking at once. Officer Brown had been found unconscious beneath

258

the window. But Tina King was safe, and with them. They had hurried directly to the hospital after finding the girl. She was alone, in a small farmhouse near the orange grove. The men had left, if there had really been six men. Anyway, it was simply to get most of the police off duty at the hospital that Tina King was permitted to work loose a badly tied rope.

There was more I wanted to ask Travers—The Hidden Hand. But the opportunity was gone. Too much noise, too much excitement, and too much questioning of each other in the bedlam that went on by the door, under the square of cardboard which bore the letters SILENCE.

One man only followed the instructions of "Silence." Old Benevolence simply leaned back in my arms and died, as quietly and as easily as any good citizen. Two or three low gasps, and he slipped over—his head resting gently on my arm.

I didn't need the young doctor to tell me he was dead. I've lived too close to death not to recognize it when I see it. I let him drop to the floor, and stood staring down at him—the flash in Captain Rogers' hand now upon the dead criminal's face.

"Strange—queer, ain't it?" Captain Rogers muttered. "Howard Quincy Travers! He's been coming here for years— a couple of homes. An eccentric but charitable gentleman. What—what do you make of it?"

I didn't answer at first. I was still staring down at Travers and at his wide, lifeless eyes.

"Damn it," I said, half to myself, "his eyes are blue—pale— but blue just the same."

"Yes, yes." Rogers looked at me queerly. "He's robbed and killed—and what good does it do him now? He can't take the money to hell with him."

"He can't, eh?" I turned sharply on Rogers. "Don't you believe that—he took a pile of mine." And I stopped dead. But certainly The Hidden Hand—alias, Howard Quincy Travers—alias, Old Benevolence had taken a bunch of my jack to hell with him. Where was my promised pay for bringing to justice The Hidden Hand—where was the unlimited fee I was to name? Yep—he had put it over on me in fine shape. I looked again at the white, dead face. But had he put it over on me? For he was dead—and I—

"Better take a look at this dig in my side, Doc." I turned to the young doctor just as Tina King burst into the room.

There's no use. You can't keep the sex interest out of life. She was clinging to me and crying softly. And I—what was I thinking, with that frail young, lovely body close in my arms? Well—truth is truth. I was thinking that I should have collected the money for the death of Beekman while Old Benevolence was pulling that "heart stuff" early the previous morning. I'm entirely too soft-hearted myself. That's my trouble.